LIFE IS BUT A DREAM

LIFE IS BUT A DREAM

A Novel

DAVID EARLE

ISBN: 978-0-9858479-1-3

Cover by Wendy Hoag Design, Inc.

For Mom and Dad,
who never stopped believing in me

Time present and time past
Are both perhaps present in time future,
And time future contained in time past.
- T.S. Eliot

ONE

"Happy birthday!" his fellow workers cheered as Roger Owen entered the conference room. There were no balloons or streamers, only a large sheet-cake with white frosting and one lit candle in the center, as well as cans of soda, a couple gallon jugs of punch and two bags of ice all placed at the far end of the conference table.

Roger, a handsome black man dressed in relaxed business attire, minus tie with an open collar and rolled up sleeves, tried to express a look of surprise despite having heard whispers all morning long of an impending party that was to take place later in the day. Following an out-of-tune sing-a-long of The Happy Birthday Song by everyone present, Roger reminded them all with a warm smile that his birthday would not be until tomorrow.

"And tomorrow's Saturday. So we're hitting you with this today" a voice cried out.

"Yeah. You didn't think we'd let you sneak out of here without acknowledging you're now *forty*?" said another.

"Not until tomorrow" Roger protested in good humor as he made his way across the room towards the cake. "So don't go calling me forty just yet. Let me savor the last hours of my thirties while I still can."

After a remark jokingly made from a person in the group, something about one candle as opposed to forty and a reference to the Fire Marshall, Roger snickered along with all of the others who were reacting with laughter before blowing out the tiny flame. Cheers and applause went up along with beckoning for a speech.

Roger Owen was never one who felt comfortable speaking before a large number of people. Even though his position often required him to conduct meetings in front of a number greater than those gathered around at that moment. And so there was a bit of hesitation that preceded his impromptu response.

"Okay. A speech. Wow. *Forty!* Guess I better start planning some sort of a mid-life crises for myself."

A feeble attempt to inject some comedy to his *speech* succeeding with only a faint laugh by all.

"Your best years are just ahead of you, Roger. Take it from me" called out Charlie, an elderly coworker who should have retired a decade ago.

"Thanks, Charlie. I'm sure you're right....Well, as most of you know, I'm a man of few words. Except when the project is showing more signs of falling behind schedule. Then I always have *plenty* to say. But nevertheless, all I can say here and now is, thank you, and....let's all have some of this cake."

The "project" Roger spoke of was the construction of the Miami Ballpark and future home of the Miami Marlins going up on the former site of the Miami Orange Bowl in the part of the city known as Little Havana, two miles west of downtown. At least a dozen large grey trailers to accommodate the administrative side of the job were placed adjacent to the enormous 37,000 seat retractable roof stadium. The numerous little offices built within three of the trailers were small and cramped in comparison to Roger's office which was the largest. A luxury afforded him because of his title as Senior Project Manager. But with the larger office came heavy burdens. July 1, 2009 marked the start of construction preparations with the ceremonial groundbreaking following eighteen days later. But hopes for a 2011 opening day had been pushed back to April 1, 2012. And keeping the 515 million dollar project on budget was an ever present challenge ever since work on the ballpark began. It would therefore come as no surprise that the end of each day always found Roger still at his desk long after everyone else had gone home. And there would be no exception to this routine of his on that October day before his birthday when his assistant Liz Ortiz popped her head into his office.

"Okay, I'm out of here" she said in her thick Cuban accent. "And you should be, too. It's six-thirty. Why don't you leave early for a change? Go start your birthday weekend."

Roger leaned back in his chair with a deep stretch and sighed, "You're right. I've had enough. Nothing that can't wait 'till Monday."

"Good. Then have a great weekend. And happy birthday again, Roger."

"Thanks Liz."

Whatever headaches brought on by the day's job, Roger left them all behind the moment he would drive off the parking lot, with that mammoth steel grid structure rising up from its foundation in the background, and head for home, north to Ft. Lauderdale. On a good day without much traffic he could make the trip in thirty minutes. But seldom was there a good day without traffic, which meant an additional fifteen to thirty minutes of time to sit and marvel over how wonderful his life is. For truly it could be said that Roger Owen loved every aspect of his life. Anxieties aside, he took great joy and pride in his work. He owned a beautiful two story home in a new gated housing community complete with a neighborhood clubhouse, swimming pool, two man-made lakes, along with fifty percent of the homes offering small boat docking capabilities for those properties where the backyards flanked one of the many canals that wound their way through the tract of homes, down through the city, and eventually spilling out into the cobalt blue ocean of Florida's Gold Coast.

Such was Roger's home, boasting a canal in the back, though lacking a boat. But a boat was something that would be forthcoming by next spring he figured. Taking his entire family out on weekend boating trips had always been a dream he often shared with his beloved wife Laura. And it was his love for her, their three children, his parents, and the brothers and sisters he was raised with in his native city of Cleveland, Ohio, that he prized above all else.

Indeed Roger's love and devotion to his family was boundless and took precedence over career, money, even himself. An admirable attribute that would not be lost the following day at Snyder Park where he gathered with his family for a picnic barbecue to celebrate his forty years of a perfect life.

This display of love was self-evident in just the way he spent most of that day recording with his camcorder each member of his family.

There was nine year old Justin, sitting proudly atop the monkey bars in a playground congested with other children.

There was one year old Natalie at play with her bucket and shovel with her mother kneeling beside her.

"Look at Daddy. Natalie, look! Look at Daddy. He's taking your picture."

Then there was Tyler, Roger's eldest son at age fourteen, slouched in a fold-out lawn chair, eyes closed, and head bopping to the rhythm of a beat blasting from the headphones plugged into his iPod.

And finally, never to be left out of a family occasion, there were Roger's parents, Josephine and George, both in their seventies, whose move to South Florida followed shortly on the heels of their son. It was a move that Roger took great delight in for reason of the close relationship he shared with them, as well as the proximity and time it allowed his children to spend with their grandparents.

After a day filled with more camcording of Roger flipping burgers on the open grill, the opening of presents, and that Birthday Song sung once again with the presentation of yet another cake, the rest of the evening belonged to Roger and Laura alone.

With Roger waiting in the foyer below, Laura descended the staircase with the kind of grace and elegance that came naturally to her and which only enhanced how stunning she looked that night. Still, being an infinitely concerned mother is something that also came naturally to her.

"I just checked on her. She's still asleep. We should be home at ten thirty. Eleven at the very latest. I gave you our cell phone number right?"

Tracy, the sixteen year old baby sitter from down the street, assured her for the second time that she had the number and then beseeched them both not to worry and have a good time.

The boys were dressed in their pajamas and sitting on the sofa with a bowl of popcorn watching the third game of the World Series. The Texas Rangers and St. Louis Cardinals were going into game three each with a win in the previous two games and Roger had wanted to watch the game along with his sons, but Laura's romantic dinner for two to celebrate his birthday had been planned for weeks and was something he knew in her heart she had been looking forward to. Besides, he reasoned, he could always read about the game highlights in tomorrow's paper, while any time spent with Laura was affectionately more special to him.

After hurried good-byes to the boys Roger and Laura headed for the front door with the family golden retriever Baloo wagging his tail by their side.

"No, Baloo. You can't come" said Roger. "Tyler..."

"Baloo. Come here boy."

It was not uncommon for Roger to reflect upon the day he and Laura met. It was, after all, what he always considered to be the luckiest day of his life.

Having arrived in the early evening at New York's LaGuardia Airport on that June Friday in 1995, Roger felt rushed by the time he at last entered the apartment of his close friend Jeremy Johnson on West 145th Street and Amsterdam Avenue. Their friendship went back several years to when the pursuit of unrestrained lascivious revelry and establishing themselves with a post college career took precedence over the thought of settling down with a wife or even a steady girlfriend. The night life club scene of Cleveland in the nineties offered far too many temptations for two handsome men in their twenties.

And so it came as a disappointment to Roger when Jeremy moved to the City of New York at the turn of the year in '95 with a lofty goal and determination of making it big on Wall Street. Yet throughout that winter and spring Roger made several trips to the city to party with his friend in the new haunts they would discover together, proving that the miles between them could not bring an end to years of wild uninhibited times and their enduring friendship.

It was at the Tunnel located on 220 12th Avenue in the Chelsea district, a huge dance club named for the tunnel-like shape of the main room, where Roger and Jeremy arrived a little past midnight - the typically appropriate time to arrive at a club in the city that never sleeps. There they were to meet up with their new buddy and native New Yorker, Anthony, who was accompanied by a mutual friend of

both he and Jeremy's, Darlene. And it was Darlene who brought along
her friend, a beautiful young lady by the name of Laura Davis.

Roger was not informed of the two ladies that would be joining
them until he and Jeremy had already entered the club. Roger could
still recall vividly the extent to which he objected to this
prearrangement and how uncomfortable he would feel being the *fifth
wheel* amid their little group. It was inside the entrance where Jeremy,
despite his repeated assurances that they were all merely together as
friends and not as "dates", as Roger assumed, was not able to convince
his buddy otherwise. But as they waited for the other three of their
party to arrive Roger eventually relented to meet and join them after
taking under his own consideration the impromptu decision he made to
fly out that particular evening and how unfair it would be of him to
expect them to change their plans on his behalf. Still, it was not until
Anthony, Darlene, and Laura arrived at the club and introductions
where made that it became evident to Roger that the discomfort he felt
certain would follow was clearly not going to develop. In fact, the
moment his eyes fell upon Laura, Roger knew that despite whether or
not they were indeed dates of his two friends there was little chance he
was going to allow this opportunity to know this incredible woman
better slip through his hands.

Her hair was longer then; shoulder length. And in a club where
the women tended to attire themselves in a way more flashy and
suggestive, Laura exuded an aura of style and grace that came not only
in part from the elegant cocktail dress she wore - an apparel that might
have looked a bit out of place on anyone else - but also in the way she
carried herself in mannerism and speech. She was a discernible
contrast, but not in a disparaging way, to her friend Darlene who was a
loud, likable and funny extrovert. Both ladies were employed as tellers
at a bank on lower Madison Avenue which accounted for how these
seemingly opposite women came to be friends outside of the work
place.

The tiny group moved to the bar area. After ordering cocktails
they sat down on a sofa where the evening progressed splendidly for all
as Darlene kept everyone in laughter with her witty, offbeat, and not-
so-candid remarks. Conversation swung from one trivial topic to
another with the only awkward moment coming when they all decided
to take to the dance floor. Roger hesitated, uncertain if Anthony's
suggestion that they dance was meant to include him as well. But the
uneasiness of that moment left when Darlene took Roger by his hand

and dragged him up from his comfortable seat and onto the massive dance floor where under circular color washes of lights they all danced facing each other in a ring, as friends, and not paired off as dates.

The Tunnel, a former railroad freight terminal, was a unique club that got its name from the tunnel-like shape of the main room where train tracks from the early 1900's once ran through the sunken area of the dance floor. The dance floor featured several dance cages and boasted an exceptional sound system and state of the art lighting that played host to some of the best DJ's of the time. Although the club attracted a predominately gay audience, there was still a strong following of straight club goers as well as members of the hip hop community. On the dance floor they would all mass together under a fusion of light and sound where on packed nights the number of bodies would swell to well over a thousand. Such was the case on this particular evening. So congested was the dance floor that it became impossible to move an inch in either direction. The shoulder to shoulder dancing eventually became too claustrophobic for every one of the friends to deal with. So when a *"time out"* hands signal was called by Anthony, they all mutually agreed to squeeze their way back to one of the rooms. The tunnel was not only distinctive for its long narrow space, but also for its multiple rooms and several levels. These rooms varied in decor that changed frequently. There was common knowledge of a V.I.P. room in the basement, and the Kenny Scharf Lave Lounge that typically drew a more exclusive clientele. Still, there were several other lounges throughout, each with their own special character; from S&M dungeons to Victorian libraries, yet all offering plenty of dark corners for illicit activities. And it was in the Victorian library lounge where they were lucky enough to occupy a recently vacated sofa and chairs.

Of this party of five Laura spoke the least. But her consistent smile and sincere attentiveness towards the others demonstrated that she was in no way bored or disinterested in the company she was keeping. This observation was not lost on Roger who could not stop himself from studying her intensely for her beauty, her allure, her unwitting magnetism. At times when realizing he had become transfixed on her he would look away, but only momentarily, for his yearning to gaze upon such loveliness was far too powerful to resist. There was no mistaking the fact, however, that this coveted and often time come-hither stare was by no means a mutual exchange. Roger never once mistook her lack of interest in him as a sign of rudeness, for she was too far above having such a flaw as rudeness in her character.

In fact, it was to the contrary that he found her exceedingly polite by the way she listened and responded to his every question with intentness and always with that bewitching smile. But following each of her answers she would ever so subtly turn away from him and towards the others.

Am I just plain boring? Roger began to speculate.

He would repeatedly conjure up other comments that he hoped would dazzle her. But nothing he said could produce a meaningful or even trivial conversation. As time went on Roger began to feel an embarrassment over his blatant efforts to win her over that he could only assume his friends were by now all privy to.

Alas, the evening drew to a close with no headway made towards igniting a spark of interest from her. And at a time in the morning when a majority of the Tunnel patrons were heading downtown for after hours at Club Shelter on Varick Street where the party would continue until ten or eleven in the morning, Roger and his friends decided instead to call it a night. As good-byes were made outside of the club no phone numbers were exchanged with the promises of staying in touch. Yet Roger knew that the memory of Laura would haunt him a lifetime.

Roger spoke hardly a word throughout the cab ride back to Jeremy's apartment. Jeremy, on the other hand, having consumed more drinks than his friend, drifted back and forth from petty chatter to nearly dozing off. He might have passed out completely the moment of crossing through his doorway if it had not been for the ringing from his telephone.

"Hello?" he answered rather loudly. "Hey, Darlene. No, just got in. You're at Laura's?"

This came as no surprise to Jeremy. Knowing that Darlene was living in Queens and Laura in Chelsea, it seemed only likely to him that Darlene would stay the rest of the evening at her friend's home rather than cope with the subway at that early morning hour.

With the mention of Laura's name, Roger's attention was immediately seized.

"Of course he's here. Oh *really*? Hold on."

Jeremy reached out to him with phone in hand and hesitated a moment before a broad grin swept across his face.

"Guess who wants to talk to you?" He then mouthed the name, Laura.

This, naturally, came as nothing less than a complete surprise to Roger who scurried up from the sofa he had just sat upon.

In her small confined apartment Laura silently objected to Darlene's urging to take hold of the phone. Her reluctance to speak with him was not due to the misperceived feelings Roger had received throughout the evening. For the fact of the matter was that her emotions at first sight of him ran as deep as his towards her. But it was Laura's shy and nervous reaction while in his presence, augmented by his unwavering stare that caused an erroneous impression in her manner. Nevertheless, from the moment she left the club with Darlene it was none other than Roger whom she repeatedly spoke of with adulation as well as regret for not being more conversational.

"Hello, Laura" came his voice over the phone.

Laura rolled her eyes and dithered as she thought hard for a cleaver response.

"Hi" was what she came up with.

An awkward silence followed. Roger figured that after all the vain attempts at dialogue he tried but failed to spur at the club, it was now her turn to make an effort.

"I guess you made it home alright?" she finally asked but immediately cringed over what she figured was a ridiculous opening question.

"Back to Jeremy's place, yeah. No problem."

"Well, that's what I meant. Jeremy's place." Unsure whether or not he was being facetious she nonetheless drew in a deep breath and moved on to her next question.

"So when will you be flying home?"

"Sunday."

Roger was certain she already knew the answer to this question, for Darlene had asked it in her presence shortly before they all departed the club. But for the first time he was able to detect a slight nervousness in her voice that was never there earlier and all at once realized the possibility that their feelings for each other might be mutual.

"Will you be coming back to New York again anytime soon?"

At that point it took every ounce of control in Roger to prevent himself from yelling out in jubilation. This was undoubtedly his chance, his *moment* to assert an equal amount of nonchalance and boldness into an opportunity that may never come again.

"Perhaps." *A perfect nonchalant response*, he thought. *And now for the bold attack.* "Will you have dinner with me tonight? Just the two of us?"

It would be their first dinner of many. A point in time where their lives changed and there would be no looking back.

Throughout the remainder of that year Roger would spend nearly all of his weekends in New York - even driving when he could not afford to fly. Laura, in turn, would also make her fair share of trips to Cleveland until that January day the following year when they married with a vow that whichever direction their lives would take them they would go the journey together.

They settled in Cleveland where the birth of their first-born came in the early part of 1997. Then a move to Florida less than two years later shocked both his family and hers. But job opportunities in construction, warmer winters, and his love of the ocean and dream of someday owning a sailboat for his growing family all played a part in their decision to head south.

So it would be, sixteen years, four months and three children later since that first dinner date together in New York, Roger and Laura where once again on their way to another dinner. Dining at the indoor-outdoor *Tuscan Grille* restaurant called Mancini's on Las Olas Boulevard had always been a romantic experience for Roger and Laura on many special occasions, and this particular evening was certainly no exception. They chose to sit indoors where throughout the candlelight dinner they spoke mostly of their future, such as taking Baloo to the vet on Monday to have a microchip identification system injected under his skin.

"I don't know, babe" said Roger, warily to the idea. "Do you think it's really necessary? I mean, he already has his tags."

"But you know what the shelter told us when he was picked up. They said that if by some reason he loses his collar, at least with that microchip they'll be able to scan it to trace his owner. I read it's only the size of a grain of rice, they inject it just under the skin surface and he won't feel a thing."

They also spoke of taking care of the Christmas shopping early this year.

"Well the kids are easy enough to buy for" said Laura. "But I haven't the faintest idea what to get your parents or mine this year."

"What about getting my folks a ceramic soup tureen? My Mom mentioned the other day that she broke the one they had."

"We gave them a ceramic soup tureen last Christmas."

"You don't suppose..."

"Gee, I hope not. That soup tureen wasn't cheap."

They also spoke of the far future, tossing around ideas as to where the family might go for next summer's vacation.

"You know the kids will have no complaints if we go to Orlando again."

"Yeah, but we go there every year" said Roger. "I was thinking of us all going to a different kind of park next summer. A *national* park. Like Yellowstone or the Grand Canyon."

And of course Roger spoke of that boat his heart was set on buying in the spring.

"I can't decide whether we should get the Hunter 326 or the Beneteau 331."

"Well honey, *that* decision I'll leave entirely up to you because I know nothing about sailboats."

Following the main course Roger's strawberry swirl cheesecake was placed before him with a single lit candle protruding from its middle. He had hoped the other waiters would not gather around their table to sing Happy Birthday to him *again*. But they did, much to Laura's amusement. Roger simply cringed and then smiled politely until they were finished.

———————

After dropping Tracy off at her home with a request that she pass along his regards to her folks, he entered his own house, flicked off the foyer light and headed upstairs. Walking down the hall towards the master bedroom he stopped to peek in on each of his children. In Justin and Tyler's dark bedrooms he found both of his sons fast asleep. He then entered the nursery where he crept up to Natalie's crib, looked down upon his sleeping angel, her head lit by the glow of a night light, and gingerly, lovingly, caressed her little head.

Laura was keeping herself awake with a book when Roger entered and began to undress.

"It's over" he sighed. "Can I say it's over?"

"Depends what you're talking about. As long as you're not referring to the two of us."

"I'm talking about this birthday. This whole build-up to turning forty. It's over. Done with. Time to embrace middle age and move on."

Laura closed her book and chuckled.

"You laugh" he continued. "Wait until forty rears its ugly little head at you."

"It's only a couple years away and I'm not dreading it in the least. It's a number that means nothing as long as you're happy. And *I'm* happy. Are you happy?"

Crawling into bed next to her he responded first with a kiss.

"Couldn't be happier. Thanks to you."

"Good answer."

With another kiss that immediately grew passionate, Laura's book slid off her lap and onto the floor.

Hours later the entire home was as silent as a tomb except for the faint ticking from a small mantle clock in the living room, the one surrounded by a few too many framed family photos. In the kitchen Baloo was asleep on his doggy bed, as was the family cat Bagheera, curled up in a tight ball on the sofa.

While the children slept without a stir, in the still of their own room Roger and Laura, with their heads nestled down into their soft pillows, lay snug beneath the covers in deep motionless slumber.

TWO

The dreamless black gradually gave way to a growing brightness that penetrated his eyelids. Brighter, brighter, and brighter still until Roger's mind told himself that he was now awake and that it was time to open them.

In doing so his mind also perceived that the light was much brighter than what he was normally accustomed to when awakening. So much so that he had to squint until his eyes adjusted to the view above him, a stark white ceiling with the glare of florescent lighting that seemed to envelop the whole room. *But whose room?* Roger thought.

He rolled his head over to his right where his eyes gazed upon a lady, a rather young lady, sitting in a chair positioned against the wall near the far end of his bed. She was dressed only in white, what looked to be a uniform of some sort, and was staring directly at him. Almost immediately upon noticing her she rose to her feet and approached him, looking down upon his face and directly into his eyes. The strangeness of it all left him speechless. And then, without hesitation, she hurried out of the room through what had been a closed door.

I must still be dreaming, Roger assured himself. But in looking about the tiny room his senses began to tell him otherwise. Everything appeared extremely sterile. Even the scent of the room was sterile, yet he had never known of a dream where the sense of smell was evident or even possible. The room was also unusually bare except for several computer-type objects to each side of him towards the head of the bed. They seemed to be of a medical purpose, monitors and the like, though dissimilar from anything he had ever seen before. Nevertheless, despite having no professional knowledge of medical equipment he reached the vague conclusion that he must be in a hospital room.

But how did I get here? And why am I here? his mind began to question. *Did I have a heart attack during the night? Did I fall down the stairs in the dark? Where's Laura? Why isn't she here? The kids! Are they all right!?*

Through the same door from where the lady had left the room entered an Asian man, roughly in his late thirties, who by all appearance struck him as being a doctor. The same lady in white followed this doctor, a nurse he figured, along with two others, male and female, although he could not determine whether they were doctors or nurses.

"Well now, look who finally decided to wake up" said the doctor in a congenial voice as he moved straight towards him until the flashlight in his hand was shining into his eyes.

"My name is Dr. Ozawa. And can you tell me what your name is?"

"Roger Owen."

Dr. Ozawa lowered his flashlight and looked up at the others in the room who were all exchanging mutual glances at one another as if quite puzzled over the response given to his name. Apparently they already knew the patients name, but the name spoken was not the name they expected.

However, no one present was more puzzled than Roger himself. For just as the words left his lips he immediately recognized the sound of his voice as not being his own.

Dr. Ozawa resumed his examination of the patient. "Okay...*Roger*, now can you make a fist with your left hand for me please?"

Roger did as he was asked but also repeated his name twice, still bewildered as to why he sounded the way he did.

"Roger Owen. Roger Owen."

The voice sounded deeper. Older. And this time he detected a definite British accent.

"Good. And now if you can do the same for me with your right hand" Dr. Ozawa continued.

Roger complied as he further tested the perplexing sound of his voice.

"Mary had a little lamb with fleece as white as snow. Everywhere that Mary went the lamb was...."

"Now I'd like you to wiggle your toes for me and also tell me what year it is."

"What's wrong with my voice? What happened to my voice!?" said Roger in a tone of growing panic.

"Your voice sounds fine" the doctor reassured him. "Now why don't you tell me what year it is?"

"I know the sound of my voice. I'm not crazy. The words I speak are my own, but the sound..."

He stopped short from completing his thought as suddenly previous questions flooded his emotions.

"Where am I? Why am I here? Where's Laura? I want to see Laura!"

As he struggled to raise himself from the bed Dr. Ozawa called on the others to help restrain him. A rush of pain shot throughout his torso, but still he contested.

"Professor Hamilton, please!"

"*Professor!?*...Who?....What are you doing!?"

Ozawa and the male nurse held down Roger's straining arms against his protests and pain while the female nurses wrapped leather straps, already attached to the metal bed frame, tightly around his wrists.

Looking down at his bound wrists Roger discovered a terrifying sight - his hands were that of a white man.

"What happened to my hands? Oh God, what's happened to my hands!? Untie me!"

Roger struggled and twisted his body in a desperate effort to free himself as the male nurse fought to hold down his feet. Dr. Ozawa removed from his coat pocket a devise that could only best be described as resembling a penlight, approximately five inches long. He pressed one end of the device against Roger's temple and then clicked a tiny red button located midway on the cylinder. Instantly Roger's body went limp followed in seconds by a deep induced sleep.

The amount of time that had lapsed until Roger awoke never came into question when he opened his eyes. His first thought was a mere second of relief that what he had just experienced was only a nightmare. But the now familiar sound of Dr. Ozawa's voice made it immediately clear to him that the nightmare, if it *was* that, was regrettably not over yet.

"He's coming to" Roger heard him say in a soft voice. "He'll be perfectly coherent. But very relaxed. No more rage or outbursts like before."

"Hello. Can you hear me?"

The voice spoke to Roger with a soft gentleness that immediately made him think of Laura. His eyes followed the sound of her voice until they gazed upon a beautiful young woman - late twenties or perhaps early thirties he figured - seated in a chair by his side. Her skin looked soft and her hair a pale blonde that flowed over the front of one shoulder. Her eyes were sincere and caring. And her smile warm and trusting, so much so that for the first time Roger felt somewhat at ease despite his puzzling circumstances.

Her name was Jessica Wynn, but she introduced herself only as Dr. Wynn. And unlike those still present in the room from earlier who were all attired in white coats, her clothes were of a non-uniform type and instead, dressy-casual in style, yet quite dissimilar to any fashion Roger had ever seen before.

"Would you mind answering a few questions for me?"

How could he refuse, coming from such a lovely face? He nodded, feeling too fatigued to speak.

"What is your name?"

"Roger Owen."

"And what year is it?"

Roger paused a moment having noticed for the first time what appeared to be a small tape recorder in her hand.

"2011" he finally answered.

Quick glances were exchanged by everyone in the room except from Jessica whose eyes remained fixed on Roger as the smile left her face and her expression grew more serious.

"Can you tell me who is President of the United States?" she asked.

"Obama" said Roger.

More than one mouth was suddenly agape as a long silence followed. Jessica then turned to Dr. Ozawa and suggested that it would be best at this point if she could have some privacy with the patient. Dr. Ozawa nodded in agreement and turned to the others who followed his lead out of the room. But as the last two nurses filed through the door he overheard one nurse whisper to the other:

"Was there a President Obama in 2011?"

"Don't know. I'd have to look it up" came the answer.

Recalling a favorite animated story watched repeatedly by his children, Roger began to relate to how Alice must have felt after falling down that rabbit hole into a wonderland of bizarre characters who made no sense. *But Alice was only dreaming, right?* He could not remember how the story ended.

"Where do you live, *Roger*? What city?"

"You say my name like you don't believe me."

Roger's observation elicited no response from the doctor.

"Okay. Then why don't *you* first tell *me* where the hell I am?" he continued.

"Massachusetts General Hospital."

"*Massa*...How?...Why am...?"

He stopped short from completing his sentence when upon glancing down at his hands he became reminded of the fact that they no longer resembled his own.

"A mirror" he requested apprehensively. "Bring me a mirror so that I may see my face."

Baffled by his request, Jessica hesitated.

"Please" Roger begged.

She looked about the room, as well as the restroom, but failed to find a mirror that was not attached to a wall. Turning to him almost apologetically, she suddenly remembered a compact mirror she kept in her valise. Jessica retrieved the mirror and held it in front of his face.

"Lower" he instructed her until the reflection of his face came into view. What he beheld struck him numb with disbelief. It was the face of an old man. A white man, with sad blue eyes and short cropped silvery hair.

"What is it?" asked Jessica, noting his sudden look of dismay. "What's wrong? Tell me."

But Roger could not find the words to speak as he gazed transfixed on the reflection of this unfamiliar face in the mirror. Every inclination coming from his five senses was telling him that this was not a dream, despite trying so desperately to convince himself that it was.

Unable to further consume or comprehend anymore of these unexplainable surreal happenings, Roger elected to turn his face away from both the mirror and Jessica in the hope that just maybe by ignoring his dire state he might fall asleep and awaken with Laura by his side, Baloo and Bagheera on the bed looking down at him with that familiar desire in their eyes to be fed, and the sounds of mischievous giggles and laughter resounding down the hall from the children's rooms. But this, as he would soon discover, will never be.

Patient appears to suffer from total amnesia as a result from the trauma sustained in the fall - so appeared the words on the computer screen as Jessica's voice dictated notes on her latest patient.

What is clear, however, is that the patient is experiencing acute depression of bipolar disorder and a dissociation of his true identity. This might be a temporary case of the patient thinking he is someone he knows, met, or may have heard of incurred by his injuries. Although the fact that he believes the present year is 2011 makes this an unlikely scenario. More probable in this situation would be a diagnosis of Multiple Personality Disorder, an uncommon condition in which two or more independent and distinct personality systems develop in the same individual when there is a splitting off from conscious awareness and control of thoughts, feelings, memories, and other mental components in response to circumstances that are painful, disturbing, or in some way unacceptable to the person experiencing them. This patient may

or may not have been diagnosed with this prior to his accident.
Therefore further questioning and examination is necessary before a
positive diagnosis can be made and the proper treatment determined.

Her notes on Professor Sydney Hamilton, also known as Roger Owen, would suggest nothing from the ordinary in regards to the knowledge, professionalism, and dedication she would pour into every one of her patients. Therefore, in keeping with these ethics in her practice one would never assume that there was ever indeed a prior connection between this particular patient and herself.

"Are these really necessary?" were Roger's first words when Jessica entered his room. He sounded cross, and he had sound reason to be for he was referring to the straps that still bound his arms to the side railings of his bed.

"They most certainly are *not*" replied Jessica, sounding even more irate than he at this indignity put upon her patient.

"Would you please?" she said to the female nurse sitting in a chair keeping watch over him. But the facial expression on the nurse showed signs of reservation. And before she was able to voice an explanation for her reluctance Jessica jumped in with a reason that all but sounded more like a reprimand rather than a request.

"He's every bit as well my patient as he is Dr. Ozawa's. Now untie him immediately and then leave us alone."

The nurse wasted no time as she scurried from one side of his bed to the other doing exactly what she had been told.

"I'm so very sorry. There was no reason for you to be restrained like that. I should have realized that yesterday and had them removed right then. But I'm sure Dr. Ozawa felt justified in having done so under the circumstances..."

Jessica stopped short of completing her sentence when remembering the presence of the nurse still in the room but on her way out.

"*What* circumstances?" asked Roger after the nurse had left.

Jessica hesitated and then decided not to answer that question just yet. It was too soon, she felt. But Roger's patience at getting to the bottom of these *circumstances* that brought him there, why he had been bound like a wild animal, and why he sounded and looked completely different from the person he is, or was, had vanished in his sleep. He wanted answers *now*.

"Look. That little lady was placed in here so she could get me a bed pan or urinal whenever I needed one. Unfortunately on one occasion she wasn't quite fast enough. Now I *know* this isn't a dream. So why don't you then tell me *what* it is, Doctor? Why am I here? How did I end up in Massachusetts? Where's my family? And most puzzling *and* disturbing, *how* did I become a white man?"

The last question caught Jessica off guard. She was not expecting it and had to take a seat in the chair.

"What ethnicity *are* you, Roger."

"Now you're talking to me like I'm crazy. Listen here, there's nothing wrong with me aside from suffering a deplorable lack of answers. Something we're both obviously suffering from come to think of it. So why don't we play a little game? For every question you answer of mine, I'll answer one of yours? Agreed?"

"Agreed."

"Fine. I'll start. With an easy one too. You mentioned I'm in Massachusetts General Hospital. Why?"

"You had an accident. A fall. From the third story window of your apartment. You suffered a coma that lasted five days. Remarkably though, your other bodily injuries were limited to bruised ribs, a dislocated shoulder, many contusions, a few lacerations and scrapes. But no broken bones. You're very lucky."

"How is it this fall turned me white?"

"I believe it's my turn. What ethnicity *are* you, Roger?"

"I'm black. I am a forty year old black man with a wife and three kids who went to sleep the other night in his bed next to his wife in his home in Ft. Lauderdale, Florida. Yet I woke up in a hospital bed in Massachusetts in the body of a gray haired old white man with a British accent... My turn. How?"

"I wish I could tell you. I really do. But that's what I'm trying to figure out." She hesitated only a moment before continuing with an approach that she hoped would reveal the truth. "Roger, may I please speak with Sydney Hamilton?"

Roger rolled his eyes back, practically amused, and shook his head. "So you think I have one of those split personalities? Is that it?

Look, I don't *know* who this Sydney Hamilton is. I only know who *I* am."

"And so do I. You are Sydney Hamilton. History Professor at Harvard University. Your identification, your place of residence, your place of work, the people who know you, all attest to this fact. You're Professor Sydney Hamilton. And the year is 2125. *Not* 2011."

After a long pause it seemed surprising that the only words Roger could conjure up would be; "You don't say?"

If his response sounded placid, even a bit blithe, he really did not know himself why he said it considering the seriousness of what he had just been told. Truth, perhaps, in that humor sometimes presents itself as a means of coping with dire news or situations.

Once again he saw in the doctor that same genuine look of concern he saw in her the previous day. And with that he realized right then and there that his only hope of learning exactly what happened, and to make any sense of it, would mean that he would have to bury any hostility and be completely forthright in giving her as much information of himself and his life leading up to that fortieth birthday as his vivid memory would permit.

And so for the following two hours Roger recalled in explicit detail, or as best he could, everything about his life, from his earliest childhood memories up to the events of the day that led to his one hundred and fourteen year long sleep. He left nothing out, feeling that everything he said would be relevant to proving his sanity and that what he was telling her was indeed the truth and not a mere fabrication from some apparent fall.

He told her his birthday and the hospital where he was born. He spoke of his childhood and the home where he was raised. He gave her the names of his parents, brothers, sisters, wife, and children, even the names of his pets. He informed her of the schools he attended. The degrees he earned. His occupation and where he was working. He described his house and every room in it with remarkable clarity. He even told her the year and model of the car he drove.

Jessica listened intently to his every word while recording the entire session for later study. So captivated was she by his oration of this life over a hundred years ago, along with the love and poignancy with which he spoke of it, that she never interrupted him nor went into any further description of the other man in his life he knew nothing of.

Could such a sudden glow appear on the face of a man who does not believe in what he says is the truth, she wondered?

But that glow would eventually dissipate amid the recollection of his last moments awake in the twenty-first century, a memory of he and Laura making love and the sad realization that it might have been their last time. After this point Roger could no longer continue and Jessica felt it would be inconsiderate to try.

Although much was learned in those two hours, no answers were discovered as to what happened and why. But Jessica promised before she left that those answers will come eventually, though it may take some time. She then informed him of the tricyclic drug she would be prescribing for his depression, and that he should not expect to see her again for another four days. She apologized, explaining that a family reunion on the west coast for her parents' wedding anniversary would make it impossible to meet again anytime sooner, something she immediately regretted telling him upon realizing too late that mentioning "wedding anniversary" and "family reunion" to a man in his state was like throwing salt on an open wound.

Before leaving the room Jessica bade him goodbye, but Roger remained silent.

It was by chance that Jessica happened to meet up with Dr. Ozawa who was passing by Roger's room.

"And how's our Professor doing today? Still thinks he's living in the twenty-first century?"

"Apparently so."

Careful not to breech any doctor patient confidentialities by disclosing exactly what he told her, but keeping it in mind that Professor Hamilton is Dr. Ozawa's patient as well, she merely explained that the information he offered her about this other person he believes he is was so startling in its detail that it would be inappropriate to conclude that amnesia and a failure to recall the correct date as the only diagnosis.

"There's something more here. Much more" she added suspiciously.

"Split personality?"

"I'm not sure. Could the personality of an individual who only exists in the patients mind know *so much* of a life that never truly existed and at a time in history he most certainly never lived through?"

"Well, I don't know exactly what he told you about his personal life. But as far as thinking that he's from the year 2011, keep in mind that our patient is a *history* professor. And from what I've heard, an acclaimed one at that. So wouldn't it be plausible for a man of his education to know more details of our history than say, you and me? Think of it, if I were some eminent Egyptologist I'm certain I could paint a pretty accurate picture of what life was like during the time of the Pharaohs and even convincingly place *myself* in that picture if I erroneously believed I was actually there."

Dr. Ozawa's simplistic explanation sounded convincing. However, there was something that Professor Hamilton, or rather Roger Owen, spoke of that sounded equally persuasive. His occupation and degrees as a General Contractor, Building Inspector, and Structural Engineer were claims that could not be ignored considering the obvious knowledge behind the words he used to describe this part of his life. She felt a strange need to get this point across to Dr. Ozawa in Roger's defense.

"And I'm somehow certain that he'd be able to hold his own in a one-on-one conversation with another Structural Engineer if put in that situation" she added.

"Unless construction has changed in the past hundred years. We know it has since they built the pyramids, the Parthenon, the Wall of China. So how would a Structural Engineer of today be able to dispute claims made by a historian on how they were constructed?"

Jessica felt no desire to continue playing devil's advocate with Dr. Ozawa. He was not there to hear the words from their patient. And by restricting herself from going into too much detail, how could he possibly understand the peculiar circumstances that were making it impossible for her to draw any immediate conclusions?

"Well, it sounds like you've got a lot of sessions with him ahead of you" said Dr. Ozawa after sensing by her silence an unwillingness to continue the subject. "I'm discharging him tomorrow. Will he be going home or to a mental hospital?"

Jessica was taken aback by this decision of his.

"The man just came out of a five day coma and you're ready to release him?"

"His physical injuries were remarkably minimal. And during those five days his body healed ninety percent. Now I'll admit that psychologically he needs continued help, but physically speaking I see no reason for him to remain here and take up the use of a much needed hospital bed. And if he's going home then I'll take personal responsibility of arraigning the best day care nurse to assist him however long it be necessary."

"Home? His only home is a house in Ft. Lauderdale in the year 2011. Sending him to some unfamiliar apartment here in Boston would be - "

"The right thing to do" Dr. Ozawa interrupted. "Perhaps doing so will bring back his memory. But if your psychiatric intuition disagrees then I guess that leaves only one other place for him to go."

Jessica, nevertheless, did not back down, but instead asked him to compromise with her by letting him stay for the following four days until she returned from this ill-timed though obligatory trip. After some reluctance Dr. Ozawa finally agreed.

It would be, however, an agreement that he would fail to keep. For at approximately three o'clock the subsequent morning the door opened to Roger's room casting a glaring light from the outer corridor. The two large figures that stood in the doorway were silhouetted against this light making it impossible for Roger to distinguish their faces. Still, he figured at first, that it was only the night nurse coming to take his vitals. An annoyance that would awaken him every two hours. But *two* nurses? Before a sense of alarm could pervade his half-asleep consciousness one of the shadowy figures withdrew from his pocket the same type of penlight-like device that Dr. Ozawa had used on him previously and proceeded to use it on Roger in the same manner, pressing it against his temple until the click of that little red button sent him into a deep state of unconsciousness.

Someone snoring was the first sound Roger heard before he opened his eyes to the sight of another hospital room. Yet this room was far larger than the one he occupied before. So large, in fact, that he found himself sharing it with seven other roommates. There were four occupied beds directly across from him, one occupied bed to his left, and two more occupied beds to his right. The room was dark and all present appeared to be asleep. At least this was certain for the one doing all the snoring across from him, second bed to the right.

When an attempt was made to raise himself up for a better look, he realized that once again there were straps binding him to the bed. Only this time, along with his feet and arms being bound, his entire torso was also constrained by a large leather belt. *What now?* was his first and only thought as he exhaled a deep breath and closed his eyes with a hope against all hope that perhaps the next time he awakes he will find himself in his own bed and in the arms of his dear Laura.

But in the final hours of darkness there would be no sleep for Roger. His mind had become overwhelmed with images of all that he had experienced since he opened his eyes to this bizarre nightmare and the now frightening uncertainty of what may lie ahead.

"Breakfast time!"

The words coming from the young black male orderly startled Roger at first. With his eyes closed and his thoughts blocking out the sounds around him, his approach with a tray of food was never noticed. Nor did he recognize that the snorer had long since ceased his insufferable droning.

"Well, it says nothing here about you bein' violent, or a danger to yourself and others" he continued to say while glancing over Roger's chart - an illuminated paper-thin screen that he held in his hand. "So I suppose these straps are sort of pointless."

He replaced the chart back into its holder from where it came. At this same moment the man in the bed directly to Roger's right awoke from his sleep and immediately launched into a conversation with himself, speaking rapidly with words and sentences that made no sense whatsoever.

With the room now well lit by its overhead lighting Roger was better capable of surveying his surroundings than he had been able to earlier in the dark. The ceiling was high and the walls painted white. The building was noticeably older than the prior hospital he had been in, but only older by 2125 standards. It was still decades ahead of the type of structures familiar to him as a builder.

"Now where am I?"

"Look around" said the orderly. "If you still don't know then chances are you're in the right place."

Roger glanced about the room again, this time studying the other male individuals who were beginning to stir awake in their beds. One man, lying in a fetal position with his back facing Roger, was weeping softly, while another man sat up in his bed with his arms folded and began to rock nervously back and forth. Then there was the fellow who could not move at all because he too was bound to his bed by the same type of bondage that Roger was presently being released from. And still there was the talkative one to his right who amazingly seemed to defy the need to take a breath as he rambled on without a break or pause.

"I'm *not* crazy" Roger made firm.

"Says you and everyone else who occupies a bed in this place" came the amused reply.

"Where's Dr. Wynn? I want to see Dr. Wynn."

"Ain't no doctor by that name on staff here. But don't worry, I'm sure one of the other doctors will be around to pay you a visit sooner or later."

"Look, you gotta find her and get a message to her for me."

"Oh yeah? And why should I do that?"

A moment of hesitation on Roger's part passed before he decided to attempt a different approach with him.

"'Cause you and me, we're the same. On the outside I may look like this old white dude, but on the inside I'm black. Just like you, bro. I'm black just like you. You *gotta* help me."

At first the young orderly was taken aback by his statement, but then a broad grin emerged as he quickly found the humor in its absurdity and began to laugh.

"So you think you're black?"

"I don't *think*. I *know*."

"Well now, if this don't beat all. I thought I've heard everything working here. But *this*...First of all let me explain something, I'm black on the *outside*, *not* on the inside. We're *all* the same on the *inside*. It only took several hundred years for this country, and the rest of the world for that matter, to realize this. And now you come off here talkin' in a way like no one's talked in nearly a hundred years? Who do you think you are?"

"Not the person you see! That's what I'm trying to tell you!"

Roger's loud retort, for merely a moment, brought about the attention of the other patients in the room. The man rocking stopped long enough to look up; the other ceased his weeping and glanced over his shoulder; and the chatterer paused only for an instant before continuing his incessant babble. Roger's head then settled back into his pillow as he gazed up at the ceiling in exhaustion and sighed.

"I'm Roger Owen. A black man born in the twentieth century."

The young orderly appeared puzzled over the old man's assertion. He looked at him in wonder and tried to understand why this new patient would believe this of himself. Then he promptly remembered that he was indeed just that, a patient. And all the patients in this place have but only one thing in common.

"You're crazier than anyone else here. And you know *why* you're crazier than anyone else here? See that dude at the end? The quiet harmless looking one who never stops praying? He thinks he's Jesus Christ. There's another guy up on the third floor who thinks he's Mohammed. A couple years ago we had a Buddha in here. And I can't even begin to count how many other religious and historical figures have passed through those front doors into this place. I hear that five years ago they even had a guy in here who claimed he was God, until one of his roommates killed him because he blamed God for the pandemic that wiped out his family. But you, you're a different case altogether. You don't claim to be anyone famous. Just black. Not even a *famous* black man. Just a man named Roger who happens to be black. Like me."

Unexpectedly a big smile graced his face.

"And for that I like you" he continued. "Yes sir, I actually do like you. You don't believe you're someone famous like so many of the others here do. You only believe you're someone like me. And I appreciate that a lot, Roger. I *do*. Now you enjoy your breakfast. And if you want more, you just let me know."

Roger felt unconvinced that the orderly truly believed a single word he told him, yet also a little content in that someone had finally referred to him by his actual name. But as the orderly began to walk away something he had mentioned begged for further explanation.

"Excuse me. What "pandemic"?" Roger asked.

The question stopped the young man cold and seemed to astonish him.

""*What pandemic?*" Man, you *are* from another place in time."

The orderly shook his head and turned again to walk away.

"Hey" Roger called out, stopping the orderly once more. "Does he ever stop?" referring to the talker on his right.

"Yeah, he'll stop. After he takes his medication."

As the orderly made his way for the exit Roger noticed him shaking his head and muttering to himself in disbelief, *"What pandemic?"*

The home of Jessica's parents was a sprawling ranch house both spacious yet homey nestled on the outskirts of St. Helena in California's Napa Valley, a valley rich in vineyards that was still producing wine just as it had done a hundred years ago and a hundred and fifty years before that. Built in the late 1990's, her parents bought the dwelling because of their mutual love of period homes, and for what they felt would be the perfect place to raise their family.

After spending her first day settling in, relaxing and enjoying the closeness of family and hours of conversation that seemed to hasten by, it was not until the end of the second day, a full day dedicated to running around town with her younger brother and preparing for the anniversary party planned for the following day, when she was finally able to find the time to further research the topic of split personality. In the quiet of her room, little changed from the day she left for Boston to complete her education at Harvard, Jessica mulled over an overload of information on the subject. But something did not add up in regards to what she was reading and its relation to her patient, Professor Hamilton. It was the incredible depth and detail he offered her on his life so many generations ago. After listening over the two hour recording of their session while jotting down significant dates, names, and places, she decided to do some investigative research with the information laid out before her. But it was late in the evening and she could barely keep her eyes open. It would have to wait until the next morning before the scheduled noon party was to begin.

It would be another restless night for Roger, due in no small part to his snoring roommate. He wondered how it is that even into the twenty-second century there is still no definite cure for snoring. *Or perhaps there is,* he surmised. *But stopping crazy people from snoring isn't worth their effort.*

He had no way of knowing what time it was when the night nurse opened the door to his room. Nor was he able to make out the face of the shadowy figure that stood next to him. After the nurse pointed in his direction the figure entered the room alone and made certain the door closed completely shut behind him. There was only the pale glow from a night light plugged into a wall socket at the far end of the room, and yet the mysterious figure made no attempt to turn on an additional light. Instead the figure made his way towards Roger's bedside in near darkness. Silently, like a phantom, the figure approached his bed. But even then he still could not make out a face, it was just too dark. He *was*, however, able to distinguish what appeared to be a long heavy coat being worn by the visitor.

"Now what?" asked Roger.

But no response was given. It was then Sydney noticed that in the hand of the stranger he held that same penlight size sleep inducing device that was by now all too familiar to him.

"Oh not again" Sydney groaned.

No sooner had the words left his lips then he was once again off in a deep sleep.

"Breakfast time!" came the now familiar wake up call.

Sydney opened his blurry eyes and focused them on the same orderly from the other day.

"And how's my *brotha'* feeling this morning?" asked the orderly who then immediately broke into a hearty laugh.

In his drowsy state Sydney was able to offer no more than a subtle grin.

"Looks like *somebody* had a good sleep last night" said the orderly.

"Yeah."

"Sit up now. I've gotta good breakfast here for you this morning. Scrambled eggs, two sausage links, a blueberry muffin, and orange juice. Mmmm-mmm."

"Why'd they put me to sleep last night with that thing?"

"Why'd *who* put you to sleep with *what* thing?"

"That thing the size of a pen. They press it against my temple and boom, I'm out."

"I have no idea what you're talking about. I work the morning shift. What goes on during graveyard shift is none of my business."

"I'd still like to know why they did it."

"How well have you been sleepin'?"

"I haven't had a good night's sleep since 2011."

Again the orderly broke out in laughter. "You must've been one tired son-of-bitch then. And it seems to me that would explain why they did what they did to help you sleep. Now c'mon and sit up. I've got other patients to feed ya know."

Sydney did as he was told and the orderly rolled a food tray up to his chest.

"Now what's that you got on your neck?" asked the orderly having noticed a small but plainly visible raised red spot on the bottom left side of Sydney's neck. "Looks like a mosquito bite."

Sydney felt the site in question with his fingers. Indeed it was raised, and tender to the touch. "But it doesn't itch" he said.

"Then it's probably a little spider bite" said the orderly. "The cold drives them in lookin' for someplace warm. Well, enjoy your breakfast, Roger. The nurse will be around later with your medicine."

Across the country three thousand miles away Jessica's morning consisted of a hearty breakfast and excited chatter of the day's upcoming event and final preparations. It was not until after Jessica had dressed for the party that she found an hour of spare time to sit down with her computer to do the detective work that had been on her mind from the moment she awoke. In actuality she really did not know what it was that she would be setting out to prove if any correlation at all were to be found between the Professor and the information he offered her.

Searching public records on an individual and investigating that person's history is not a time consuming effort, even when the individual lived over a hundred years ago. Before the dawn of the computer age one only had written records, journals, books, photographs and even paintings as the only reference of information on those who lived before us. And even those sources covered only the mere tiniest spec of the overall populace in the history of humanity. But then along came the computer, that electronic brain that could permanently store a reservoir of information on every human being who lives or has lived within the civilized world during this technological era. Records of our birth and death and everything that has transpired in our lives in between, from who we married, our children and grandchildren, our parents and grandparents, our health and interests, where we lived, worked, shopped and played, even where in the world we have traveled has all been electronically documented and archived. And because of the capabilities available for eternally saving this information there has never been any need to dispose of it. It may not be what George Orwell envisioned in his novel *1984* when he coined the phrase *"Big Brother is watching you"*, but it can be concluded that Big Brother, through a profusion of resources, has been taking notes on us and storing those notes for posterity.

Jessica began by going right to the core of her investigation, her subject, a man named Roger Owen born on October 22, 1971 at University Hospitals. From that point, which was verified, she branched out to seek corroboration with the other particulars related to this man as told to her through her patient, Professor Hamilton. Little by little, bit by bit, she would find that everything he told her bore truth and accuracy.

Through her excitement there also lay confusion as to what it all meant until a knock at her door interrupted her focus.

"Company's arriving. Are you coming?" asked her brother, Tom.

"Yeah. I'll be right out."

She knew that concentrating on a party would be impossible at this point. She *had* to piece together a rational, or at least plausible, explanation for these findings. She trained her attention to the moment when Roger Owen went to sleep on the night of his fortieth birthday in the year 2011, and when Professor Sydney Hamilton awoke from a coma remembering nothing of his present life, but recalling only a past life. His *present* life. And a *past* life. But not just *a* past life.... *His* past life.

All of a sudden, like a great wave, a revelation of understanding poured over her. So powerful was it that it knocked her back into her chair in stunned amazement. With her mouth agape only three words were able to come to mind as she whispered them in a heavy sigh.

"Oh my God."

THREE

Certainly no tea party. And yet the room is filled with Mad Hatter's.

Recalling once again Alice's Adventures in Wonderland, this thought crossed Roger's mind in a futile effort to find some humor in an otherwise humorless environment. The room, or *social area* as it was referred to, was approximately the size of a high school auditorium. There, most of the nonviolent patients would be allowed to congregate during the day to *socialize*, though one would never really find much interaction going on. Aside from those who paced nervously about, the majority of them simply sat. Some carried on in the mannerisms characteristic to their mental illness, while others expressed little more than a vacant stare or look of paranoia. Still there were others who by all appearances seemed to be no more insane than Roger himself. These few would bide their time with a book or engage themselves in conversation, usually with a fellow patient who would behave oblivious to the other individuals' prattle.

Roger decided as early on as his first day there to speak as little as possible, figuring that the more he told them of himself the more he was bound to convince them that he was crazy. The only person he chose to converse with was the young orderly. Even if the young man did not believe a word of what he had told him, at least there was a sense of security in knowing that an orderly did not make the decision as to who should stay and who could leave.

Roger also fought hard against the willingness to believe that Dr. Wynn had betrayed and abandoned him to this *hell*. The moment his anger would begin to emerge from the thought of such a notion, he would remind himself repeatedly of her explanation for being away and the promise she made to return in four days. But life in an insane asylum would prove to be the longest four days Roger had ever experienced in his life - past or present.

Having come to terms days ago with the fact that this experience was anything but a dream, he spent most of his hours awake trying to theorize his own explanation of what happened. What brought him to this very real place over one hundred years in the future? And why in a body that was not his own? The only answer he could conjecture was that somehow, while asleep, his soul or spirit left his body and time traveled through a sort of wormhole - relying on science fiction phrases - and entered into the body of a man whose spirit had left, having given up the body for dead, thus leaving Roger's spirit a place to inhabit. Science fiction? Indeed. Did it make sense? Of course not. But then nothing of these bewildering circumstances made any sense.

So there he sat in the center ring of this demented circus until the voice of a hysterical woman brought his attention around to the outside corridor and the nurses' station where he found his savior, Dr. Wynn, embroiled in a dispute with the staff. Because of the thick glass partition separating the social area from the outer hall her words came across as muffled, although her body language was quite explicit with arms waving and the palm of her hand pounding down on the counter one, two, three times. Before long one of the staff doctors arrived on the scene only to have Jessica's identification and some loose papers thrust in front of his face. Roger could not help but find the whole spectacle just a bit comical. A still moment followed as the papers were read, and then, in unison, everyone turned their attention squarely on Roger and nodded. Roger responded with a slight wave as Jessica rolled her eyes back, shook her head, grabbed the papers, and marched into the social area. He immediately noticed a large bag she was holding that was stuffed with clothing.

"Professor Hamilton, I am *so* sorry. I had *no* idea this was going to happen."

"Pleasant trip? I hope your parents enjoyed their party."

Without recognizing the hint of sarcasm in his voice Jessica continued to apologize in earnest. "This is disgraceful. You never should have been sent here. I assure you that the person responsible for this has not heard the end of it from me."

"Apology accepted. Now if you could pull whatever strings that need to be pulled in order to get me out of here I would greatly appreciate it."

"I've already taken care of that, in case you hadn't noticed. What happened to your neck?"

"One of the patients here thinks he's Dracula."

Jessica's eyes widened in horror.

"I'm kidding" he assured her. "It's just a spider bite. I think."

Jessica shook her head. "I'm taking you out of this bug infested place. Are there any personal items of yours you need to gather up?"

"Personal items? How would I know what belongs to me if I don't even know who I am?"

"Well I figured you wouldn't have any street clothes with you so I took the liberty before coming here to gather up an outfit from your home. Your housekeeper was kind enough to assist me. And I also brought with me what I believe is the answer to what we were searching for."

"I do hope it's better than what *I* was able to come up with. Tell me."

"Not now. Let's first get you out of here."

City parks change little from generation to generation. Trees grow bigger and the city skyline surrounding them may change dramatically over the ages, but the parks themselves for the most part stay the same.

Although once the grounds for a cow pasture, public executions, and military training during the revolution, Boston Common, a fifty acre park nestled in the heart of Boston and America's oldest with its beginnings dating back to 1634, has seen few alterations to its present appearance in the past three hundred and seventy-seven years. So is also the case with Public Garden, a smaller adjoining botanical park to the west of Boston Common, separated by Charles Street, that was founded in 1837.

On this frigid February day, with the Elms and Maples bare of leaves and a good six inch layer of snow covering the ground, it was no surprise to find both parks void of any people. But for Roger, after spending a week in a hospital bed as well as in that windowless mental institute, the cold crisp air felt exhilarating and the sunshine upon his face unimaginably wonderful.

As he stood by the iron gated entrance to Public Garden at Arlington Street waiting for Jessica to return from a sidewalk hot dog vender nearby - *Some institutions are destined to always be with us*, he thought - Roger looked back at the park behind him and up at an imposing statue of George Washington atop his horse situated on an immense pedestal bearing his surname. He found it to be a small and peculiar comfort to see something older than himself still around. This same comfort was felt in a greater degree as he looked to the buildings directly across the street that flanked each side of a Parisian-style boulevard called Commonwealth Avenue. A boulevard 240 feet wide, with a 100-foot-wide central mall that divided the avenue in two opposite traffic directions, offered a park-like setting with benches, elm trees, and statues memorializing the once famous but now forgotten. The four, five, and six story Victorian structures, circa nineteenth century, were at one time aristocratic mansions boasting ornate facades and fanciful bay windows, but had since - even long before Roger's time - been broken up into luxury condos and apartments. Although not the residential showplaces found on Commonwealth Avenue, the stone buildings still reminded Roger of the old brownstones from the same era found in Chelsea and that night he brought Laura home after their first date.

In that predawn hour when the city belongs to the street sweepers and the fellows who deliver the newspapers, Roger held no expectations that he would be invited up to Laura's apartment, nor did he wish to say good-night to her from the inside of a taxicab, so he asked the cab driver to let them off at the corner of West 21st Street and Ninth Avenue where he could escort her for the short walk back to her building.

Both felt the evening had been a perfect success. Following a romantic dinner and an off-Broadway play, the warm evening was too pleasant to resist a stroll that would end at an all-night-diner where they continued to tell their life stories over coffee and a shared slice of coconut cream pie. And with the admission of their mutual attraction towards each other they were finally able to dispense with any nervous behavior and open up with an abundance of stimulating conversation.

"Well, here we are" she said, coming to a stop at the foot of the steps that led to her apartment building door. "I certainly had a wonderful time."

"Same here."

"I can't believe how fast the evening flew by."

"Yeah. Guess I'll just have to pick you up earlier next time."

It was Roger's way of inviting her on a second date. To which she sweetly replied;

"Yes. Earlier would be better."

What followed was that typical awkward hesitation that comes before that first goodbye kiss. Once their eyes locked, however, Roger moved in smooth and sure of himself. The kiss was subtle, tender, lasting longer than either one of them anticipated.

"Good-night" she whispered softly.

"Good-night."

Roger waited until she was out of sight behind the door of her building before leaving. He then proceeded down the sidewalk with a certain lighter-than-air dance to his every step and a feeling in his heart that this was the start of something big.

Jessica returned from the vendor with two hot dogs, handing him one and keeping the other for herself. He paused a moment, happy to see that this all-American favorite was still around.

"It's called a *hot dog*" she thoughtfully pointed out.

"Yes. I know. We ate them back then, too."

He grinned in amusement at her embarrassed smile.

The two strolled silently into the park, eating their hot dogs, while Jessica wondered how best to broach her theory and how he might react to it. Ahead of them, past the Washington statue, was a foot bridge built in 1867 that spanned over a small shallow lake, or *Lagoon* as it has always been known, that was now frozen. They did not cross the bridge but instead turned to the left taking a pathway cleared of snow towards the Lagoon's edge.

"Now again, which of those buildings behind us is the one you said is the home of this Professor?" he asked.

"You live in that building" pointing to the north side of Commonwealth Avenue. "The one with the red bricks and black trim. On the third floor. But before taking you there I first wanted to share with you my belief on what happened to you. You see, there's a chance that once you see the inside of your home, and those surroundings that *should* look familiar to you, the memory of who you are now might possibly surge back and the man you were *then* may fade away forever."

Roger looked at her perplexed. Feeling a bit nervous, she paused a moment and took a deep breath before continuing.

"Do you believe in reincarnation?"

Roger thought about it and shrugged his shoulders.

"Can't say I do. Can't say I don't. Something I never really thought about."

He stopped and looked at her with a vague expression.

"You're not saying... But reincarnation means someone who has had a *past* life. Not someone who is experiencing a life in the future. That doesn't make any...."

Taking a seat on a park bench along the Lagoon's bank, Roger's brow tightened as he tried to comprehend what she might be suggesting. Jessica sat down next to him studying his every reaction.

"Roger Owen *was* your past life. It's Sydney Hamilton's past life. What I believe happened is that your fall and the resulting coma brought to surface the memory of this past life, every detail of it up to a certain point, that point being Roger Owen's fortieth birthday. And then when you, Sydney Hamilton, awoke from your coma you were no longer able to recall who you are in this present life, but only the *memory* of a life you lived in the past."

She took a moment to let it all sink in before proceeding.

"You really are a psychological phenomenon. I don't know of any documented cases where a patient not only recalls but actually takes on the persona of a past life in the conscious mind rather than in the subconscious. You're fully awake in a sort of perpetual state of deep subconscious recollection that would normally take an expert hypnotist to bring out."

Roger stood and shook his head, refusing to believe her words because they sounded more probable than his own now seemingly ridiculous interpretation of events.

"It can't be. What proof do you have of this...this *theory?*"

"I'm afraid there is no hard proof when it comes to reincarnation. For most believers reincarnation is spiritual. A *transmigration of souls.* A characteristic found in at least four different Asian religions. In fact, eighty-five percent of the religions on this planet cede an underlying belief in reincarnation. But religion is based on faith. And science doesn't dwell on faith, it dwells on factual evidence. And the only evidence there has ever been with cases of reincarnation has been the detailed facts of lives lived often centuries ago through that same subconscious recollection by individuals, like you, living in the present."

"I still say it doesn't make any sense."

"It's the only thing that *does* make sense considering that everything you told me about Roger Owen is true. He really lived. And what I found most compelling of all for a doctrine that has always lacked any hard evidence is that you, Sydney Hamilton, were born on December 8, 2059.... Roger Owen *died* the same year on that same day."

With all living things death is the one certainty we commonly share. But what very few experience is being told the exact day they will die. A profound revelation that would assuredly come as a hard emotional blow to anyone. But to be informed of the day you *died* is beyond comprehension. The enormity of it sent Roger's mind swirling, practically in a daze. His life was over. Finished. This meant that the same would also be true for his wife and family as well. The thought was unthinkable. He then felt a sudden rush of hostility towards Jessica for informing him of this in a way he felt was heedless to his feelings.

"How can you sit there and tell me this with so little disregard to my feelings?"

Jessica, realizing immediately her lack of sensitivity, rose from the bench with a barrage of apologies while Roger continued to vent.

"You've just told me that I'm not only dead, but the actual day I died as well. No remorse. No compassion. No discretion to the fact that by what you're telling me means that my family is dead as well."

"I'm sorry!" she cried out in a voice louder than his that he finally heard. "It's difficult for me to look at you and not forget that the person I see on the outside is not the same person on the inside, but rather someone else. I'm sorry. I'm truly sorry. If you'd feel better talking with a certified Past Life Regression Therapist I can contact the International Board for Regression Therapy - "

"No!" Roger interrupted. "I don't want anyone else to know about this theory of yours."

After taking a moment to compose his thoughts and emotions, he tried once again to comprehend his plight.

"If I am to believe what you're telling me, that everything I've experienced from the time I was born to the time I went to sleep that night,...every recollection of my being right down to the most minuscule detail, is all simply a memory of a past life I lived one hundred and fourteen years ago,...then unless you've mastered time travel in this century there really is no hope that I will ever be able to go back."

"I'm afraid that's true. It's impossible."

He grew anxious. Fearful of her truth while refusing to believe it.

"No. This I won't accept. If I can't go back by whatever means brought me here then I'll find another way. There's *got* to be another way."

"We're talking about a *memory*, Professor. Buying these hot dogs at that vendor just a short while ago is now a part of my past. It's become a memory. But I can't travel back in time to relive it over again."

"Yes, however, you *can* physically go back to that vendor. As long as he's out there you can go back again and again and again!"

All at once the dire realization of what she was trying to make him understand became all too clear.

"But you're still living" he said softly. "Whereas my life has already ended.... So how can I physically go back to my Laura...and my children, if they only exist in my mind? Tyler, Justin, my beautiful Natalie."

And with that the feeling of total loss of his loved ones came crashing down upon him.

"Oh God."

Practically in a stagger he crossed a few feet through the snow over to the edge of the Lagoon where his trembling legs gave out from under him, dropping him to his knees. Jessica was uncertain whether to rush over to comfort him or leave him be. She decided it would be best to allow him this moment alone as she watched him look up to the heavens before bowing his head in grief.

Upon opening the door Jessica allowed Roger to enter first.

"Is that you, Dr. Wynn?" asked Mrs. Deere before emerging from the kitchen.

A warm, cheerful, slightly heavyset lady in the same age range as her employer, Mrs. Deere began her career as the Professor's housekeeper nearly ten years ago. On appearance one would say they look like the perfect couple. But their relationship was strictly professional with the only emotional bond being the lonely void that was filled through each other's company.

"And look who we have here. Welcome home Professor."

This long awaited moment for Jessica and Mrs. Deere, a moment of whether the Professor would recognize a person he personally knew prior to his accident, brought a tense feeling of anticipation. They both studied his eyes hoping to find in them a glimmer of familiarity. But through his eyes he saw nothing. The moment proved anticlimactic, prompting him to merely respond in kind as he would to a stranger on the street.

"Thank you."

"I have a pot of hot tea steeping for you. I'll be right out with it" she said, turning in haste towards the kitchen.

"Uh, thank you again, but I really don't care for hot tea. A cup of coffee would be nice if it's not too much trouble."

"No trouble at all. I'll have it for you in a jiffy."

Mrs. Deere smiled, gave a concerned glance to Jessica, and then promptly entered the kitchen where out of view from the others she took pause as her eyes welled up with tears.

Roger looked at Jessica, nodded in the direction of the kitchen and mouthed the words, *"Who's she?"*

"Mrs. Deere. Your housekeeper. She's worked for you for nearly ten years" she whispered. "Not even familiar?"

He shook his head and then went about closely observing the aspects of his surroundings. The sitting room, dining room and study were distinct individual areas, but not separate rooms closed off from one another. Only the kitchen was out of sight by means of a two way door, as well as the Professor's bedroom located down a short hallway. He immediately found comfort in this spacious apartment. Though this was not due to any recall of memory, but rather a marvelous sense of acknowledgement of things from his era and before. For Sydney Hamilton's home was not adorned with possessions of the present, which for Roger meant all things unfamiliar to him in the future. Instead the dark paneled room was filled with antiques and artifacts from centuries past. He likened it to a private part-museum, part-library, for all around there was also an enormous abundance of books. Books everywhere. Packed on shelves, stacked on tables, covering every subject from every period in history imaginable.

"So many books."

He ran his finger down the length of one such tall stack of books.

"I've never been much of a reader" he added.

There were seven books that stood out for being conspicuously placed together, but separate from the others. He immediately noticed that these seven books were written by the same author - Sydney Hamilton.

"A writer, too."

One particular shelf caught his attention for its impressive collection of cameras. Old Kodak and Ansco box cameras, a Folding Brownie, a Field Camera and Imperial Triple, a Graflex, several Bell & Howel's, a 1960's Polaroid, a 1970's Instamatic and a conspicuously out of place Nikon Coolpix L24 digital. It was this camera he grabbed with a smile and playfully tossed in the air.

"I have this very same camera."

Jessica gasped. "Uh, I'd be careful with that. It's an antique you know."

"And I thought turning forty made me feel old."

He gently returned the camera to its place on the shelf and once more did a quick glance about the room.

"Nothing?"

"I feel like an intruder" he quipped.

"There now, I told you that wouldn't take long" said Mrs. Deer as she came through the kitchen door holding a tray with two cups of coffee, a creamer and sugar bowl.

"And I prepared yours, Professor, just the way you like it - cream with two lumps of sugar. Although I failed to ask how you would like yours, Dr. Wynn. So I just brought you a little bit of both in case you have a special way you like to drink it."

"Thank you, Mrs. Deere" said Roger and Jessica simultaneously.

"Now if you'll excuse me, there are just a few things I need to pick up at the grocery store for tonight's supper. I'm making lamb chops."

She looked directly at the Professor with a smile, expecting a reaction. But none was given.

"Your favorite?" she continued.

"Oh yes, of course. That sounds delicious. Thank you."

But his response was given only in politeness to the kind lady.

"Very well then, I'll leave you two alone. I won't be long though."

They bade her goodbye as she slipped out the door with a large purse and heavy coat.

"Is she *always* here?" he asked.

"No. She arrives in the morning to make your breakfast and stays until after your supper has been served."

Roger appeared to accept this arrangement with a nod and then looked down at the coffee disappointedly.

"I drink mine black."

"Then you can have mine. I happen to drink it with cream and sugar. Though with only one lump."

He smiled as he picked up the coffee cup and saucer.

"And the lamb chops?" she asked.

"Oh I like lamb chops. Fortunately. Although I wouldn't call them my *favorite*."

There was one table at the far end of the room that caught his attention for not having any books whatsoever on it, but instead a gallery of numerous framed photographs on display.

With cup and saucer in hand he strolled over to the table. The photographs seemed to peak his interest in a way that nothing else in the room had up to that point. There were photos of the Professor as a very young man and as he appeared throughout the different ages of his life, always with the same beautiful woman by his side. There was a wedding photo of the two, telling him that they were obviously husband and wife - at least at one point. And there were also photos of what he assumed to be their daughter, from baby photos on up to those of a young woman with a husband of her own and their child.

He set his coffee cup down enabling him to pick up a few of the pictures for closer study.

"It's your....*his* family" she finally said, breaking the silence.

"So I figured. Is this his wife?"

"Her name is Margaret. But everyone called her Marge."

"*Called?* I take it she's no longer alive?"

Jessica shook her head.

"And the rest of his family? Where are they?"

"Dead."

"Not *all* of them!" he said with astonishment.

"Sadly, I'm afraid so. He lost them all to the pandemic."

"The pandemic. This pandemic has been mentioned to me once before. What pandemic is this that would take a man's entire family?"

"It took more than *his* family. Millions of families perished. Whole *generations* were wiped out. It began ten years ago during the summer of 2115. An unusually hot summer as I recall. In its four month duration it took the lives of over one hundred and fifty-two million people worldwide. A pandemic on a scale the world hadn't experienced since the influenza outbreak of 1918 when original estimates put the death rate at twenty-one to thirty million. But Epidemiologists later revised that number to at least fifty or possibly one hundred million deaths globally.   But unlike the 1918 flu pandemic, where the origin began here in the U.S., the origin of the 2115 pandemic was in Brazil, from which point it quickly circumnavigated the earth. As far and fast as man could travel, so too did the virus. Large cities were the hardest hit. Hospitals ran out of beds for the infected. Makeshift morgues spilled out onto the streets. But the virus spread to even the most remote regions of the world as well, obliterating entire village populations. Not a single nation on the planet was spared. When taken into consideration the world population eight hundred years ago its death ratio exceeded that of the bubonic plague, or Black Death as it was better known, that began in Asia in 1346, and then swept over Europe by the following year. And whereas the estimated thirty million who perished in the Black Death happened in a period between 1346 and 1350, the pandemic of 2115 hit within a period of four months causing panic and hysteria on unprecedented levels. How do I know so much about these past pandemics? During those four months, while bodies were piling up on streets faster than they could be buried, the public was inundated by the media with the history of previous pandemics.   The years 1918 and 1346 were ingrained in everyone's mind. This time the flu-like symptoms came from a virus that was virtually unknown until 2115. But just like the 1918 virus that killed more people in one year than the Black Death did in one century, the 2115 virus hit hard and killed fast.   It wasn't uncommon for a person to board a jet, a train, or even a subway feeling mildly fatigued, only to be found dead upon it reaching its destination. The only people you'd find not wearing a surgical mask as a preventative measure against contracting the virus were those already dead by it.   In that short period of time economies over the world collapsed because people were too frightened to go to work or even step foot out of their homes, except for food. Public events were canceled. Restaurants closed. Travel came to a standstill, except for those desperately trying to flee the cities, which most did by any means other than public transport because all travel by air, rail, and sea was halted in an effort to stop it from spreading further. It didn't matter if you were young, old, middle aged, rich, poor, healthy or not, the virus didn't discriminate. It knew no boundaries. It crossed all races and cultures. Although to this day doctors have never been able to figure out why some individuals escaped infection of this highly contagious virus, especially in households where the mere breath of one infected is all that it would take to pass on the airborne microbes to another. But some lucky ones, as best they can figure, must have had an auto-immunity to the virus."

"Such was the case with this Professor?"

"Apparently. Mrs. Deere informed me that his grandson was the first from his family to die from it, followed by his only child, his daughter, then his son-in-law. A couple of months later his wife eventually succumbed to it. He lost his entire family, but he lived on."

"Something I can finally relate to in this man" he said softly to himself. "And what about you? How did you and your family manage?"

"I was still living at home with my parents at the time. And fortunately for us they lived, and still do, in a home protected from the nearest human by acres of vineyards. When news first broke about the virus and how fast it was spreading, my parents took immediate action by stocking up with all the necessary provisions to keep us quarantined from the outside world until it ended and the danger of coming in contact with others was finally over."

"And how *did* it end?"

"Like with previous pandemics throughout history, this one just ran its course. Ending as suddenly and mysteriously as it began."

There fell a moment of silence as Roger tried to grasp the enormity of what she was telling him.

"Horrific" came the only word he could think of.

"Yes. That's one event of his past that you're lucky not to remember. But before he lost his memory and you surfaced, what happened to him and his family was a part of his past that he *wouldn't* stop remembering. He was never able to let go of it and move on...except into this place. According to Mrs. Deere, after it was all over and life, for the most part, gradually got back to normal, the Professor moved out of his home in Chestnut Hill where he and his wife raised their daughter and into what he called "this modest dwelling" closer to the university campus. It was then he hired her and the two have rarely spent a day apart ever since. She went on to explain to me that with the loss of his family and the loss of her own husband twelve years ago, you two have helped alleviate *some* of the loneliness in each other's lives. Although their relationship, she assures me, has always been strictly platonic and professional. Part of this reason, she believes, is because of the sorrow that has overwhelmed him over the past ten years. He would just teach, study, write, seldom smile, never laugh, and never allow himself to grow close to anyone. Then he suddenly grew even more despondent than usual, leaving Mrs. Deere and the investigators to suspect it was a suicide attempt through that window."

The mention of suicide brought a natural reaction of surprise from Roger.

"Suicide!? You told me he fell."

"I told you it was a fall because I didn't feel it would be wise to lay suicide on you during our first meeting."

"Well you sure saved up an awful lot to lay on me today, Doc. The loss of two families that I'll never see again. Pandemic. Death. Is there anything else you've left out? Fire, flood, famine?"

Once again Jessica started in with a string of apologies as Roger moved directly over to the supposed suicide bay window.

"This window?" he asked, interrupting her.

"Yes. That's the one."

He unlatched the window lock and opened the frosted windowpane casement allowing a frigid rush of air to enter. Peering over the windowsill he was unable to see the ground three stories directly below due to the thick foliage of an enormous bush that hugged the side of the building. He did not take long to examine the apparent scene of the incident before merely shaking his head, closing the window, and then turning to Jessica and stating rather matter-of-factually;

"This wasn't a suicide attempt."

Taken aback by his assertion, Jessica took a moment before responding.

"But the change in his demeanor preceding it was witnessed by people he knew..."

"Did he leave a suicide note?" he interrupted once again.

"No."

"Then killing himself was never his intention, even if he *did* jump. He surely would have known that the thick bush directly below the window would break his fall substantially. It doesn't surprise me that he only suffered a dislocated shoulder, some bruises, a few scratches - "

"And a coma" Jessica injected, wanting to make certain he not think lightly of his injuries.

"Of course. Which, if not for that, I would not be here...In mind at least."

"So you're saying he fell?"

"I'm not saying he fell. The space between the floor and the bottom sill is too high for him to simply fall over unless he was *sitting* on the sill with the window opened and lost his balance. But then one would have to ask why would he be doing that when the outside temperature is below freezing? Certainly Mrs. Deere would have mentioned it if this was a typical behavior of his."

If he did not jump and he did not fall this left only one other word to explain how Sydney Hamilton would end up going through that open window to the ground below. They both knew what that one word was but neither one of them would speak it. After a moment of contemplating the absurdity of such a notion, Jessica shook her head and refused to accept the possibility.

"You're speaking as Roger Owen. And obviously Roger Owen can look out that window and determine that that fall wouldn't kill him if he wanted to commit suicide. But Professor Hamilton evidently thought it would."

"Roger Owen never had a reason in his life to consider suicide."

It was the first time Jessica heard him speak of himself in the third person.

Shortly afterwards Mrs. Deere arrived back with a bundle of groceries. No other mention was made regarding Roger's or Sydney's families, or the pandemic, nor the incident at the window. Mrs. Deere joined the two of them for supper, as it had become the customary thing for her to do with the Professor less than a year after her employment began. Conversation over the meal - which commenced with Cream of Asparagus soup, lamb chops with Rosemary and mint jelly, braised root vegetables and a fine 2105 vintage Burgundy - was kept light and mostly between Jessica and Mrs. Deere, often drifting from current events that were happening in the world to asking questions of what life was like in the late twentieth and early twenty-first centuries,..yet always careful not to bring up his family. Nevertheless his family was always in the forefront of his thoughts. For this reason he said little and ate even less, trying to eat just enough so as not to appear rude or ungrateful for the effort Mrs. Deere had put into the meal. Although he managed to find a hearty appetite for the dessert of rice pudding, of which he had plenty of room for seconds.

Jessica stayed long enough to help Mrs. Deere with the clean up that followed, and then left, leaving Roger at last alone in these unfamiliar surroundings he was expected to regard as home.

It had been a long and emotional day, from the time he awoke in the asylum, to the park, and then ending it here at this man's apartment. He could not remember when he had ever felt so exhausted or emotionally drained. He entered the bedroom and felt no reservations of wanting to crawl under the covers of this man's big comfortable looking bed - after a week sleeping in hospital beds - but had his own nightly routine of things to do before doing so. He felt it best to familiarize himself with where things were kept. Opening the closet door he found it orderly and well stocked with clothes. *Old man clothes* he thought to himself. *I'd never wear any of these.*

He moved over to a dresser and began opening drawers which made him feel like a snoop or a prowler and a trifle uncomfortable. There, in one drawer, he found pajamas. Roger was always a boxers or briefs man when sleeping, except on those beautiful nights when he and Laura would make love and the two of them would sleep until dawn with their naked bodies pressed snugly against each other. But the Professor was obviously a pajamas man, perhaps so as not to offend Mrs. Deere who would arrive at sunrise each morning. It took him awhile to decide whether to put them on or not. They were not his, yet on the other hand they *were*, and had been worn on the body he was in probably numerous times. That rational won out and he eventually dressed himself in the pajamas.

Next he went to the bathroom to finish preparing himself before bed. He looked at his reflection in the mirror and studied his new features with great scrutiny. *So old*, he thought. *And I thought turning forty was difficult.*

He noticed that the swelling and redness on his neck caused by insect bite had dissipated. It was also no longer tender to the touch where only a light pink spot remained. But when it came to his next ritual, brushing his teeth, he was faced with another uncomfortable challenge greater than putting on the pajamas - putting the toothbrush that belongs to another man into his mouth. Again he told himself that the toothbrush had already brushed the same teeth he was looking at in the mirror. It was not someone else's toothbrush but *his*. He rolled out a fine line of toothpaste and brought the toothbrush to his lips, but ultimately could not bring himself to placing the toothbrush into his mouth. With that he dropped the toothbrush into the waist basket and went to bed.

As he laid on the bed in the dark room he found it impossible to fall immediately asleep despite his fatigue as the memories of his family, his parents, brothers and sisters, children, and of course Laura, and the thought of never seeing them again dominated his weary mind. He began to weep uncontrollably from his sorrow until slumber came at last.

He never left the apartment during the three days that followed. Where would he go? Even if it were still 2011, Boston was not a familiar city to him, and getting lost would be an excitement he felt he could very well do without.

By the second day he actually looked forward to Mrs. Deere's morning arrival. He welcomed the company and her constant chatter on simple subjects such as who she stopped and talked to in the park, the price of this or that, and her own memories of how things used to be back in the early second half of the twenty-first century, or "the good old days" as she fondly referred to it, when she and her husband were a young couple. He would listen politely and intently to her every word, but rarely offered any dialogue of his own. To him it was all enigmatic, and Mrs. Deere sensed this, but he enjoyed the feeling of normalcy it brought him, and she felt that by carrying on as usual might eventually begin the processes of bringing back bits of his memory little by little. He was also grateful for her eagerness to accommodate without question his simplistic little requests, such as buying him a new toothbrush.

Throughout these days he occupied the rest of his time with browsing through more photographs as well as the books written by the

Professor.   Or he would gaze out the window to observe the pedestrians, all bundled up under layer upon layer of clothing with often only their eyes peeking through under the rims of their hats and above the mufflers wrapped snugly across their noses and mouths. To and fro he would watch them scurry along the frozen sidewalks, carefully with every step not to slip on the occasional patch of ice, as they would make their way to wherever their destinations may be that will bring them immediate warmth.

It was on the second day of watching these hearty soles brave the freezing climate when he noticed a peculiar sight. It was a man dressed in a long black coat and a matching color hat standing in the middle of the Commonwealth Avenue Mall directly across from his building. He was uncertain of his age for the distance was too great. But there was no mistaking that this mystery man was staring at the building. He stood motionless with his hands in his coat pockets, never once diverting his attention away from the building in front of him. In fact, it was not long before Roger began to suspect that the man was looking directly at *him*.

"Would you like your afternoon tea served here or in the study, Professor?" came Mrs. Deere's voice, momentarily drawing his attention away from the window.

"Here would be fine, Mrs. Deere. Thank you."

Afternoon tea.   What I wouldn't give instead for a shot of strong Cuban coffee - he thought to himself, remembering this afternoon practice at his job site that was such a traditional part of the south Florida community where in thimble-sized cups, *un cafecito*, a powerful blend of sugar and caffeine would give the workers that much needed jolt, or *mule kick* as it was referred to in his office, to get them through the rest of the day.

Turning back towards the window he saw that the mystery man was gone. No sign of him could be found in either direction from his panoramic viewpoint three stories up.

One of the pastimes he found most awe-inspiring was the electronic device that he was not surprised to find still around a hundred years later - the television. With no remote controls to frustrate oneself over, it took Mrs. Deere's assistance to instruct him how to turn the television on by simply saying, "Television on." Although it was not the innovation of voice activation commands that so amazed him but rather the 3-dimensional images that the screen projected. Yet this was not achieved in the holographic sense, for there was still a flat screen that he likened to looking at a fish tank where, depending on from which angle it was viewed, he would see different aspects of the picture. For example when viewing a news program he would look at the screen from his far right and see the left side of the anchor persons face looking straight ahead. When viewing it from his left he would see that same anchor person's right side. An on-the-scene report of an accident or incident would bring the event more seemingly live into the home, only in miniature. The same could be said regarding other programs such as situation comedies, dramas, concerts, and stage productions which brought to him the feeling of being in a theater where a live theatrical performance could be viewed from different angles depending on where one sat.

From the kitchen door ajar only a crack Mrs. Deere could not help herself but to spy on him and observe with humor the odd sight of this man she had known for ten years as being invariably serious and somber, carry on like a young child full of wonderment as he would move about left to right, up and down, and every other which way possible while studying something so common and that has been around for so long as 3-dimensional television.

The highlight of each day of his, however, would not come from anything seen on television, but would be the expected visits made by Jessica. Her presence, just the sight of her, would warm him from within with a feeling of security and comfort like that of an old friend amongst strangers, even though their total days together could be counted on one hand. Perhaps it was because she knew as much of what was going on with him as he did himself. She believed in him and who he is...or *was*. Therefore there was a sense of not being alone, of being in this together, and knowing that she was going to do what she could to bring resolution to the matter, whatever that resolution may be.

On the third day since he arrived at the home of Professor Sydney Hamilton, Jessica, showing a growing concern over his inability to remember anything of who he is in the present, offered a solution that might bring back his full memory. Reasoning that if under hypnosis many have been able to recall a past life, then quite possibly under hypnosis one might also be able to remember everything about their present life and awake with that memory still intact. And since hypnosis was a field of intense interest and study during her years majoring in Psychiatry she would be eager to test this theory on him if he was willing.

Roger felt immediate reservations towards accepting this proposal. Not because he did not believe it *would* work, on the contrary, for it was the belief he felt that it would work that prompted his reluctance to accept.

"Look around us and you see a room full of photographs. Memories of this man's life and family. But what do I have to remind me of the life and family I loved so, yet no longer have? Nothing. No photographs. No mementos. Only what's up here. In my memory. Now if you can't guarantee me that if when I awake from this hypnosis I'll still remember every intimate detail of my life as Roger Owen, as well as the life of this Professor, then I'll have no part of it. I'd rather go on living my life with only these cherished memories of my loved ones than to lose that forever just so that I can live out what's left of this old man's life, knowing more about the people in those photographs, the tragic means by which he lost them, and the loneliness and sorrow he carries with him every day."

The following day Jessica took Roger to the downtown district to join her in lunch at one of her favorite restaurants. Her vehicle, like all vehicles of the time, took owner voice recognition and commands to an astonishing level. By telling the vehicle computer the exact address or place of one's desired destination - example, *"work"* or *"home"* - the vehicle would go into a sort of *auto-pilot* mode and drive itself to that destination while obeying all the traffic laws, adjusting for variable weather conditions, and stopping appropriately for other vehicles, pedestrians or additional road obstacles, thus reducing vehicle accidents dramatically. The driver would only need to sit back and enjoy the ride. Perfect for city driving or long road trips. Of course, if the driver did not know his or her exact destination, one could simply disable the autopilot and drive the vehicle manually - or rather the *"old fashion"* way.

It was his first outing out since he left the asylum, and his first hard look at the extent to which mankind had progressed towards technical advances and structural achievements. As he looked out the window of Jessica's vehicle and marveled at the sights and sounds surrounding him he was reminded of the feeling he got as a child when his folks took the family to Disneyland and the riveting impact Tomorrowland made upon his young impressionable mind.

The topic of hypnotism weighed heavily on Roger's conscience ever since the subject was brought up the previous day. He decided to choose their luncheon to broach the issue once again, only this time he had a radically different approach to her proposal. And assuming that she too would find his idea outlandish, he decided it would be best for him to begin their conversation tackling yet another more simpler issue.

"You know, I'll never get used to you calling me Professor. It's just not *me*."

"I'm sorry you feel that way, but I'll never be able to look at you and see anyone else but Professor Hamilton because.....Well, I'll just never see you as Roger."

"You were going to give a reason. *"Because"* why?"

Jessica looked down at her menu in an effort to hide her blushing face.

"The corned beef sandwiches are delicious here. They really pile it on with the corned beef. Do you like corned beef, Professor Hamilton?"

"Why Dr. Wynn I do believe you're skirting the question."

"And what question would that be again, Professor Hamilton?"

"You were going to give a reason as to why you can't see me as anyone else but Professor Hamilton. Because....?"

With a sheepish grin she lowered her menu and looked directly at him.

"*Because*...you were *my* Professor."

His reaction at first was puzzlement. Then with a cock of his head and a finger pointed at himself he grinned.

"Yes, you" she continued. "Not only did I begin my practice in Boston, I also earned my degree here. At Harvard. And one of my courses was World History."

"And I was your teacher?"

"Professor" she was quick to correct.

"Then you were my student" he said with a broad smile, deriving a bit of humor from the coincidence of it all.

"Well, yeah, that's typically how it goes. Professor. Student. Student. Professor. Are you ready to order now?"

"Tell me, did the student ever have a secret crush on this Professor?"

"Professor Hamilton! Please don't refer to us in the third person. I'm here and you're right there and..."

Flustered and blushing even more prominently than before she recoiled back into her menu. Roger, on the other hand, surprised that his jest might have actually bore some truth based on her reaction and not wishing to embarrass her further, decided to withdraw his questioning on the subject.

"Nevertheless" she finally spoke up. "It's for that reason why I can't look at you and think of anyone but Professor Hamilton."

"Understood. But I'll still never get used to being called Professor. So I'll tell you what. How 'bout a compromise? If you can't call me Roger, you may call me Sydney, on the terms that I may drop the doctor and refer you by your first name....Whatever that may be."

"Agreed. And it's Jessica."

"Jessica. A pretty name at that."

"Thank you....Sydney."

"I like that, too. Doesn't it feel so much better dispensing with all the formalities of titles and such?"

"Yes it does" she said with a smile.

"So why didn't you tell me you were a student of mine?"

"Because I was hoping that just maybe you might remember me. But after seeing how you didn't even recognize Mrs. Deere, not to mention your entire family, then who was I to think that you might actually remember the face of one of your many *many* students from several years back?"

This resolution over their names and the ensuing lighthearted revelation made by Jessica brought about a closer feeling towards her than he had felt before, and ironically the same type of closeness she had hoped for in years gone by. From that moment on their conversation over lunch continued on the same carefree path until Sydney found the appropriate moment to revisit her hypnosis theory.

"But I thought you were explicitly against it" she said with surprise. "You mean to tell me you're willing to let me hypnotize you?"

"Yes, but in a way that I hope and believe will produce a different outcome than the one you theorized. I want you to bring me back to my fortieth birthday as Roger Owen, actually the morning after, so that I can resume living the life I can't remember."

"I'm not sure I understand."

"It's simple really. If it's possible for you to bring back through hypnosis all the memories of Sydney's life, then why shouldn't you be able to bring me back to my last memory of being Roger and then let that memory continue its due course from that point forward?"

Her expression told him he was correct in assuming that she would find his idea outlandish, but he was not prepared for her outright opposition to it.

"You mean, rather than just remember everything of Roger's life up to the day he died, you're wanting instead to continue living his life through memory just as if it was really happening? The same way you experienced it before?"

"Exactly."

"But in order for that to work, *if* it would work, you would have to be kept in a perpetual state of unconsciousness."

"Yes. I know. That seems to be the only way."

"But that's impossible."

"Why? If people can be kept alive while in a coma - "

"Because it is unethical for anyone to be placed in a coma purposely" she interrupted. "It's just not done. Besides, what about Sydney? What about his life? Because you don't remember it doesn't make it right for you to take away the remainder of this man's life that other people *do* remember, and know, and love."

"But what kind of a life would you be bringing back to him? A life of loneliness and sadness? To hell with everyone who knows him, what about Sydney? What would Sydney want? And what about me? What about Roger? Let's not dismiss the fact that the life that ended for me was a life I loved and want to go back to. This isn't my world. My world is with my family."

Jessica paused long enough to contemplate his argument and finally accepted his reasons for wanting to take this bold move. However, it did not sway her opinion as to whether it would be the right thing to do.

"And what happens when Sydney dies? What happens to the life you're reliving in his mind?"

"Who can say? Who can explain why reincarnation even happens? Why does it happen to some and not others? Or does it happen to everyone but only a few can recall their past lives? And if that's true then what about heaven? Where does heaven fit in? There are simply hundreds of questions without any definitive answers. But one thing I do know for certain, and that is that my life wasn't even half over. I lived a long life. I grew old. And I want to experience everything I missed out on getting to that ripe old age."

Jessica thought about it further but ultimately could not be moved to accept his reasoning for going through with it based on her ethics as a doctor.

"I'm sorry. Putting a person's mind into an eternal state of sleep until the body eventually dies,..we just don't do that sort of thing. Not even in the twenty-second century."

The finality in her tone cast a gloom over the rest of their luncheon that would stay with them throughout the ride back to his home.

Before reaching their destination, Sydney - having come to terms with the fact that he should now resign himself to that name - asked Jessica to let him out of the vehicle at the stoplight on the corner of Tremont Street and Boylston - the South-East end of Boston Common - so that he may walk the remainder of his way home through the park. He had to assure her several times over that this surprising request was not on account of him being angry with her. For this was undeniably the truth. How could one possibly be angry when looking into the eyes of such a sweet and lovely face? Or find fault with someone who believes and honors her ethics so faithfully?

Although she did not attempt to talk him out of this impromptu trek of his, she did express her concerns.

"Have you any idea of the distance from here to Commonwealth Avenue?"

"I've walked one end of Central Park to the other. Boston Common can't be much greater than that."

"And suppose you get lost? How will you be able to contact me since you refused to bring along your mobile?"

"I didn't bring it because I wouldn't know who to call. Nor would I know anyone who might try calling me."

"In this day and age we have something called GPS...."

"Global Positioning System. Yes, I know what it is. We had them during my day and age, being a standard app in smart phones, or *mobile*, as you refer to it. Really, there's no need to worry. I promise not to get lost. I just need some time alone, and with Mrs. Deere there...."

And then as if on cue to further her case, light snow flurries began to fall.

"Now it's snowing. You really don't want to walk back with it snowing, do you?"

"I've walked through snowy conditions before. I *am* originally from Cleveland, let's not forget. Born and raised" - which sounded rather bizarre being spoken with such a prominent British accent.

"Now don't worry" he continued while stepping out of the vehicle. "I'll phone you when I arrive home. And *don't* follow. I'll be fine."

Although not feeling completely secure with this bold step he was determined to undertake, she reluctantly realized that it was nevertheless a step he *should* take in order to begin the processes of reacquainting himself with his surroundings.

After crossing the Tremont Street intersection he then entered the park. With not a single person in sight Sydney felt complete solitude as he set out along a path that would take him towards the center of the park. It was the solitude he had hoped to find in order to contemplate the issues of what transpired over lunch. The bitter cold did not take away from the pleasure he was deriving from the utter silence and stillness surrounding him. And the fresh snow blanketing the ground filled him with a tranquil feeling that justified his reason for embarking on this little solo adventure of his.

To his left he passed an old burying ground where a tight cluster of skewed headstones were surrounded by a wrought iron fence. Further along to his right he passed Parkman Bandstand, an early twentieth century round structure with a dome covering. But the serenity he felt would end too soon when suddenly he was overcome with the unnerving sense of being watched. Yet looking ahead and over his shoulders in both directions he found no one there. He did not stop, but he did, however, slow his pace as paranoia, a trait he was unaccustomed to, began to set in.

It's only your imagination. There's no one else around, so he kept telling himself. And with the only movement as far as his eyes could see being the snowflakes, which were becoming larger and denser as they floated and swirled their way downward, he gradually grew convinced that it was indeed just that - his imagination.

Pressing onward and picking up his pace with a renewed sense of calm, Sydney passed a great Civil War monument to his right. It was at this point he made a sharp turn to his left towards Charles Street. Across this street lay the entrance to Public Garden and beyond that the foot bridge.

That wasn't so difficult, he thought proudly to himself over his accomplishment for not getting lost. In the distance, at the opposite end of the bridge, he could even see the large statue of Washington on his horse.

After crossing Charles he began his way over the foot bridge. Midway across he glanced down to the frozen lagoon where a gaggle of Canadian geese had gathered below him. When he looked back up he was suddenly stopped dead in his tracks, for directly ahead of him at the end of the bridge there stood a dark figure. Sydney immediately recognized the lonesome stranger as the same man he had noticed from the previous day staring at his building. He was dressed the same, black coat and hat, and stood gazing at him in the same manner, with hands in his pockets. This time, however, he was much closer so that Sydney was able to distinguish the man's age as being approximately in his late forties or early fifties. His face was sullen, cold, with pale ash color skin and beady eyes that were set close together. An altogether sinister looking fellow that summoned a wary feeling in Sydney that told him to avoid this person, that he was dangerous. Although he could deduce no reason to support this intuition, he only knew that he needed to get away from him, to where there are other people, which meant out of the park.

Wanting not to provoke a chase, Sydney ever so subtly turned away from him and started back with a steady pace in the direction of Charles Street. He looked over his shoulder to see if the man was following. He was. So Sydney increased his stride only to look around again to find that the mysterious man was quick to do the same. Upon reaching the end of the bridge Sydney abruptly decided to take a quick left and head down a flight of steps that led to the base of the bridge and a pathway that ran alongside the east bank of the lagoon. At this time Sydney did not dwell on the question of who this man is. There would be time to contemplate that later. But several things were certain. If the Professor knew who this man was before the coma, he had no memory of him now. And it was obvious that this mystery man did not have conversation on his mind. There would have been opportunity for that had he just knocked on his door rather than staring at his building from across the street. Nor was this person settled on merely observing him from a distance, as evident now by his ongoing pursuit. No, this man was definitely after him and it was not Sydney's intention to find out why with no one else around to turn to should he need help.

When Sydney reached a split in the pathway he looked over his shoulder again to find his pursuer following him down the same steps. He hesitated a moment before choosing the path to the right which lead towards Charles Street and what appeared to be the busy intersection of another thoroughfare. He picked up his pace and kept his focus straight ahead at the park exit before him.

Beacon Street was not the bustling horde Sydney had hoped to find when he finally reached its intersection with Charles Street. Perhaps it was on account of the weather. Nevertheless, he was relieved to find at least *some* pedestrians out and about. And when he looked around to discover his pursuer was gone, he breathed a sigh of relief. *It worked*, he thought to himself. *Whatever it is he wants, he's not going to mess with me with other people around.*

But this false sense of security was not to last. Having barely walked a quarter block due west towards his home on Commonwealth, he once again came face to face with the mystery man standing straight ahead of him on the same sidewalk - hands still in his pockets and that same menacing stare.

The bastard knows where I live and took the left path to head me off.

Sydney knew better than to chance passing him, regardless that they were not alone. So without hesitation he crossed Beacon while heading in the opposite direction back towards Charles Street and away from his home.

I'll find another way past him.

He noticed that the man had crossed Beacon as well. It was obvious that he was not going to give up so easily.

Feeling that his only hope for finding safety would be if he could make it home, Sydney knew he would have to wind his way through various streets leading in that direction in a desperate effort to elude the stranger. So before coming to Charles Street he turned on to a far smaller road called River Street. And what he discovered upon rounding that corner left him dumbfounded. Suddenly he found himself back in time. *Way* back. Much further than whence he came. The dark narrow street with its uneven brick sidewalks, gas lamps, and red brick buildings resembled to him something straight out of America's colonial past. Yet this was not another time warp he stumbled into but rather a historical quarter of Boston known as Beacon Hill. Although not going quite as far back as colonial times, it was nevertheless a well preserved and protected area dating to the first half of the nineteenth century.

But there was no time to waste by slowing his stride in order to take in the visual appeal of it all. A leisurely tour of this unique neighborhood would have to be saved for a later date, he told himself as he hurried around a corner continuing eastward onto the much wider Chestnut Street. Once again, however, he was faced with the unsettling feeling of being on a street void of any other pedestrians. And this uneasiness was only heightened with no sight of the mystery man behind him. Surely this person knows these streets better than he and could suddenly emerge from around any corner or alley at a moment's notice. Nevertheless, he continued up the slight incline of Chestnut Street and past Charles until he stopped to catch his breath and reevaluate his strategy for losing the one who is after him while finding his way back home. Fearing that at any moment his pursuer might round the corner onto Chestnut Street, Sydney decided it would be best to take full advantage of this maze of tree-named streets that were both long and short, uphill and downhill, by weaving his way in and out of them in a roundabout direction that would lead him home. He was wishing he had brought that mobile phone to summon Jessica. But it was too late for regrets now. He had to remain focused on his surroundings and the direction he needed to follow or he would surely find himself lost.

He crossed the road onto West Cedar Street, a narrower street with another incline, and then made another turn eastward onto Acorn Street. What he found was most certainly the steepest and narrowest of all the streets thus far, barely wide enough for a single vehicle. *More fitting for a horse and buggy*, he thought. To the left was a brick wall with evenly spaced doors that he could only presume led to some sort of courtyards on the other side. To his right the brick facade was residential with entryways and numerous shuttered windows and flower boxes. Despite the very short length of Acorn Street, the snow flurry had grown so dense that in these nearly white-out conditions he was unable to make out where the cobble stone road ended. Yet the five gas lamps on the street flickered dully in the opaque light. A truly eerie sight all around. In spite of this he continued to run up its center until suddenly it came upon him once again that now familiar black silhouette standing directly ahead of him at the street's end.

Stopping abruptly, Sydney's feet slipped on the cobble stones made slick by the thin layer of snow. Down he went, flat onto his back. When he swung his body around to stand he saw that the mystery man had not made a move towards him. He just stood there, hands still in his pockets, glaring down upon him. If his sole intention was to drive Sydney mad with fear, he was gradually succeeding.

"Who are you!?" Sydney yelled out while still on his hands and knees. But the man said nothing.

After picking himself up he yelled again to the man.

"What do you want from me!?"

Once more there came no answer. Slowly, Sydney began to back away.

"I don't know who you are!"

Still not a word was spoken nor a single step made in his direction. The man simply remained motionless. Sydney cautiously turned his back on him and proceeded a couple steps before looking over his shoulder to find, to his surprise, that the man was gone.

Like a cat-and-mouse game with the Cheshire Cat - now you see him, now you don't.

And Sydney did not care to find out where the game might lead him next. So in a quick pace, rather than a run, he backtracked his way towards Beacon Street. If the man failed to make a move on him on a lonely road, then what were the chances of him doing so if he crossed his path again on a crowded street? But another face-off with the mystery man would not occur again, much to his relief.

When Sydney finally arrived at his home he was breathing hard and perspiring. The arduous trek left him feeling for the first time the limitations inherent with this sixty-six year old body.

"Good heavens! What on earth...? You're perspiring as though you've been running" said Mrs. Deere.

"I have. Thought I'd take a little jog in the park."

He decided ahead of this moment not to share his experience with the mystery man with Mrs. Deere, figuring it unnecessary to burden the poor lady with yet another worry, as if trying to cope with a stranger in the body of someone she has known for ten years was not upsetting enough.

"Well I can definitely see you're still not thinking like the Professor. He *never* did any sort of exercises."

"I can tell."

"He'd sit in that chair at his desk all day if it wasn't for his occasional classes, or me urging him to come to the dining table. Now why don't you change out of those soggy clothes into something warm and dry and I'll fix you a nice hot cup of tea."

And for the first time that cup of tea was precisely what Sydney desired.

Although the images of the mystery man were never far from his thoughts, Sydney tried his best to stay focused over the suppertime conversation. This eventually became easier to do when he decided to question Mrs. Deere on the state of the world in the year 2125. With all the questions he received from Dr. Wynn and Mrs. Deere regarding what life was like in his time, he never took the opportunity to question them likewise, for his way of thinking had always been preoccupied with how he could go back to what once was.

Throughout history there has been a relatively equal share of good and bad events. And what Sydney learned was that the past hundred years were no different. On the down side, wars had come and gone. He was not surprised by this. In a world where wars had been fought since the dawn of history, he sadly reasoned that when it came to war and peace there was little change one can expect over a mere hundred years. Then there was of course the pandemic, but he wished not to hear anything further on that subject, nor on whether terrorism continued or of any catastrophic natural disasters that may have occurred. He wanted instead to hear of the good that mankind has achieved in the future.

He was surprised to learn of the peace that finally came to some nations and the alliances that were signed between others. And he was happy to hear that it had become a far more accepting world towards varying ethnicities, religions, cultures, individuals' preferences and diversities.

Another topic of his interest was just how far we had come in space exploration. Although Mrs. Deere admitted to "not being up on all that space stuff," she *was* able to tantalize him with some insights into how far space exploration has come. Mars had been colonized by a group of scientists. But it was still a small colony in number. And where civilian space travel is quite common - circling our own planet only - vacations to the red planet by the leisure traveler was still a thing of the future, although NASA, other world space agencies, and the travel industry had been in talks about it for years. She also spoke of a planet finder telescope that NASA launched into the far reaches of our galaxy long before she was born. This telescope discovered the possibility and even *probability* of life on other planets and moons, but being that they are so many light years away, sending a space craft to these galactic worlds is something still far reaching due to the inability to travel faster through space. However, all other means of travel on earth had certainly become faster, more streamline and supersonic, even by rail as well as again by air. Also bridges and tunnels now connected land masses, islands, and continents where it was once pure science fiction to think it possible in his day.

People also typically looked younger longer and lived greater life spans, whereas at his age of sixty-six he was now considered middle-aged. And many of the ailments and miseries that accompanied the aging process were now a thing of the past. And although some vaccines and antibiotics would lose their effectiveness against diseases and infections, they would be replaced by new vaccines and antibiotics. In fact, medical science had made extraordinary advances with preventative medicines and cures. Even AIDS had long since been eradicated. But where one virus was conquered others materialized, which brought the conversation around full circle back to the pandemic.

Mrs. Deere was quick to skirt the subject knowing the somber relevance it held for the Professor, despite his incapability of remembering it.

"Good heavens! One can so easily forget just how much has happened in the past hundred years until you take a moment to think about it. And you know, discussing all of these things that have changed since your time gives me a fair idea as to what life must have been like for my great grandparents. My father and mother, nor even *their* parents for that matter, never spoke to me of things of that long ago. Only of the times as far back as they themselves could remember. But even that is beyond the years you last..."

She stopped short from finishing her sentence when she realized it would conclude with a thought that would undoubtedly upset him.

"Listen to me ramble on" she said apologetically while spontaneously clearing the table. "Here I am talking about my family generations as if it would interest you. Sometimes I just talk and talk and never know when to shut up."

"It's okay. Really. I'm a happy listener."

And he meant what he said. For listening to Mrs. Deere would bring back memories of his youth back in Cleveland when he would listen to his own grandmother as she fussed away in the kitchen over the preparation of a meal or special dish, all the while chattering about relatives he had never heard of or met.

But this time during Mrs. Deere's endless prattle she said a word that would suddenly brighten Sydney's emotions, fill him with a new hope, and cause him to momentarily forget the mysterious man that had tormented his psyche earlier that day.

Generations. What might have become of his own generation? Surely of his three children he must have *some* descendants living somewhere. A direct physical link to his past. No longer merely a memory, but rather an actual connection to a member of his own family that would then allow him to integrate himself into becoming a part of that family. *If* they would buy who he is. That, however, would remain to be seen. First he would need to recruit Jessica's assistance in finding them. But bearing in mind her stubborn refusal to go along with him and his hypnosis proposal, he worried what her reaction might be to helping him find his relatives.

"Would you like another bowl of rice pudding?" asked Mrs. Deere.

"Yes, I would. I never realized how much I love rice pudding."

"It's always been the Professor's favorite as well" she said with a smile.

Sydney never spoke a word of the mystery man to Jessica the following day. He felt it would be an unnecessary worry at a time when he preferred her focus to be on the task he was only too eager to request, but doubtful she would accept. Nevertheless, he was not hesitant this time about bringing up his latest idea. In fact, Jessica had no sooner sat down on the sofa after having just arrived when Sydney immediately launched into what he wanted and his reasons why. He never looked at her once, but kept his attention fixed on the window until he finished his exhortation. He did this in part because of the mystery man he was certain he had not seen the last of, and also by reason of the disapproving faces he was convinced Jessica would make before he would be able to finish. But this assumption of him was wrong. She made no faces and left him rather speechless with surprise when she matter-of-factly stated, "I think it's a great idea."

Perhaps she will be less agreeable after I ask for her help, he thought to himself.

"And if you like I'll be glad to help you with your search in any way I can."

With his whole planed argument for going through with this now utterly useless, he could do little more than divert his look away from the window and squarely on her with a broad smile.

"Thank you."

Jessica's reason for being supportive and even willing to assist him was two-fold. The most apparent reason to her was that he was so obviously determined to find his family that he would do it with or without her regardless of what she said. The other less apparent reason was that deep down inside she had come to adore the Sydney Hamilton with the mind and personality of Roger Owen. Not long ago she held a crush on the Professor for reasons, she recalled, that had more to do with her attraction for distinguished older men than it did for his obviously profound intelligence. His striking silver hair noble looks would leave her spellbound with adoration every day in class. But where his appearance would have this moving affect on her, his humorless, always serious, and often somber demeanor left her feeling at other times the complete opposite - nothing. Unaware of the personal tragedy that changed him from the happy individual he once was, she could only look at him and wish that he possessed this one essential missing quality.

Now there was an entirely different Professor. One who insisted on being called, Sydney. One who was easygoing, nonchalant, smiled, and even laughed on occasion despite his own valid and complex reasons for feeling despondent. This was the man she eagerly looked forward to visiting each day. The man whose company she felt both mystified and at ease with at the same time. The man she hoped would never change. And perhaps this direct present day human link to his past would be the one thing to assure her that forgetting it he never will.

After some gleeful discussion over what her plan will be for finding his family - a task she felt should not prove too much of a challenge considering the rather simple steps by which she found the history on Roger Owen - Jessica did not prolong her stay knowing that she had other appointments to fulfill before she could sit down at her computer and embark once more on her investigative digging.

Sydney saw her to the door and watched her as she made her way down the hall towards the elevator.

Flames. Magnificent billowing flames of amber and gold soaring upward 'till they filled the night sky with dancing sparks and plumes of orange-gray smoke.

Sydney awoke from this dream in the middle of the night - his pillow damp from the profusion of sweat on his brow. Although every aspect of the dream remained extraordinarily vivid in its detail, he could not understand its meaning or the tremendous feeling of sadness that overwhelmed him because of it. So intense was this sadness that he began to weep uncontrollably while his stomach ached with the kind of pain one exclusively associates with deep anguish. As the images of those flames replayed in his mind these feelings only intensified. Curling up in the fetal position and clutching his pillow he cried and cried all the while wondering the obvious question - *Why?*

FOUR

The hours spent at the computer drifted late into the evening and filled up most of the following day for Jessica. But come dusk she was finally able to make that phone call to Sydney that she had located Roger Owen's nearest living relative.

In her conversation the next morning with Cyrus Owen, Roger's youngest son Justin's great great grandson, she made no mention of the true connection her "friend and acclaimed Harvard Professor" has with his great great great grandfather, only that he has a "significant affiliation with him." The last thing she wanted to do would be to scare him into thinking Sydney was some crazy man whom he should be wary of. Any hasty opinions before understanding fully the concept of reincarnation would undermine the trust, belief, and acceptance that they set out to achieve during their meeting with Cyrus Owen.

Although he had never lived in New York City, Roger's visits with Jeremy and subsequent courtship with Laura allowed him, to a limited extent, to feel fairly comfortable knowing his way around Manhattan, from the Upper West and East Sides all the way down to Battery Park. And so it came as a surprise to him to see just how greatly the cityscape had changed. The skyscrapers that were once so familiar to him and what made this city the most recognizable city in the world were, for the most part, nearly all gone. Newer, higher reaching towers of steel, concrete, and glass now stood where only the memory of others had been over a hundred years before. There were, however, some landmark buildings that still remained. The Chrysler Building and Empire State Building had endured as vestiges of a bygone era, although their visibility no longer dominated the skyline. They were now lost amidst the dense overabundance of surrounding superstructures equal to their height. This was likewise way down below in the shadows of these giants where many other buildings had been saved from the wrecking ball through Historical Preservation.

Some of the major thoroughfares throughout the city were also unrecognizable with their second tier expressway levels reminiscent of the Elevated Trains, or "El's", from yesteryear. Though in this day and age they were explicitly used for vehicles with the sole purpose of bypassing pedestrian crossings and enabling direct entrance and exit access to the garages of those monolithic hi-rises.

Unlike Commonwealth Avenue and the Beacon Hill area of Boston, he found that many of the quaint residential brownstones had not survived the ravages of time and were sadly replaced with modern three and four story dwellings. This was the case when Sydney and Jessica arrived by taxi - different model but still yellow - at the home of Cyrus Owen on West 15th Street between 8th and 9th Avenues in Chelsea.

"Now remember what we discussed" Jessica overcautiously emphasized before stepping out of the cab.

"I haven't forgotten since you reminded me six blocks back" he said with a grin. "I'm to say very little and let you do all the talking. You're going to first explain to him the theory of reincarnation and then tell him of my *supposed* leap out of a window..."

"*Fall*" she interrupted. "We don't want him to think you're suicidal. That will lead him to a preconception that you're mentally and emotionally unstable."

"Of course. Even though I don't think it was a fall either. Nevertheless, you'll tell him about my *fall* out of a window and my awakening from a coma with the detailed *knowledge* of his ancestor. Not his *memory* because we want him to draw his own conclusion. Mustn't throw *too* much at him all at once and expect him to believe it. Now whenever you feel your confidence in me has been put at ease what do you say we march up those steps, ring that bell, and see what happens next?"

After a quiet pause a wry smile appeared on her face as she took the initiative to finally exit the cab.

The day was sunny and cloudless, yet the temperature was markedly more bitter than what they had experienced over the past couple of weeks in Boston.

"So much for global warming" Sydney commented as they both waited for a response after buzzing the door.

"Hello?" came a young man's voice from the speaker box.

With her teeth already chattering so fiercely her lips could hardly form the words to speak. "Hello. It's Dr. Wynn and Professor Hamilton."

"Oh, yeah. Come on in. Second floor, number three."

The door opened to a foyer and such a welcomed relief of warmth that they both found it necessary to pause a moment to warm up.

"Holy shit, it's brutal out there!"

Sydney's remark came as a shock to Jessica and brought forth from her a burst of laughter.

"What's the matter? Why are you laughing?"

"It's what you just said. If you only knew the Professor as *I* knew him back in school, that choice of words would have never come from his lips. Very stiff, proper Englishman, you know" she quipped with a mocking British accent.

"Is that why you developed a crush on him?"

His quick lighthearted comeback drew an abrupt cease to her laughter.

"Shall we proceed?" she said while leading the way past him towards the elevator.

"Let's take the stairs" he suggested. "It'll warm us up."

Sydney took the lead as they headed up the stairwell until he stopped at the top landing and hesitated a New York minute allowing Jessica to pass.

"What's the matter? Are you nervous?" Jessica asked.

"Perhaps a little. But not nearly as nervous as you." Again flashing that grin she now realized could allay any anxieties or fears she may hold.

One final hesitation followed before Sydney knocked on the door of his kin. His initial observation at first sight of Cyrus, who swung the door open with the greeting of a warm hello and a big smile, was his notably lighter skin. *Some interracial branches have evidently sprouted from our family tree*, he assumed with a hint of delight, for Roger had always been impartial when it came to race. It was how his parents raised him and siblings to be. And yet despite an occasionally overheard racial slur or those equally racist scowls that had been ingrained in his memory as a youngster in the seventies, he remained indifferent to the prejudices of others, deducing that the mind-set of those type of individuals is on account of their ignorance and therefore should not be cause for him to bring judgment upon others of a different color as a whole.

Cyrus, a handsome young man of twenty-six, showed notable exuberance and an unmistakable measure of excitement.

"It's nice to meet you both. Come in. May I take your coats?"

Both Sydney and Jessica were never sure how they would be received. Would he be distant and suspicious of them? Or cynical and rude? But as they removed their coats they also shed any misgivings they previously harbored by means of his friendly politeness.

Their mutual first impression of the small dwelling itself was not that of wealth but rather of a person struggling to get by. Jessica thought the furnishings looked secondhand. Whereas Sydney was struck with a recollection of his own apartment going back to his college days as Roger Owen. They were both quick to also notice the television as being turned on, but the volume of the newscast he had been watching was set to mute.

"Now it was you I spoke with on the phone so you must be Doctor Wynn."

"That's right. It's a pleasure to meet you in person, Cyrus."

"And you're Professor Hamilton. The man who has much to tell me about some distant relative of mine."

"Your great great great grandfather Roger Owen, to be exact."

"I never knew I had a great great grandfather Roger."

"Great great *great* grandfather Roger" said Sydney, feeling it necessary and important to correct him.

It was at this moment when a lovely young lady entered the room from the kitchen holding an infant. And there was no mistaking the fact that she was well on her way towards giving birth to another in the near future. Sydney immediately thought of Laura, not so much for any sort of resemblance that the woman bore to his beloved, but more for the way she looked entering the room carrying a little girl that appeared to be the exact age of his precious Natalie.

"Hello" she said while placing the child in a play-pen.

"Hey babe, this is Dr. Wynn and Professor Hamilton. I'd like to introduce you two to my wife, Sarah, and our daughter, Jasmine."

After an exchange of mutual hellos, Sydney strode directly over to the play-pen with his heart gushing.

"And aren't you just the prettiest little girl! Look at those big beautiful eyes! How old?"

"Thirteen months" said Sarah.

"I knew it! She's the same age as my Natalie."

"Your granddaughter?" she asked assumingly.

"My daughter."

Jessica drew in a deep breath, worried over where this might go if he divulges too much too soon.

"And what have you got here? A little pony?" he asked as he playfully picked up a small stuffed animal toy only to have it quickly snatched by the child and clutched so dearly to her heart.

"Oh yes, that's her little pony and no one else's" Sydney laughed.

"How many children do you have?" asked Cyrus.

"Three."

Before he might begin telling them their names and when they were born, Jessica felt an urgency to jump in with a change of subject.

"We're very grateful to you both for allowing us to come here to share with you something that we're sure you'll find quite interesting about your relative, Roger Owen."

"Oh please, the honor is all mine" said Cyrus. "I read about you on the internet, Professor, and I was *very* impressed with what I learned. Not only are you a great historian, but you've also written many books."

"Apparently I have."

"How many have you had published?"

Stumped for an answer, Sydney turned to Jessica for assistance.

"Seven" she was quick to say. "Along with numerous essays and articles."

"*Very* impressive" he reiterated. "I'm a writer myself."

"Oh really?" said Sydney with genuine interest. "Have you had anything published?"

With that question the smile left Cyrus' face. Jessica noticed too that Sarah's expression shifted to one of pessimism and discouragement.

"Well, not yet" he answered, trying hard to hide his sadness with the face of optimism. "But it will happen. Just haven't found that one-of-a-kind story."

"Are you working on anything now?"

"Actually, no. Since Jasmine came along, and with another one on the way, Sarah has had to quit her nursing job and I've had to go back to working at the warehouse, often pulling double shifts in order for us to...."

Cyrus stopped himself from completing his thought knowing that it was a touchy subject of much agitation between he and Sarah. After pausing a moment he then continued with a lighter air in what was an obvious attempt to change topics.

"So, my dear mister history professor, what is it about my great great *great* grandfather Roger that brought you here from Boston to tell me? Was he some unsung hero? Or perhaps some infamous outlaw?"

"Oh good-heavens no. None of the above. He was just an average ordinary hardworking carefree man who loved and cherished his family very deeply."

Cyrus reacted disappointingly to this. Perhaps hoping that in Roger Owen he might have found that long sought after one-of-a-kind subject to write about.

"Then I don't understand. Why would a person such as you, someone who has written about legendary figures, find something to tell about a man so average and...un-remarkable?"

"I wouldn't call him *un*-remarkable" Sydney responded in a way more sad than defensive. "To his family I'm sure he was *quite* remarkable. A remarkable husband. A remarkable father. A remarkable son."

Cyrus, however, remained unmoved by his sentiments. Jessica, on the other hand, saw this as the perfect moment to launch into her well planned narration on reincarnation.

"But it's *how* he came about learning so much about your ancestor that is what's so *truly* remarkable here."

"Turn it up" interrupted Sydney in reference to the television. "Turn it up" he said again.

"Mute off" came the command from Cyrus while they all watched on as Sydney moved in closer to the 3-dimensional image on screen of an immense stadium known as The Miami Ballpark.

"Oh my Lord, would you look at that! I don't believe it! They *finally* finished it! And it turned out great. Why it's *beautiful*, don't you think?"

At that very instant his proud smile melted as the super structure, following the rippling sound of loud explosions from within, came crashing down in a magnificent cloud of concrete dust. It was only then that Sydney took note of the news anchor's voice describing the scene.

"And with a series of explosions a familiar site of the Miami skyline vanished in a cloud of dust today, even after ardent protests by a group calling itself the, "Preserve Our City's History" failed in their efforts to save The Miami Ballpark from demolition by having it declared a historic landmark. The hundred and thirteen year old Ballpark had declined over the years into a state of deterioration and disrepair, ultimately forcing its doors to close five years ago. After a vote by city trustees it was decided that a move to restore the stadium would be too costly. As of yet there has been no decision what the city plans to do with this prized property, only that it will continue to be used for a public purpose."

"Television off" Sydney muttered grimly.

A hushed moment followed until Sydney finally shook his head and smirked, "And they said it would stand for the next two hundred years."

"Did you once work at that stadium?" asked Cyrus.

"*Work* at that stadium? Hell, I helped build it!"

It seemed for an instant that even one year old Jasmine was struck with the same silent look of bewilderment shared by her parents. Whereas with Jessica, whose jaw dropped the second those last four words left his lips, stammered in a hasty and desperate attempt to rectify his slip-up.

"Da...What he meant was..."

"Oh let's not beat around the bush about this" Sydney continued so nonchalant. "The truth of the matter is, I'm your great great great grandfather Roger. And that stadium, or what's left of it, is where I worked during its construction from the year 2009 to the night of October 22, 2011 when I went to sleep and didn't wake up until a hundred and thirteen years and four months later, to be exact."

Jessica's face dropped into her hands as she shook her head. For both Cyrus and Sarah, they appeared to be waiting for a punch-line until it gradually became clear that their guest was serious in believing what he had just told them.

"Honey, the kitchen" said Sarah trying to subdue her developing alarm. But Cyrus made no response, as though, perhaps, still waiting for that punch-line.

"Honey, *please*, the kitchen?"

As though hearing her for the first time, Cyrus turned to her and then back to their company.

"Excuse us."

After they disappeared into the kitchen Sarah quickly returned for Jasmine, mindful of not leaving her alone with them.

Within the seclusion of their tiny kitchen Cyrus and Sarah's alarm *did* emerge, though they kept their voices down to a controlled whisper.

"Cyrus."

"I know."

"That old man is nuts."

"I know."

"What are you going to do about it?"

"I don't know."

"What do you mean, you don't know!?   Throw him out! Throw them *both* out! She's probably as nuts as he is!"

"I can't just throw them out."

"Why not!? My God, Cyrus, you heard him. The old man thinks he's Rip Van Winkle!"

In the other room Jessica also maintained control of her voice as she laid into Sydney over his impromptu mess-up.

"I can't believe how you completely ignored absolutely everything we discussed in regards to how we were going to approach this! No sooner do I get past 'hello' then you start spouting out about how you built a ballpark that was constructed over a hundred years ago and that you're actually his dearly departed great great... great great..."

So flustered was Jessica that she found it impossible to complete her sentence.

"Okay. Yes, I admit I jumped a little ahead of the plan. But when I saw that stadium I simply lost for the moment my sense of discretion."

"Well, now because of your loss of discretion they're not going to believe a word we tell them!"

"Shhh...I'm trying to hear what they're saying."

"They're probably on the phone with the police! And I really can't say I'd blame them!"

For a moment they both ceased with their banter so as to listen intently to the indecipherable muffled whispers coming from the kitchen. When in short time Cyrus and Sarah eventually emerged, Cyrus wore a false smile to mask any hint of misgiving. Not so with Sarah. Her look bore no secret to the suspicion and anxiety she felt not only towards Sydney but with Jessica as well.

"Uh....Sarah and I just remembered that we have to be somewhere, like, right now. So unfortunately we're going to have to reschedule this little get-together for another day. Hopefully we're not too late getting to where we have to be....right now."

Jessica merely nodded her head expecting completely this sort of action from them. Sydney, on the other hand, was not so willing to let it go at that.

"Look, I'm really sorry for throwing that at you all at once like I did. It's just that I wasn't thinking straight as a result of this flood of emotions hitting me so suddenly. Emotions brought on by meeting you. Seeing your daughter who reminded me of my own little Natalie. Watching The Miami Ballpark, that I helped build, get blown up..."

Jessica rolled her eyes back and shook her head, whereas Cyrus and Sarah reacted with confusion, especially in lieu of his last sentence.

"If you could just spare us five minutes to allow us to explain how this all came to be" he continued.

"You say you're a doctor" said Sarah, point-blank at Jessica. "Is *he* your patient?"

"Actually, yes" Jessica answered with a bit of reluctance.

Cyrus and Sarah only had to look at one another to convey they were both thinking the same thing upon hearing this admission. And with that Cyrus began to slowly usher Sydney and Jessica to the door.

"I don't know if either one of you believe in reincarnation" Jessica was hurried to say. "But what happened with my patient - Professor Hamilton - makes a strong case in proving the validity of the reincarnation theory."

"That's nice" said Cyrus trying his best to be polite.

"After waking from a coma Professor Hamilton was unable to recall anything of his life as Professor Hamilton. *However*, he was and still is able to remember every detail in the entire life of a man named Roger Owen who lived over a hundred years ago. A man he had no knowledge of prior to his coma."

"My life up to the age of forty that is" Sydney added.

"Fascinating" Cyrus responded sarcastically.

"It certainly is" Sydney continued. "Try to imagine how you'd feel stuck in the body of a man you know nothing about in a time that's so far ahead in the future."

"I can't. I can't imagine it at all. But we'll get together again and you can tell me all about what it's like. I have your number and we'll stay in touch. Good-bye."

After shutting them out Cyrus leaned against the door and exhaled a drawn out breath. He paused a moment in thought of what they had told him and then looked at Sarah with uncertainty.

"Do you really think we did the right thing having them leave?"

But Sarah remained unconvinced to feeling otherwise.

"Oh Cyrus, *please*."

No words were said between Sydney and Jessica as they made their way to the bottom level. Even as they stood on the sidewalk waiting for a passing cab, with a distinct distance between them, the silence remained until Sydney finally spoke out optimistically.

"I think that went over well."

"You've *got* to be kidding."

"I admit it could have gone a little better."

"He threw us out, Sydney!"

"Well I hardly expected him to start planning a family reunion."

Jessica shook her head and turned away from him.

"Look" he continued, "something such as this will take time. We should have never gone up there trusting that he'd believe right away everything we tell him. We may have to return again and again until he gradually begins to understand and ultimately embraces the truth of the matter."

"Have you ever heard of a Restraining Order, Sydney? Or didn't they have those back in the twentieth century."

"I know what a Restraining Order is. That's why we have to go about this delicately."

"*We?*"

"Don't tell me you're bailing out on me? Not now after coming this far. This is when I need you most. Yes, I'm sure he thinks

I'm a nut-case. That's why I need you to be the voice of someone he can trust."

After waving down an approaching taxicab Jessica turned to Sydney and spoke with a sincere empathy.

"Give it up, Sydney. You would have had to have been deaf and blind not to realize that not only do they have no desire to even *consider* hearing us out, but I think they were in fact a little afraid of us as well."

Sydney reacted slowly when it came to following Jessica into the cab. Once inside, after their destination was given to the driver and the cab was on its way, Sydney responded calmly.

"I'm not the kind of guy who gives up just like that. It means too damn much to me to feel a part of a family that was once *my* family in another life. Turn left" he instructed the cab driver.

"Left? But our hotel is on Broadway."

"And then make another left on twenty-first. There's something I need to see."

She did not question him further, feeling that his reason for wanting to see this street might be personal.

Turning onto West 21st Street, Sydney leaned forward and peered far ahead in anticipation of what he hoped to find. It had been sixteen years in Roger's life since he had last been on this street. Within that short period of time he would not have expected much to change. But now, in the year 2125, he had already bore witness to the extent which things have changed all around him in little over a century. He knew the odds were against him that it would still be there. But still he hoped. And then, optimism. The entire 21st Street block between 9th and 10th Avenues appeared to be spared from future redevelopment.

"Stop!" Sydney exclaimed. "Stop here!"

And there it was. On the center north side of the block, Laura's apartment building. The old brownstone had survived the ages. Forgetting his manners he said not a word to Jessica as to the significance of the building he was looking at. For he suddenly found himself lost in the excitement of seeing something for the first time that was an actual physical part of his past. In this strange new world where even the old was unfamiliar to him, here was something that was a part of who he is, or rather, who he was. It surprised him to find that little had changed in the way the building looked. He studied every detail of the brick facade, the low wrought iron fence that flanked each side of the stoop where he and Laura had bid many a fond farewell kisses, and the window to the left of the entrance. This was Laura's apartment. He almost expected to still find her curtains hanging in the window.

This building held a deeper emotional bond to him than merely being the place where Laura had lived when they met. For it was beyond that window where he and his beloved made love for the first time. He could still see the heavy rain that pelted the building that late summer eve when they stepped out of the taxicab, both already drenched after having been caught unprepared for the sudden downpour. They hurried up the steps of the stoop laughing the whole time. Once inside the apartment they no sooner closed the door when their laughter gave way to their passion with an embrace and kiss that seemed to match the intensity of the lightening thunderstorm raging outside. Finally separating for a moment, Roger reached over to flick on the wall light switch. But Laura gently lowered his arm from doing so. It was then he knew, they *both* knew, that tonight would be the night.

Her bedroom was dimly lit by the flickering light of three candles. There was no need for music - the sound of the rain and thunder offered a perfect ambiance that no vocal or instrumental could outdo. On her bed the desire for one another they held inside since the day they met would finally be expressed. They explored each other's naked bodies with tender kisses and yielded themselves to each other completely in the bliss of making love. For Roger and Laura there was never a previous time in their lives more beautiful, yet there would come many times thenceforth that would equal it.

Across the city a hundred and thirty years away, Sydney sat in a chair in a dark and lonely hotel room gazing out a window at the twinkling lights of the metropolis spread out before him while visions of that night haunted his memory with mixed affection and sadness.

In a room down the hall Jessica also laid awake in bed, but the reason for her restlessness was due, naturally, to a different cause. Thoughts of what transpired earlier in that day between her and Sydney brought about heartfelt emotions that up until this point had been suppressed, not only for the obvious ethical reason between a psychiatrist and patient, but also for the uncertainty of what such a disclosure might have on their growing relationship. Still, with these moments of lighthearted banter and friendly spats, as experienced earlier that day, becoming ever more frequent, Jessica was developing a concern over her feelings towards Sydney. Feelings that were deeper than a dreamy student "crush", as Sydney had so tauntingly put it. She realized also that she was falling for not one man, but two. The looks of one and the personality of another.

It was a sleepless night for Cyrus and Sarah as well as they quietly stirred under the covers in the darkness of their bedroom.

"Are you awake?" Sarah finally asked.

"Yup. Haven't slept a wink."

"Same here."

"You're thinking about him, too?"

"Of course. I wonder what he was trying to pull over on us. Pretending to be the ghost of one of your ancestors."

"He never said he was a *ghost*."

"Well, something like that. One of the oldest scams in the world, if you ask me. Pretending to be some *clairvoyant* who has one of your dearly departed relatives speaking through him. And then once he hooks you into believing it he'll expect you to *pay* him to have further conversations with this *Roger*. Total scam."

Cyrus clicked on his bedside lamp and looked at her with amusement.

"He never said he's clairvoyant either, Sarah. Where are you getting all this? Weren't you listening? He never said anything about being clairvoyant *or* a ghost. They just spoke of reincarnation."

"Oh. And you believe in that?"

Cyrus chose not to answer, opting instead to turn the questioning on her.

"Well, I thought you believed he was just plain nuts?"

"No. I'm thinking now he's after something. He and his sidekick."

"His *sidekick*, as you call her, is an employee of Massachusetts General Hospital and the Professor *really is* a Professor of History at Harvard who, by the way, has had more books published than I probably ever will. I already told you all this, babe. I researched them both before allowing them to come here. They're not out to scam us. *That* I'm sure of."

"Then what *do* they want?"

Cyrus took a long pause before attempting to answer.

"I don't know. Maybe if I had let them explain before throwing them out so soon..."

"Don't even go there, baby" Sarah was quick to interrupt. "You did the right thing by getting rid of them. Now turn out the light."

Sarah rolled over on her side leaving Cyrus to hesitate in thought before reaching for the lamp switch. Still, he could not bring himself to end these thoughts as simply as turning off a light.

"He wakes up from a coma remembering nothing of himself, only that of a past life he says he lived."

"The light, Cyrus."

"If it's not true, then why would he choose me? Why would he choose an ancestor of mine who wasn't famous? Someone who was just an average ordinary guy? Don't you think that's odd?"

With that Sarah rose up, reached over her husband, and turned off the lamp. A long silence followed until a small voice emanated the darkness.

"It's possible. Don't you think?"

"*Good-night*, Cyrus."

Sydney eventually fell asleep in his chair but awoke later that evening in a heavy sweat. He had been weeping in his sleep again from the same dream of flames that he had dreamt before. The dream was identical in every aspect - nothing more to it, nothing less. The mysterious anguish that followed was repeated as well. He crawled into bed, clutched a pillow, and wept some more until once again he was finally able to succumb to sleep.

Sydney was still asleep when Jessica knocked on his door at eight in the morning. Blurry eyed and tousled he dragged himself over to answer it.

"Oh my!" came her immediate reaction. "I guess I wasn't the only one who had a restless night. Well, nothing that a big breakfast with lots of coffee can't fix. Get yourself together and we'll walk over to this cute little place close by that I found in that in-room magazine."

"You want us to walk somewhere in that cold?"

"Can you think of a better way to wake the body up? Besides, I heard on the weather this morning that it's going to be warmer today. Actually *above* zero!"

Sydney scratched his head and yawned, but made no effort to move.

"C'mon sleepyhead, if we eat and pack soon enough we might be able to make the eleven o'clock back to Boston."

"Boston? Who's going back to Boston?" he asked, finally becoming more alert.

"Is there *another* reason you want to stay in New York?"

"No. Just our *original* reason for coming here."

"Sydney, I know this must be hard for you to accept, but you've got to face the fact that the Owen's want nothing more to do with us. To pursue this further would boarder on harassment."

"After just one meeting you're ready to throw in the towel? We can't possibly leave without so much as a phone call to find out if they'll see us again. I can't and I won't give up on him so easily. I told you that yesterday."

"How long then? How long are you going to give yourself with this *quest* before you let it go?"

"I don't know, Jessica. I can't answer that right now. But if you want to go back to Boston, then by all means feel free. There will be no hard feelings from me if you do. You've done more than enough already. You've helped me find my kin, and for that I'm eternally grateful. Now the rest is up to me from here on."

"What about what you told me yesterday? About this being when you need me the most? And how you need me to be the voice of someone he can trust?"

"I do. That hasn't changed. But if you need to return to Boston, then I want you to know I understand."

Jessica exhaled a deep aggravated sigh. But before she was able to grow too agitated Sydney flashed that grin that he now knew had a disarming effect on her.

"But if you're not in *too* much of a hurry to get back home, I'd still like to have breakfast with you at this cute little place you found."

The grin worked. Jessica shook her head in acknowledgment of her own weakness and drew in a breath on the verge of responding when suddenly her mobile phone rang.

"Hello? Yes. Good morning to you too. Uh, sure. What time? Okay. We'll see you then."

She ended the call and looked at Sydney with an unmistakable look of surprise. So surprised was she in fact that it took a moment before she could share with Sydney who the caller was and what it was in regards to.

"That was Cyrus Owen. He wanted to know if we could stop by his place. Says he has something he wants to show us."

FIVE

There were no apologies made by neither Cyrus nor Sarah when Sydney and Jessica entered their apartment for the second time. Although unlike the last time, Cyrus offered them to take a seat and make themselves comfortable and even brought them each a cup of coffee. The exuberance and excitement Cyrus had greeted them with the day before was notably absent, but so too was the uneasiness and suspicion he had shown them when they left. Instead, Cyrus exhibited politeness and an overwhelming eagerness to listen and learn from his guests. Not so, however, was the same measure of hospitality displayed by his wife. Sarah quietly sat in the background the whole time, cradling her daughter, while making no attempt to conceal her chilly skepticism.

When asked by Cyrus to explain again "this stuff about *reincarnation*, and how it is that you think you're my great great great grandfather", Sydney and Jessica happily gave a detailed account of the events that ultimately brought them to his door.

The dialogue began with Sydney describing the happenings of that final day. A full recount of everything he did leading up to that point in time where he fell asleep on the twenty-second night of October in the year 2011.

Jessica stepped in at this point to tell of Sydney's accidental fall out of his third story window, as it was described to her, and of his waking from a coma with not only total amnesia, but also with an impassioned belief that he is somebody else. She went on to relate how after her first meeting with her new patient she hypothesized his condition as being a Multiple Personality Disorder, until she began to delve deeper into the past life of this man named Roger Owen.

"And while she delved, I sat in an insane asylum for four days. Courtesy of that Doctor Ozawa."

Although Jessica had really not planned to go there, she was nevertheless relieved to see that Sydney's admission of being briefly institutionalized had not fazed Cyrus in the least. *Of course, after everything we've told him so far, what could possibly faze him now?* she thought. But in her peripheral vision she *did* notice Sarah rolling her eyes.

Carrying on, Jessica spoke of the correlations she discovered in her research with the life of a Roger Owen and the Roger Owen Sydney Hamilton claimed to be. And how at first she asked herself the same question that she presumed must have crossed Cyrus' mind; if she was able to learn of this information on a man who lived over a hundred years ago, then why not the Professor as well? But that question would continuously be answered with another question....Why?

"Why would the Professor here jeopardize his esteemed career, his honorable reputation, his whole way of *life* just to play out some well acted charade? And furthermore, why would he pick an individual who lived a basically average life that wasn't historically noteworthy in any way?"

"You never told me you thought that" said a surprised Sydney.

"Well, I did. Briefly."

Again she saw Sarah rolling those big brown eyes of hers. Undaunted, however, by her subtle incredulity, Jessica was at last able to launch into her teachings on reincarnation and how she came to the conclusion that Sydney's condition was based on this theory. This led Sydney to finalize with the now obvious reason for him wanting to connect with Cyrus. An actual blood descendent to his past life.

After they had both finished speaking there fell upon the room a heavy silence in anticipation of Cyrus' response. Jessica chose not to look over at Sarah, figuring that she was no doubt rolling her eyes again in disbelief. Besides, it was Cyrus' judgment that mattered most to Sydney, and what mattered to Sydney is all that mattered to Jessica.

Finally, Cyrus' serious attentive look gave way to that same broad smile he had greeted them with the previous day along with one simple word that seemed to sum up his verdict over all that he had just been told.

"Fascinating."

Although Sydney and Jessica were pleased and relieved not to be escorted once again to the front door by their host, they were nonetheless a bit baffled over his reluctance to expand upon his thoughts beyond that one word, and even more so by that smile. That smile that might have been saying, you *both* should be institutionalized, or, I believe you and who you say you are, or, perhaps an ulterior motive hidden in that smile that mattered not whether he believed in them at all. Regardless of what was going on in that mind of his, Jessica finally spoke up with a reminder of what he had mentioned to her over the phone.

"Didn't you say there's something you'd like to show us?"

"Yes. Absolutely. It's not that I forgot. I just wanted to hear you two out completely before showing it to you. And now that I have, I'm even more certain that you'll..." He stopped short from finishing his sentence and sprung from his chair. "Well, you'll see."

From the dining table he picked up what appeared to be a shoe box and one single shiny metallic looking card. He sat back down in his chair and placed the box on the coffee table enabling Sydney and Jessica to look inside. What they saw were several dozen more similar cards, some silver and some gold. Some had label stickers pasted on one side with handwritten dates or an individual's name, while others had no such labels at all. Jessica knew immediately what the cards were, but Sydney, on the other hand, was expectedly puzzled.

"Don't ask me how this box full of family images ended up in my possession. I've had them for so long I really can't remember which of my relatives tossed them over onto me. But because they're family pictures you just don't throw stuff like this away. So they've been gathering dust in the closet over there until this morning when I got to thinkin' maybe there's something on one of these that will show this great great great grandfather Roger of mine. But since most of these were never labeled I had to insert each one of them and do an audio search on any mention of the name Roger."

"He couldn't fall asleep. So he started in on that" said Sarah. "And then he called in sick so he could meet with you again." And then, mumbling under her breath she added, "As if we can really afford for him to take a day off work."

Choosing to ignore her testy remark, Sydney perked up with an eager interest.

"And what did you find?"

Cyrus held up the single silvery card with no label that was set aside outside of the box.

"This. The name Roger is mentioned seventy-two times. And when I looked at the dates that appear on the images I found that the earliest date goes back to the 1980's on what I guess they used to call video. Although there are a whole lot of other images that I think might date back even further that offer no dates and no sound at all. These images often appear a bit fuzzy, sometimes jerky, and occasionally have white spots that emerge for a few seconds at the end of a scene."

It took a moment before Sydney realized what Cyrus was talking about.

"Eight millimeter! Of course! My Daddy's old Bell and Howell. He bought that camera before I was even born."

Glancing at each of the faces in the room, Sydney could see that they were all confounded over what he was talking about.

"Film" he continued. "Eight millimeter film camera."

Cyrus and Jessica nodded, yet Sydney felt a bit certain that they were still not in complete understanding of what he was saying.

"Anyway," proceeded Cyrus, "the images progress onto digital and high definition, but fall short of appearing in 3-D, so everything looks really flat. And when I did a search on the last image recorded by the date shown, I came up with 2059. These dates definitely fall into the time period of when my ancestor Roger Owen lived. Therefore, I have little doubt that *this* is his recorded life."

"May I?"

Cyrus handed Sydney the card. Sydney studied it closely. It was the same size as a credit card and just as thin, but not as light or bendable. It seemed to be made of a substance that might render it unbreakable.

"From cradle to grave" Sydney commented in amazement. "My entire life all on this one little card. Makes my whole existence feel so insignificant."

"There's over a hundred and twenty hours of viewing on that card. I wouldn't call that an insignificant life" said Cyrus.

"A hundred and twenty hours? And my name only came up seventy-two times?"

"I did an audio search on the name *Roger*, not Dad, Daddy, Son, Grandpa, Dear, Honey, Babe, or whatever the Misses might have called him, or any other variations on his name. Just Roger. And actually, when you think about it, seventy-two is quite a lot when you consider how seldom people's names are mentioned on a home camera."

Sydney's eyes remained fixed on the card he held between his fingers as if beholding his own immortality. Snippets of his life captured for posterity, or anyone else who might discover it and learn about the man he used to be and the people he loved.

"Please?" he said softly as he timidly offered the card back to Cyrus. The look on his face said the rest.

"Absolutely."

Cyrus took the card and inserted it into his computer.

"But you should know" he continued, "whichever ancestor of mine took the time to download all of these images, he or she never put them in any sort of chronological order. You can tell this by the dates shown and the quality. It really jumps around a lot."

After a couple strokes of the computer keyboard Cyrus brought their attention around to the television.

"*Television on*" he said. "We can watch it on this."

Sydney drew closer to the screen - closer than the others.

It began with a birthday. Roger's birthday. This he thought was ironic considering his last memory of that life also fell on a birthday. But on that eight millimeter film footage Cyrus referred to as "a bit fuzzy" and "sometimes jerky" was a little boy celebrating his third birthday. He could tell it was his third by the number of candles on the cake in front of him. Surrounding him were neighborhood children and siblings.

"Bobby, Zach, Andy, Calvin" he pointed out by name. "Brianna, Kailyn. I don't know who that boy is or those two girls. But my brothers and sisters are all there. Your great great great Uncles and Aunts. There's Will, Alisa, Kimberly, and Evan. As you can see I'm the youngest."

What followed would be a montage of other joyous events in Roger's long life with Sydney narrating throughout, but not in an effort to prove validity to his story, for at that moment it did not matter to him what anyone believed. Rather, it simply came as a natural response for him to reminisce out loud while he mesmerized over the images flashing before him.

"Oh now would you look at that. Christmas in the old house. Always my favorite time of year. Look at me jumpin' up and down, all excited over those presents under the tree. By the looks of me there I'd say I'm either six or seven. And look at that Christmas dinner. Mama sure knew how to whip up a big holiday feast. Oh my Lord, and there's Grandma Esther and Grandpa Joe. And even Aunt Emily and Uncle Russ. Such a clown was Uncle Russ. Always makin' us kids laugh. And there's Mama and Daddy. Your great great great *great* grandparents George and Josephine. Mama used to tell me she was named after Josephine Baker, a black singer of the twenties who became famous after she moved to Paris. Mama even followed in the shoes of her namesake and sang with a swing band for a short time. Ended up marrying the tenor sax player,...my Daddy. They played clubs all up and down the eastern states, but never made it big. Or as Daddy used to say, *we never became famous, but we sure had a hell of a lot of fun tryin'*. When they finally decided to settle down and raise a family he got a job working as a pressman at The Plain Dealer newspaper....Oh and what's this? If I'm not mistaken I do believe that bundle of joy in my Mama's arms is *me* going home from the hospital only a couple days old. My big debut! Cute baby, wasn't I?"

Sydney expected he would see Laura. But he was not prepared emotionally for what would be the first image of her to appear. The sight of Laura in her beautiful white wedding gown took his breath away. His only word, "Laura."

After the scene switched to both Roger and Laura exchanging their vows at the church alter he resumed his narration.

"Isn't she beautiful? Everyone we both knew was there for our wedding. There's my brothers up there and my best friend, Jeremy. There's Darlene."

Jessica cared little about the other people he was pointing out. Her eyes became fixated on Roger himself. She never knew what Roger looked like, and this was her first sight of him as an adult. At last she was able to place a face to the personality of the man she was falling in love with. As she leaned forward to scrutinize his every feature further she became aware of two things -how handsome Roger was, and how amazingly a bit of jealousy could prevail in her towards a bride in a wedding that took place over a hundred years ago.

The next image was a flash to the future Roger could not remember beyond his fortieth birthday. At the helm of a sailboat out at sea he saw himself surrounded by his children.

"Those are my kids! Tyler, Natalie, and your great great grandfather Justin. And that must be the sailboat I dreamed of getting someday. I see I chose the Hunter 326. What a splendid choice she is! Exactly as I envisioned her."

Following shots of a family Thanksgiving dinner when Justin was still in a highchair came another image beyond his recollection of his children dressed in their Halloween costumes from the year 2012. Tyler and Justin were dressed as a Ninja and Spiderman respectively. But it was Natalie in her princess costume that brought forth Sydney's melancholy comment, "My princess. Always my little princess."

A leap back to more eight millimeter footage presented Sydney with memories of a family vacation to Disneyland. Sydney estimated the year to be either 1978 or '79. This ironically segued into a trip to Disney World a little more than thirty years later with Roger and his own two sons and a then very pregnant Laura. Following this were scenes of that trip to a national park, the Grand Canyon, as he suggested that final night.

It was sometimes dizzying how often the scenes jumped from one period in time to another. A scene of Tyler and his Prom date jumped to Roger in his college graduation gown.

One of the most poignant moments on screen was the images of Roger as father of the bride. His little princess was now a beautiful young lady.

"Unbelievable. Why just look at her. Looks just like her mother. I wonder who she married? I hope he was somebody I approved of."

If that was one of the most poignant scenes, certainly the most haunting were the scenes that followed.

"Snyder Park. My fortieth birthday. That was the last day I remember before going to sleep that night and waking up in this century."

The images brought a chill to his spine. In his mind it felt as though the scenes were taken just a couple of weeks ago. But in reality a span of a hundred and thirteen years and four months had passed since those scenes were shot.

Sydney grew noticeably somber following these Snyder Park scenes. And with a series of post-October 22, 2011 clips of an Easter egg hunt, a couple of graduations, family Christmases, and a dance recital, he became less talkative. There was little he could find to say upon viewing this half of his life.

A shot of Roger and Laura in Paris brought within him a bizarre feeling. They were much older. In their sixties at least.

"I'd say we aged rather gracefully, don't you think?"

Several clips of Roger, at approximately the same age as those taken in Paris, showed him with several small children fishing on the shores of a lake.

Could those be my grandchildren? he wondered.

In a small motorboat on the lake he found himself fishing in the company of two men he *presumed* to be his two sons.

Sydney's speculation as to who the children were was confirmed in the image to follow. It was a group shot of what appeared to be a family reunion. Roger and Laura looked noticeably older still as they sat surrounded by my Natalie, Justin, Tyler, their spouses, and numerous grandchildren. Too many to count in the short time the image appeared, for suddenly it cut away to a shot of Roger and Laura sitting on folding chairs outside of a recreation vehicle. This particular image reminded him of that shot taken of his parents on his fortieth birthday in Snyder Park.

An overwhelming sadness began to invade Sydney's spirit with the realization that by some cruel twist of fate he had been robbed from living out in his memory this second half of his past long and happy life.

A panoramic view of that unfamiliar lake followed and ended on a pleasant little cottage along its shoreline. With the next shot Sydney finally surmised that this must be the place where he and Laura would spend their retirement. On the covered porch of this cottage overlooking the lake Roger and Laura, well into their eighties, sat side-by-side on a two person patio swing.

"Grandma, Grandpa, look this way" came the voice of a grown woman.

When Roger and Laura looked directly at the camera and smiled, Sydney noticed they were both holding hands.

Sydney felt his throat tightening and the tears welling up in his eyes. He wondered to himself just how much more he could take. He wanted it to end, but could not bring himself to ask Cyrus to make it stop.

The *coup de grace* came with the next image of Laura and Natalie. Natalie was but only a toddler, just as he last remembered her. Mother and daughter sat in an inflated child's wading pool with Natalie merrily splashing her arms in fits of laughter.

"Natalie, where's Daddy? Do you see Daddy?" asked Laura.

The tears in Sydney's eyes began to stream down his face. Jessica, Cyrus and Sarah became swept up in Sydney's outpouring of emotion as they watched him intently.

"Where's Daddy?"

"I'm here" Sydney whispered through his tears.

He began to weep just as Natalie suddenly stopped with her splashing and looked directly into the camera.

"I'm here, baby" he said softly again.

With tears in their eyes, Jessica cupped her hand over her mouth as Sarah held closer to her bosom her sleeping child.

Natalie reached out her arms to her father as her mother continued to speak.

"You want Daddy to pick you up?"

Completely lost in the moment, sobbing uncontrollably, Sydney reached out his hand to touch the screen.

"I'm here" he said, the words choking his throat.

"Let's sing for Daddy" said Laura as she took hold of a tiny plastic toy boat in the pool.

"Row, row, row your boat,

Gently down the stream.

Merrily, merrily, merrily, merrily,

Life is but a dream.

Come on, Natalie. Sing with me. Let's sing for Daddy.

Row, row, row your boat,

Gently down the stream.

Merrily, merrily, merrily, merrily,

Life is but a dream. "

"Stop it!" Sydney cried out. "Stop it, please! I can't take any more!"

"Television off" Cyrus commanded.

Sydney stood and hurried to the window where, with his back facing the others, he wept.

There was no mistaking the fact that everyone was deeply moved by his reaction. But before either one of them could say something or make a move to comfort him, Sydney regained his composure as best he could and turned to them. In a barely audible whisper he then apologized.

"I'm sorry."

With that said Sydney immediately crossed over to the coat rack, took his coat and hat, and solemnly left the apartment.

Cyrus rose up to follow after him. But Jessica gently held him back. Her assuring nod told him that she would take that responsibility upon herself. Saying not a word she then donned her coat and departed.

For a moment Cyrus and Sarah were left speechless as they looked at one another bemused over what they had just witnessed.

"Wow" was the only remark Cyrus was able to utter in an effort to break the silence.

Sarah stood and placed Jasmine in her crib as her husband searched for other words to continue.

"That was... I don't know... I just don't know... He certainly sounded *convincing*. But I know what you're thinkin'. You're thinkin' anyone can throw out a bunch of names and make it sound like he knew each and every one of them personally. And maybe you're right. Still I just can't understand why this Harvard Professor would..."

"He is who he says he is" Sarah interrupted as she turned around facing him.

For the moment Cyrus was again stunned into silence.

"What? Are you being serious or sarcastic?"

"I'm *very* serious. You saw him. How can you still have any doubt that he's not the person he says he used to be?"

"Well now if this don't beat all. After the sermon you gave me last night about him being a fraud, and now you, the cynic, Miss doubting Thomas, believes everything he's told us."

"I know what I said, Cyrus. And I continued to feel that way right up until I witnessed his love and grief over that child. I'm a parent and what I saw was something only a parent could feel. It wasn't just what he said, or his tears, it was his heart. I *felt* the man's heart. I *felt* it breaking at the sight of his child who he'll never see again. Tears and actions can be faked, but you can't fake the heartbreak over a lost child."

"Excuse me, but need I remind you that I too am a parent? And although I must admit he gave a powerful performance..."

"*Performance?*" objected Sarah. "I can't believe what I'm hearing."

"Or *whatever* it was. I just can't say that I'm one hundred percent certain...."

Cyrus fell short of completing his sentence, for as unwilling as he was *not* to believe the Professor, he felt just as equally willing to believe him.

"I don't know *what* to believe anymore" he resigned himself to admit.

"Listen to me, baby. He *is* who he says he is."

The little restaurant off Times Square where Jessica had intended to enjoy her breakfast with Sydney was bustling with the noonday lunch crowd by the time they sat down to eat their first meal of the day. That surprise phone call from Cyrus had derailed their original plans, thus giving Jessica a hearty appetite when it finally came time for them to take their seats at a quieter corner table. On the other hand, Sydney's appetite was completely nonexistent following his emotionally charged visual trip down memory lane. Jessica implored him to eat something, but he refused, settling instead for a cup of coffee. The ride from the apartment to the restaurant yielded no conversation which carried over to their brunch, despite Jessica's best efforts to shed a bright side on the whole experience.

"I truly believe a door of opportunity has been opened for you this morning where before I didn't think it was probable."

Sydney said nothing. So deeply absorbed in thought was he over those images that Jessica was uncertain if he even heard a word she said. Still, she tried again.

"If there's any lingering doubt in their minds, then at least you've gained their willingness to listen to you further and allow the possibility to accept who you say you are inside."

Figuring her words were not getting through, Jessica decided to give up and remain quiet as she ate her meal until the moment came when Sydney finally spoke up.

"You already told me of the day and year I died. But I asked you not to tell me when Laura died. Now I'd like to know."

There was a hint of surprise on Jessica's face. After all that silence she thought it peculiar that he would ask this. Nevertheless, she answered his question.

"She went on to outlive you by five years."

Sydney said nothing. He merely thought about it until his expressionless face eventually produced the faintest sign of a smile. From that moment on nothing more was spoken throughout the brunch by either one of them. Jessica had at last realized that the best means of helping him cope with this might just be to let him think it all through in uninterrupted peace and quiet.

Sydney would have the rest of that day to contemplate in such quietness after arriving back at his hotel room. And as the hours passed into late evening the sadness he harbored over the loss of his family and particularly the second half of his life that had been erased from his memory, began to wane and give way to the positive side of that morning's event.

It was only days ago when Sydney was telling Jessica that he had no photographs to remind himself of the life and family he loved in his past life. Yet all that changed that morning. Not only did he now have over a hundred and twenty hours of recorded images of his entire life, but also the beginnings of a personal relationship with one of his direct descendants. And the prospects of this relationship developing only grew more likely when at eleven forty-five Sydney received a phone call from the front desk telling him that there was a gentleman in the lobby named Cyrus Owen who wished to see him. Naturally, Sydney had no objection.

Thinking for a moment that the reason for Cyrus' visit may possibly be of a private nature, he hesitated before phoning Jessica. But there was absolutely nothing in his life he had not already shared with her, and he was not willing to begin keeping secrets from the only person he trusted, who believed in him, and with whom he felt a true friendship.

The ringing phone woke Jessica from a sound sleep. She had turned in early after having an emotional morning that turned suddenly into a dull uneventful day and lonesome evening. She was not only surprised to hear that Cyrus was on his way up, but also at how quickly she had fallen to sleep after turning out the light.

Cyrus was quick to apologize for his unexpected visit at the instant Sydney opened the door.

"I know it's late. I hope I didn't wake you."

"They still call this the city that never sleeps, don't they? Please, come in."

"Wow. Nice room. Bigger than my whole apartment."

"Yes. Jessica chose this hotel. Naturally."

"Of course."

Cyrus appeared somewhat nervous with Sydney. A way he had not seen him act before. Then, as if suddenly remembering the reason he came, Cyrus reached into his coat pocket and pulled out the same type of silvery card that held Roger's recorded life.

"I came here 'cause I thought you might like to have this. It's a copy. I made it after you left."

Sydney was plainly touched by Cyrus' thoughtful gift as he took it from his hand.

"Indeed I *would* like it. It's all I have. Thank you. Thank you very much."

"I figured, if you've got the time, you might want to edit it into its proper chronological order."

"That would be quite an undertaking. And I only remember half of what's on here. The other half is as new to me as it is to you."

"You apparently know a whole lot more of what's on there than I do. And besides, all the images beyond the boundary of your 2011 memory show the date. All it takes is someone with a lot of time and a lot of patience."

"And I evidently have a lot of both. But I'm afraid I wouldn't know how. Your computers are far more advanced than the type I used."

"Then I'll show you. It's really quite simple. And when you're finished, you can make a copy for me complete with an index of who's who and what's what as it chronologically appears."

It warmed Sydney's heart that Cyrus had come to him with this offer. But one question begged to be asked.

"Then you believe me?"

Cyrus had rather hoped that question would not be put to him. Expecting instead that his mere visit alone would be enough for him to assume he did. But before his hesitation to answer the question could alert Sydney to his indecisiveness there came a knock at the door.

"Excuse me" pardoned Sydney.

Upon opening the door he was taken aback for only a second by his first sight of Jessica in a night robe and slippers. Choosing to ignore his amused grin she slipped past him allowing herself to enter.

"Hello Sydney. Hello Cyrus. This is a nice surprise seeing you again so soon.....and so late" she said while trying inconspicuously to repair her disheveled hair.

"I know it's late" said Cyrus. "But..."

"He brought me a copy of my life" interrupted Sydney, holding up the silvery card. "And he's going to help show me how to edit it into its proper chronological order."

"Well now isn't that wonderful?   And *very* thoughtful. Sydney, I'm so happy for you. I must admit to you both that I wasn't quite sure what to expect after the decision was made to contact you. And after our *first* meeting I began to think that maybe this whole trip was all just a big mistake. But I'm so glad to see that wasn't the case."

"No mistake at all" Cyrus agreed. "We've got a one-of-a-kind story here in Sydney that deserves to be told."

The words struck Sydney and Jessica like a bombshell.

"Told? Told to who?"

"He's talking about a book, Sydney."

"A story about a man who awakes from a coma remembering only his past life as someone who lived over a century ago is nothing short of brilliant!"

"I don't believe this" groaned Jessica.

"I don't think there has ever been a book written with this kind of a twist on reincarnation."

"And there never will be. Good-bye, Mr. Owen."

"Now wait a minute" Sydney spoke up, still bewildered, and still trying to comprehend what he was hearing. "I don't quite understand. You want to write a book about Sydney Hamilton's experience with reincarnation, or a book about your great great great grandfather's life?"

"I don't see what difference it makes" said Jessica. "One is inevitably tied to the other."

"True" uttered Cyrus.

"And they're *both* tied to some possibly big money if this all gets out in the form of a book" Jessica continued.

"This is also true. But there's more to it than that."

"And we don't want to hear it" she shot back. "Your admission that this is about money leaves little room for us to believe that you have some other *honorable* motive behind writing such a book."

"I can fully understand your objections, Dr. Wynn. If by my writing a book might interfere with your similar plans to publish your journals on Sydney..."

"That information is private and confidential and will always remain private and confidential! Not even with Sydney's permission would I ever think of exposing him to that kind of public scrutiny."

"My mistake. And I apologize."

"*Do* you have an *honorable* motive?" asked Sydney.

"Well, although I'm certain Dr. Wynn will not find this worthy of a book, *you*, Professor, being a historian, should understand the importance of what history can be learned by a firsthand account from an individual who actually lived during that era."

"No, I'm afraid I *don't* understand because my whole memory of what I know as a historian is in an indefinite state of blackout."

"Then allow me to elaborate. Imagine if one could read about the everyday happenings in the life of an average person who lived over a century ago? Not a historical figure surrounding an historical event. Just an ordinary guy reminiscing over what his life was like growing up back then and what a typical day was like for him and his family."

"They already have books like that" said Jessica. "They're called historical diaries, journals, autobiographies."

"True. But how often can a writer direct questions to his subject when his subject in question died over sixty years ago? Questions about how he personally felt over momentous events that happened during his lifetime? Or what he thinks of this world as it appears to him now a hundred years in the future?"

Sydney's face lit up with a look of encouragement. "Then it seems to me that to write such a book you would have to believe in what you are writing is the truth."

"Not necessarily" cautioned Jessica. "I'm sure not all tabloid writers believe that each story they write is the God-honest truth."

"You have a point" said Sydney. "Which brings me back to the same question I asked you earlier. Do you believe me?"

Cyrus took a moment and a deep breath before skirting a forthright response.

"Well,...Sarah believes you. And if you can get my ever-skeptical wife to believe in you then I'm certain that at least eighty or ninety percent of the people who read this book will also believe in you."

"I don't give a damn about what eighty or ninety percent believe. Or even if I passed the believability test from your *ever-skeptical* wife. The only one that matters to me is *you*. Do *you* believe me?"

Taking another moment before answering, Cyrus then smiled.

"Let's just say, I'm finding it more and more difficult *not* to believe you. But I'm not one hundred percent there yet."

Sydney's response to follow would leave Jessica utterly dumbfounded.

"Then I'll do it. When do we start?"

"Sydney!"

"Are you serious!?" Cyrus exclaimed sounding more like he really did not expect him to agree to it.

"I hope not" said Jessica. "Sydney, are you aware of what this type of book will do to your private life? It'll become a spectacle. People who don't believe you will mock you. Those who do will want to use you. Use you as a subject of study, or worse, as some novelty guest on talk shows."

"He hasn't even begun writing the book and you already have me doing talk shows."

"I promise you, Dr. Wynn, I won't write anything that will give readers cause to mock him. His life and his experience will be treated with the utmost respect."

"How can you promise what people will think and how they will react after they read about him?"

Cyrus found himself at a loss for a response. Jessica gently took Sydney by the arm and led him to the entry door.

"May I speak with you in private, Sydney?"

"Absolutely. Excuse us. We're going to speak in private."

Jessica opened the door.

"In the hall" Sydney added with the slightest grin.

Once in the hall outside of the room Jessica firmly closed the door behind her.

"I can't let you do this to yourself, Sydney."

"With all due respect, it's nobody's decision but my own what I decide to do with my life...Or rather, make that, *both* of my lives."

"He's an opportunist."

"He's my kin."

"He's not....! I mean he is...Or was..."

After stammering for a sensible explanation she paused a moment to reassess how exactly to put into words what she meant to say.

"I know that to Roger, who is inside you, inside your head, he *is* your relative. But what about the person you are on the outside? What about Sydney? You can't ignore what this would do to him, to his reputation and his career."

"Career? Sydney's career ended the moment he woke up with amnesia. I can't even tell you the year Columbus discovered America. History was never one of my strong points."

"Then what about the person you are now? You'll be sacrificing your privacy and your anonymity. And for what?"

"For the opportunity to spend more time with Cyrus. To educate him as to who his great great great Grandfather was. And through it all to hopefully earn the same belief in me that his wife already holds. And as for this overnight celebrity you're afraid I'll become, what does it matter at this late stage of Sydney's life what kind of new turn it takes? After all, how old am I again?"

"Sixty-six. And don't think you're in the twilight years of your life just yet. In this day and age most people typically live to be over a hundred."

"And in *my* day and age there were people known as being what we called a *flash in the pan*. Individuals who pop up from obscurity becoming tabloid celebrities until their fifteen minutes of fame is up and they're bumped out of the spotlight into the land of the forgotten by the next flavor of the month. Now if those type people still exist in this century then you can be darn certain that any fame I receive from this book will be just as fleeting. And don't think that I can't handle this scrutiny you speak of. If I can handle the experience of waking up over a hundred years into the future with the body, voice and identity of a total stranger, then I'm pretty sure at this point I can handle just about *anything* life throws at me."

With lips tightened Jessica turned her face away from him in frustration. It was clear to her that there was nothing she could say nor do that would change his decision on the issue. Finally, after what she felt was a sufficient amount of time to further express her disapproval in silence, she turned to him and relented in a calm soft voice.

"Very well. Then there's nothing more to say. We both know where we stand. But it's ultimately your will that has the final word. So let's go back inside and tell our friend the *jolly good news*."

Sydney flashed that same smile that had its way of melting the icy atmosphere between them.

"Did I mention what a lovely robe that is you're wearing?"

Jessica rolled her eyes, shook her head, and reentered Sydney's room ahead of him.

"Is everything alright?" asked Cyrus.

"Everything is fine" assured Sydney. "Jessica and I just had a few minor issues to clear up. But they're resolved now, so when would you like to begin? Shall we start tonight?"

"I'm pleased by your eagerness. However, I *do* have to work in the morning and therefore really need to get some sleep."

"As do we all" said Jessica.

"You're both right. We should all get a good night's sleep and begin afresh after you get off work."

"And I'll phone you as to what time that will be" Cyrus added as he made his way towards the door. "Oh, and Dr. Wynn, if it's no trouble, may I count on you to help me with answering some questions regarding Sydney's case?"

Jessica looked at Sydney who in turn gave her a subtle nod. Facing Cyrus again she decisively laid down her guidelines.

"I'll assist you with any questions you have regarding reincarnation. I'll also tell you how Sydney came to be my patient and on what bases I formed my theoretical conclusion for his diagnosis. But I will uphold my duty to keep all other notes and records pertaining to my patient strictly confidential. Understood?"

"Loud and clear. Now I wish you both a good night. And I'll look forward to seeing you again tomorrow."

With that same now familiar warm smile, Cyrus let himself out.

A drawn out silence followed as Jessica and Sydney looked at each other expecting the other to say something. But with nothing more left to be said Jessica simply shrugged her shoulders and headed towards the door, at which point Sydney became suddenly moved to say something honest, heartfelt, and necessary.

"Jessica, don't think for a moment that I don't respect and appreciate your concern for my well being. 'Cause I do. I do very much. But this is something I just have to do. He's my one and only link to the life I lived. The only life I know. He's my family. And to have that connection, that bond,...though it's not there *yet*, but *will* be...is all I have to live for now. Please don't ask me to sever that."

"I know that when your mind is set on something there's no hope trying to change it. But you know where I stand on this, and that *won't* change. Still, I'll be there for you just as I've always been. Even when the ridicule, the scorn, and the media circus begins. Sleep well."

Jessica opened the door and began to leave, but stopped short, turning around for one last remark.

"Oh, and it was 1492."

"What was 1492?"

"The year Christopher Columbus discovered the new world. Good-night."

With that she again turned away from him and stormed down the hall to her room.

"Good-night" replied Sydney as he slowly closed the door and leaned against it with a heavy sigh. Then, softly, he whispered to himself,

"A new world it is indeed."

Sydney *did* sleep well that night, with no dreams of flames and feelings of sorrow to deprive him of his much needed rest.

The following day was Saturday thus allowing Cyrus to devote two full days with Sydney before resuming his normal job on Monday. He ceased with the double shifts, sticking with his five in the morning until two o'clock schedule thereby leaving him the remainder of the day to pursue his research with Sydney that would continue throughout the afternoon while reserving the early evening hours for his writing.

He waited until nine o'clock before phoning Sydney with the suggestion that they meet for breakfast.

"And if she's willing" said Cyrus, "I'd like for Dr. Wynn to join us."

His purpose for requesting her company was to hopefully mend any lingering misgivings she may bear towards him and to probe whatever information he could draw from her on reincarnation.

Sure that her indignant demeanor would show little change from the night before, it therefore came as a surprise to Cyrus when Jessica not only appeared amiable and accepting of his project, but also far more eager to accommodate him with her insight into reincarnation than he expected, even offering him several web sites and book titles on the subject. But for Jessica it was not merely an attempt to appease him. She decided upon awakening that morning that as long as he was determined to write this book, and Sydney remained equally determined to assist him with it for his own personal reasons, then it would only be wise for her to assure that his book be written based on a solid knowledge of reincarnation that would hopefully sway public opinion towards believing Sydney, not only for Sydney's sake but for her own as well. Sparing Sydney ridicule was her first and foremost primary concern, but the repercussion this book might have on her standing as a reputable psychiatrist was also a daunting possibility that she felt needed consideration. And so with all objections and grievances set aside Jessica did most of the talking throughout their breakfast while Cyrus, like an astute journalist, recorded every word with her approval.

Following this first of several question and answer sit-downs with Cyrus, Jessica left the two men to begin their own such session.

"I was her professor you know" Sydney commented when he knew she was a safe distance away from overhearing him. "Of course, I don't remember having her as a student, much less being a professor. But I think she had a crush on this old man."

"You don't say" beamed Cyrus.

"But don't tell her I said so. I believe it embarrasses her."

"Strictly off the record."

"So, you're a writer. I'm not sure there has ever been a writer in the Owen family, as far as I know. Although my sister Kimberly used to write poetry. She was pretty good at it too. Perhaps there's a talent for the written word gene that has transcended through the Owen generations."

"Perhaps" Cyrus responded, though feeling doubtful inside.

"Cyrus Owen. You have the name of a writer. And a great writer you shall be someday."

"Oh really? You mean to say someone who came from the past is now telling me he can see into the future as well?"

"No. This is as far into the future as I care to go. It's all about believing in a person. And I know more than ever how important it is to have someone believe in you" said Sydney as he glanced in the direction where Jessica made her exit.

With this vote of trust in his writing ability, or stroke of his ego, whichever the case might have been, Cyrus felt confident to dig right in with the questioning of his star subject.

He began by asking Sydney to recount the last day and night he remembers as being Roger Owen. He then asked him to describe in detail the thoughts and emotions he felt when he awoke as Sydney Hamilton in the twenty-second century, and every event that took place thereafter up to that point in time when they first met.

Although this was all very much exactly what Sydney had already told him in his home the day before, Cyrus wanted to record Sydney's account so as to study and transcribe it at a later time.

After several cups of coffee that left them both feeling jittery from the caffeine, they mutually agreed to brave the cold and continue the interview with a stroll along Broadway.

As the line of questioning shifted to Roger's past, beginning with his earliest childhood memories and then progressing forward through his years, Cyrus could not help but notice the naive wonderment in Sydney's eyes as he soaked in the sights of the city all around him. Although Sydney remained focused on what he was telling Cyrus, he never once stopped to ask questions of his own pertaining to the amazing things he was seeing. Had he done so Cyrus felt it would have been an obvious gimmick of someone trying to play a part. But this was certainly not the case with Sydney. In fact, it appeared to Cyrus that Sydney was trying hard to conceal his fascination, lending further proof to Sydney's extraordinary claim of not being from this century.

It might have been the caffeine, or the engrossing testimony being given by Sydney, or the awe inspiring scene surrounding him, or perhaps it was a combination of all three that allowed both of them to lose track over just how far they had walked since they began their trek back on 44th and Broadway. As they neared Columbus Circle after crossing 58th Street, showing no signs of tiring, they were approached by a beggar. The man appeared to be in his late thirties or early forties, unkempt and dressed in squalid clothes. He spoke not a word as he reached out to them with an open palm. Cyrus chose to ignore him by maintaining a fixed straight ahead look while never breaking his stride, whereas Sydney acknowledged the man, glimpsing into his desperate face, then removing his hands from his coat pockets to show he had nothing to offer. It made Sydney wonder how it is that in a society where no one apparently carries currency, where everything is purchased on cash cards with fingerprint or iris security identification scans, what a beggar such as this man might actually hope to receive. It perplexed Sydney enough to finally bring him around to asking Cyrus this very question.

"Well, it's not like old fashion hard cash is nonexistent" Cyrus explained. "There are *some* who prefer to carry on them a few greenbacks. Usually for less than honorable transactions that they wouldn't want to be traced to, if you know what I mean. I guess you just looked like one of those type of fellows."

Cyrus laughed at the unlikelihood of the Professor being *one of those type of fellows*, while Sydney remained stolid, failing to find the humor in his response. After all, being a new inhabitant to this outer shell of a man he knows nothing of, what *is* the look he exhibits to others, he wondered?

Sydney glanced over his shoulder for one last look at the beggar and was astonished to witness the evident arrest of the man by two uniformed officers who had driven up alongside him in their patrol vehicle.

"Why are they arresting him?" Sydney asked as he stopped and turned completely around facing them.

"He's panhandling. Panhandling is against the law in most major cities."

The officers were not aggressive with the beggar, nor was the beggar defiant towards them. Instead he obediently entered the patrol vehicle as Sydney watched on with great interest.

"What will become of him?"

"A relatively good thing actually. If he's found to be mentally or physically challenged the state will see to it that he receives proper medical care."

"Institutionalized" Sydney noted.

"But if he's found to be of sound mind and able-bodied he'll be put to work for the city. Typically some sort of labor job. But he'll receive a salary, minimum wage of course, that will be put into a trust until his sentence is up, at which time the money he earned will be given to him to go towards an apartment of his own, or whatever else he may need to get his life back on track. The hope is that this type of a sentence will inspire a work ethic in him so that he won't go back to begging."

"So much for one's civil liberties."

Sydney turned away from *the crime scene*, took a few steps forward, and then stopped short from continuing. He paused in thought for only a moment before turning around once again to watch as the patrol vehicle drove out of sight.

"What's old is new again" he murmured to himself.

"What's that you say?" asked Cyrus.

"It's funny. This means of rehabilitating vagrant beggars into hard working *benefits to society* is really quite similar to a law the English government enacted, or at least attempted, during the realm of Queen Elizabeth The First. Houses of Correction, or *bridewells*, named after Bridewell, London's first house of correction, were very common throughout England at that time. And in a way comparable to your system of working for wages while incarcerated, in 1576 Parliament ordered towns to give raw materials to the unemployed and then to buy back their finished products." He then smiled and added, "What's old is new again."

Again Sydney resumed his walk up Broadway, but just as he had done so twice before he suddenly stopped and then looked at Cyrus appearing somewhat confused.

"Now how did I know that?" he asked.

Cyrus shrugged his shoulders and responded, "You're a history professor, aren't you?"

Sydney said nothing. There was no need to. His momentary confusion over this sudden surge of historical knowledge had been superseded by a strange realization of what was obviously happening.

SIX

"Here I am, a renowned and respected historian who knows no history whatsoever except for that of a man who lived a hundred years ago. Now there's irony for ya."

It was a comment Sydney made to Cyrus on the first day of their sessions. Yet as the days progressed through the first week Sydney began to display additional notable signs of a mind unfamiliar to him. And nowhere was this more prevalent than at the museums they frequented.

When not pouring over the hours of images recorded of Roger's life, and taking notes with great scrutiny to every detail of what was viewed, they would engage in long walks while conversing over memories of his childhood, and as painful as it was, Laura and their children. Sydney preferred walking over sitting during these sessions because he enjoyed the never ending *show*, as so it seemed, of futuristic marvels in every direction. And with Cyrus' urging to open up with his thoughts on what new things he saw, Sydney was able to expand on how things were in his time as opposed to how he saw everything now.

But at Sydney's request it was the museums where they spent much of their time. In Roger's life he enjoyed museums. But whether it be an art museum or history museum, they were never a high priority on his list of things to do when traveling or otherwise. So this strange desire of his to visit museums, particularly the American Museum of Natural History, which they dropped in on more than one occasion, came as a surprise to him that he reckoned was on account of the comfort he derived from being able to view objects that he found familiar regardless if they were hundreds, thousands, or millions of years before his time.

Cyrus, on the other hand, saw the reason for Sydney's museum hoping in a far more logical term. *Where else would a historian prefer to spend his time?*

Perhaps it was a little bit of both that brought them each day to those great halls and galleries of culture and learning, but it was Cyrus' assumption that appeared most probable. For Sydney's momentary display of historical acuity near Columbus Circle would prove to be only a prelude to the amazing snippets of information he would divulge regarding varied artifacts viewed throughout the museums. Information that was not made visibly known to the public. He spoke not in long statements aimed to impress, but rather short passing remarks that at sometimes sounded so blasé that he felt Sydney was barely aware of saying them.

It was also apparent to Cyrus that Sydney's knowledge of history showed no boundaries. Whereas most historians may focus their expertise on a particular civilization or era such as the Paleolithic, Neolithic, Bronze, Iron, Dark or Medieval ages, or the Renaissance period exclusively, or perhaps classical Greece, ancient Egypt, Imperial Far East, or Roman, Byzantine, Ottoman Empires, or strictly North, Central and South American societies, so it was that Sydney would exhibit an uncanny and impressive capability of offering a comment on everything.

With this subtle trickle of knowledge escaping from Sydney's lips, Cyrus began to ponder the wealth of intelligence trying to break through the amnesia that had enveloped Sydney's memory. Or perhaps, he thought, such was not the case at all. Maybe these were merely slip-ups in the charade he was so cunningly trying to pull off. But the more Cyrus came to know Sydney - his wisdom and dedication in the telling of the life of his ancestor from so long ago, and the perceptible absence of him wanting to achieve some sort of ulterior motive - the more he began to believe that this man was truly a one-of-a-kind phenomenon.

As for Sydney, his historical references would come to him on an impulse so sudden that he would actually begin speaking the words as they came to mind. This always left him feeling astounded afterwards. It was as though he was hearing them for the first time from someone else, except the words were actually being spoken through him. Still, he made no comments to Cyrus on this strange thing that was occurring.

Jessica returned to Boston during that first week of "Cyrus' inquisition" - as she lightheartedly referred to it. She did, after all, have other patients with whom she could no longer continue to cancel appointments with.

She had also hoped that this time away from Sydney would prove wrong the old saying that *absence makes the heart grow fonder*. But in actuality the miles between them only intensified her desire to be with him. And despite speaking with him, as well as viewing him over her camera phone at the end of each day, it could not equal the exhilaration his nearness to her would bring.

The thought of Sydney would never leave Jessica throughout her daily tasks. At night she would lie awake in bed and dare to imagine his arms around her, all the while trying in vain to convince herself that these mixed-up feelings were anything but love. And then, as if to prove this, she would mentally list the many reasons why.

Always topping her list would be his age. She would deduce that falling in love with a man twice as old as she as just plain inconceivable, and then recall the eligible men her own age who had shown an interest in her in the past.

Then there was of course the ethical reason. A factor she reminded herself of often. For this reason alone she felt it would be absurd to consider allowing an emotion such as *love* to permeate their professional relationship. And to cease being his psychiatrist in an effort to pursue him romantically would be futile as long as his heart fully belonged to another woman - regardless that this woman passed away sixty years ago.

After accepting these self-given reasons for shunning any romantic leanings towards the Professor the remaining feeling that always prevailed for Jessica would be, loneliness. Being strongly career oriented, perhaps overly so, she subconsciously chose to never let relationships or other such emotions of the heart enter her life. Therefore, aside from family, work associates and a few friends, Jessica never saw that being all alone was cause for sadness or concern. But all that changed when Sydney Hamilton, or rather, the personality of the long departed Roger Owen, entered her life. Now, without him near, that once unfamiliar feeling of loneliness was all she knew.

There was nothing to misconstrue how Sydney felt about Jessica during her absence. He missed her. And he was not reluctant to admit this to himself, though he made a point of never mentioning it to her, feeling it would be an improper thing to tell one's own psychiatrist. But beyond that the void he felt with her gone could not compare to the emotional turmoil that he had little idea Jessica was experiencing over him. Whereas her nights were spent lying awake thinking of him, his nights on the contrary, when unable to sleep, were preoccupied with the unsettling exertion of trying to interpret the meaning of the flames in those dreams he continued to have with regularity and the reason they brought him such profound sadness. By finally controlling this anguish Sydney was able to derive that the sadness he felt was from a sense of loss. And loss of his loved ones, he surmised, would naturally be the only plausible cause that could produce a grief in him so powerful. But in what way did those flames relate to his family? This he failed to understand.

Sydney often considered sharing this dream with Jessica. *After all, she's a psychiatrist*, he would remind himself. *And interpreting dreams should be her specialty. That Freudian thing.*

And so he decided that upon Jessica's return to New York he would finally relate his dream to her, along with the emotions that invariably followed, in the hope that she might be able to shed some understanding into its meaning.

"There's something I want to tell you. Something for you to analyze" he told her during one of their evening phone conversations.

"What is it?" she asked.

"I'd rather tell you in person."

Of course there was no reason at all why he needed to wait until then. In actuality it was a subconscious ploy to assure himself she would return - unaware that any such ploy was completely unnecessary.

Although Sydney reached the decision that he would recount his perplexing dream to Jessica, he did not feel a need or desire to mention to her his reoccurring bursts of historical knowledge. Rather, it was Cyrus who phoned Jessica with this revelation while she was en route on the train to New York. It was not the specific reason why Cyrus decided to phone her, however, he was surprised to learn that

Sydney had not made her aware of these sporadic droplets of recall he was experiencing.

"All this from a man who only a week ago couldn't tell me when Columbus discovered America" said Jessica.

"Well not only can he now tell you *when* Columbus discovered America, he can probably tell you what he was wearing the day he did it."

"I wouldn't be at all surprised if you're right about that. He was an extraordinary teacher with a remarkable depth of knowledge. And I really can't say that I'm surprised his memory of being Sydney Hamilton is slowly beginning to trickle back. I knew it would only be a matter of time before this happened. But what I didn't know was if it would filter through little by little or come all at once. Now I know. This must be what it is he wants to tell me."

"Yeah? Well here's a little something I'm sure you *won't* hear from him. The actual reason why I called was to tell you about an incident that occurred yesterday."

Cyrus went on to tell of an interesting moment that had developed during a conversation he and Sydney were having over coffee at the third floor café in the American Museum of Natural History. While taking a break from his course of questioning and Sydney's random insights into history, they settled on a topic that both could relate to; fatherhood. Like most new fathers, Cyrus had plenty to share with anyone who would listen regarding those sleepless nights of unrelenting cries, that occasional cough or sniffle that would send he and Sarah into a worrisome tizzy, that first tooth and first step, and those spontaneous smiles and laughs of hers that would warm his heart in a way unmatched by anything else he had ever known. Cyrus also informed Sydney that the next bundle of joy to be added to their family will be a boy. And he wondered in what way raising a boy will differ from his rudimentary experience at raising a girl. It was this question that brought forth a response from Sydney that would baffle them both.

"They certainly are precious moments. And you should treasure each and every one of them. For before you know it they've up and grown and out on they're own. And all too often you'll wish you could go back to those times when they were so young and adorable. But now as for boys, I can *only assume* that they might have a bit more of the devil in them than sugar n' spice, being that I never had a son of my own to draw any comparisons with."

Taken aback, Cyrus paused before inquiring the obvious question.

"But I thought you had *two* sons? My ancestor being one of them."

Sydney fell silent. Appearing at first perplexed, he then developed a wide-eyed look of fear that seemed to betray what he was feeling inside. A fear that he might actually be losing the one thing he had left in this life worth living for - the memories of his loved ones from the only life he ever knew. He also realized almost immediately another fact that struck him as contradictory to what he remembered of his daughter, Natalie. He spoke of her as a child he had watched grow into adulthood. Furthermore, the daughter he saw in his mind was not Natalie at all, but the girl in the photographs placed throughout the Professor's home. The girl he understood to be Professor Sydney Hamilton's only child.

Sydney said very little for the remainder of the day and spoke nothing of what occurred at the cafe. Nor did Cyrus question him further on the subject. Incredulous though he may have been at the onset of his book writing endeavor, Cyrus was finally convinced into believing Sydney and all that he had been told of his most extraordinary circumstance.

"It was the look on his face" he told Jessica. "That look in his eyes that told me right then that it's all true. Just as Sarah was convinced as she watched him react to those images of his daughter, it was that look in his eyes when he realized he forgot he had two sons that convinced me."

Although Sydney came to know the hotel's front desk staff on a first name basis, and he was thankful that the Professor was financially well off - according to bank statements he found at his home in Boston - to afford the sizable debt he was placing on his credit card, after nearly two weeks of living out of the same room he looked forward to any opportunity that would allow him to spend time away from this temporary residence of his. And so it was at a small hole-in-the-wall pizzeria he discovered on his own over on Eighth Avenue between 39th and 40th Streets where he chose to tell Jessica about his recurring dream.

"A hundred years later and New York *still* serves up the best pizza in the world. So now that you've heard my dream, what do you make of it?"

"Well,...that certainly is an interesting dream, for sure. And its reoccurrences along with the emotions associated with it are evidence enough that there is some sort of meaning behind it. But what that meaning *is*, is purely subjective. Twelve psychiatrists can give you twelve different interpretations. And there are literally dozens of details of the dream that would have to be factored in. Such as whether there is smoke or no smoke. And if there *is* smoke, is it heavy? Is it a controlled fire, as within a fireplace? Is it a brightly burning fire? Are you *in* the fire, or *afraid* of the fire?"

"I've already told you all the details I remember of the dream. *Yes*, it is brightly burning. It's a *blazing* fire. Like a bonfire with *lots* of smoke and with sparks flying up into a nighttime sky. And I'm not *in* the fire, but more or less *observing* it. And not with fear, but rather with a profound sadness. These details never vary."

Jessica pondered these specifics further before offering her summation with a slight shrug of her shoulders.

"Lots of smoke could mean that your ego is clouding your vision. Possibly a vision of the truth. Standing in front of this brightly burning fire might mean a victory in bringing invulnerability to a situation. And being that it's a blazing fire could signify a nostalgic regret for past mistakes. But then again, I'm just basing this on what I remember from my study of dream interpretation. I'd have to do further referencing in order to derive a clearer understanding."

Sydney appeared somewhat disappointed that her words failed to immediately offer him anything more substantial. He then felt the need to refute, rather defensively, the notion of one of her comments.

"Well I can assure you that I have *no* past regrets. My life was wonderful. Ideal. *Perfect* in every way."

"So that may be true about Roger's life. But what about Sydney's?"

"I wouldn't know. I know nothing about Sydney's life."

Jessica felt this would be an opportunistic time for Sydney to bring up his recent resurgences of historical prowess, as well as that moment when he forgot about two of his children from one life while remembering his only child from another. She waited, but he said nothing. So, she tried again.

"You know, it's very likely that in time you'll begin to regain your memory of being Sydney, and eventually lose what you remember of your past life."

Sydney leaned back in his chair and grinned.

"I see you've been talking with Cyrus."

Jessica did not answer, but instead reacted unknowingly to what he was referring to.

"So how much did he tell you?" Sydney inquired further.

"Tell me what?"

"I suppose I should have no call to be upset. There are no rules against writers talking about their subjects to psychiatrists. Only the other way around."

"Yet it would be reasonable that *I* be upset with you for divulging these changes with a writer, relative or not, before telling your own psychiatrist."

"I told Cyrus nothing. He observed these *changes* in me without remark. I began to speculate that he hadn't even noticed."

"Oh, he noticed. So for arguments sake I'll just assume that your intention was to tell me all this before finishing that last slice of pizza and ask you straight out if there's anything else you haven't told me yet but plan to?"

Sydney immediately thought of the mysterious man in black who pursued him through the park. But after considering her disgruntled reaction to learning secondhand of these most recent events to come along in him, he decided against divulging the one-time incident. For certain it would only bring out an even greater wrath in her for not being told earlier.

"No. Nothing of importance. Just the same ol' same ol' that comes with living in the body of a total stranger a hundred years in the future."

"You're being facetious I hope."

"Of course I am. The truth is it scares me to death the thought of losing the only thing I've got left from the only life I've ever known. Without those memories of the people I love, I have nothing."

In his hotel room later that evening Sydney studied with greater scrutiny the dozens of photos Cyrus had printed, at Sydney's request, from the recorded images of Roger's life.   When there was no more available room on the table tops for the photos Sydney had purchased frames for, he resorted to taping the additional prints to the walls.

Moving about the room while viewing each photo one by one he would repeat to himself the names of every individual represented.

"Laura. Tyler. Natalie. Justin. Mamma and Daddy,...also known as, Josephine and...and....*George*. Josephine and George, of course! My father's name is, George. And that's John,..no, *Jeremy!* My good friend, Jeremy. And here we have Justin, Tyler and Natalie again with.... Now who the devil is that?... *Who* is *that?*... My brother? Could it be my brother? Think! Think!"

Sydney thought hard for a moment until all at once it came back to him the identity of the strange man in the picture with his daughter.

"Oh for the love of God, it's *me!*" he exclaimed with a laugh. "It's *me!*"

But his tone grew solemn upon realizing the significance of this particular lapse in memory.

"It's me."

His eyes then darted to another picture.

"Laura and *me*."

And to another.

"And that's me again with my brothers and sisters, Evan, Will, Alisa and Kimberly... No, *that's* Alisa and *that's* Kimberly."

And on to another.

"And that's me with... No, no, that's *not* me, you idiot! That's my son, Tyler! And he's with... Oh God, I know these two people. I *know* them!"

A feeling of alarm began to escalate within him as he struggled to remember the identity of the two elderly people in the picture.

"I just spoke their names in this picture over here!" he said, referring to the previous image of his parents.

"I *know* them! I *know* them!"

Sydney's eyes remained fixated on the faces he was able to identify only seconds earlier but were now only vaguely familiar to him. A feeling of dismay over how sudden and complete the memory of these two individuals had escaped him. Eventually he drew his eyes upward to another photo that was taped to the wall. He immediately recognized the young child as his daughter, Natalie. Only in this picture she was older than when he last saw her - possibly five or six he figured. Standing outside the front door of their Fort Lauderdale home and holding the family cat, Sydney felt baffled when he was able to remember the name of the cat, Bagheera, yet continued to draw a blank when it came to the names of the two faces in the previous picture.

Ruminating fondly over the picture, Sydney was suddenly struck with a vivid memory of a past experience. He saw a young girl, the same age as Natalie in the photo, with fair skin and curly strawberry blonde hair wearing a red dress. So clear in detail was this memory that he could even make out the white polka dots on her dress. Like Natalie, the little girl was also standing beside the front door of a house. There was no doubt in his mind that this house was far older than the home he purchased new in Fort Lauderdale. The modest stone dwelling, covered for the most part with ivy, was the only structure he could see amidst a sunny backdrop of rolling green hills. The light blue shutters that flanked each of the tiny windows for some reason stood out in his mind, as did the flagstone walkway that led up a slight incline to the front door from where the little girl called out to him.

"Sydney! Sydney!"

Although the girl was young his memory was telling him that he was even younger than she.

"Sydney, come in now or else Mummy will be cross with you!" she warned.

Mummy? If the English accent failed to cast a clue as to her identity, then the word *Mummy* left no doubt in his mind that this was Sydney's sister.

The memory then left him as suddenly as it appeared. But it was not forgotten. It remained with him as he shifted his eyes onto another picture, that again of his precious Natalie, her age as he last saw her, in a toddler's swing with himself, Roger, crouched by her side. He smiled warmly at the picture as any loving parent would. But his smile would again be interrupted by still another flashback of a memory unfamiliar to him.

He saw another girl of the same age, but not the same girl as before. This girl had light brown hair and rosy cheeks. She laughed as he swung her gently. At this moment he felt a sensation of love in his heart for this child. A paternal love he had only known for his own children, Justin, Tyler, and Natalie. Looking around his surroundings he found that he was in the backyard of a large stately home. It was his home. *Sydney's* home. And there were other children all around. Apparently a birthday party celebration. He then saw the same child, his daughter, seated at a small table with the other children gathered around. Approaching the table came a woman so lovely to look at, so glowing, with an allure that went beyond her physical beauty. He *knew* this woman. Every bit of her innermost self. And it was this aspect of her that captivated his heart so. Not forgetting Laura he felt almost guilty for the emotions overwhelming him at the sight of her until at last he recognized the woman as being his wife, Sydney's wife, not for the resemblance she bore to her photographs in his Boston home, but because of the feeling in his heart. An unmistakable and unexplainable feeling. He just knew.

She placed the birthday cake she was carrying down in front of their child and led everyone in a joyous chorus of The Happy Birthday Song.

"Happy Birthday dear, Angela...

Happy Birthday to you. "

"Angela" remembered Sydney. "My dear little Angie."

At that moment his attention was brought back to the image of Natalie on her swing.

"No! It's Natalie!"

Sydney was well aware of what was happening. His memories of his life as Roger were merging with the returning memories of his life as Sydney. Or were they being replaced? It was this he feared. *I have to fight it*, he told himself. He knew his only hope against these invading memories would be his unrelenting concentration of the people and places in the images surrounding him.

"Laura! Me! Justin!" he shouted as he went about the room pointing to the pictures in a nearly overwrought way.

"Tyler! Laura and the kids! Kimberly with her husband Derik and my nephew and niece, Joseph and...and...Shelley! And those two people are my parents! Of course! Josephine and George! How could

I forget? That was at Snyder Park! And this was down in Key West!
And that was my first car! And that was the old home in Cleveland
where I grew up! And this was me at Disneyland!"

It was this image of young Roger wearing a Mickey Mouse
ears hat while standing in front of Sleeping Beauty's Castle that held
his attention in a way unlike the others. He suspected his age to be
about seven or eight. Yet it was not so much the boy he used to be that
intrigued him, but the faux castle behind him. He looked closer at this
castle until the memory of another castle, one authentic in its antiquity
and in near ruins, came to mind. He instantly knew this castle to be the
twelfth century Manorbier Castle, though he had never been there, nor
had he ever heard of it during his life as Roger. Yet the little boy he
saw himself as, the one clutching a wooden sword in his hand as he ran
alongside the exterior stone curtain wall of this fortress, was none other
than Sydney himself - also age seven or eight. Entering through the
large arched entry of a grand gatehouse, complete with battlements, a
portcullis, and even arrow-slits, he saw young Sydney charge into the
grassy inner ward where he stopped only long enough to glance around,
as though looking for something or someone. Continuing his search
young Sydney entered into a long narrow passageway and then into a
vaulted ground-level room of the main hall-block that was dark, empty,
and haunting. But still no sign of what he was in search of. He saw the
young boy continue his search through the interior of the wonderfully
ornate chapel, then descend the chapel's grand staircase that took him
once again down to the inner ward where he crossed the bright green
lawn to the age-worn steps that he climbed leading to the top of the
battlemented curtain wall. But midway on the steps the boy was
stopped by the sight of his foe emerging from a small doorway at the
top.

"Ah-ha! At last I found you, Sir Lancelot! Now draw your
sword and prepare to die!" commands young Sydney.

"En garde!" replies the little boy holding up his own wooden
sword.

Sydney charges up the steps towards him thus initiating the two
friends to commence with their gallant duel. Tirelessly they spar along
the top of the curtain wall until *Lancelot* withdraws from the battle
realizing his sword is no match for the much longer sword in the hand
of *King Arthur*.

"No fair! Your sword is longer than mine!" protests the little boy.

"It's not a sword. It's Excalibur!"

"Well, why can't I use the Excalibur?"

"Because only King Arthur is allowed possession of Excalibur. Don't you remember the sword in the stone?"

"Then let *me* be King Arthur for a change."

"No. You're Sir Lancelot."

"But I'm always Lancelot. And besides, Lancelot and King Arthur are supposed to be friends."

"Not since you stole Guinevere from me" Sydney reminds him as he points his sword to a little girl, younger than they, standing in the inner ward below next to a massive dilapidated industrial hearth with a Flemish style chimney. With her hand raised to the level of her eyes to shield the bright sun she looks up at them, unaware as to why the duel for her honor has come to a sudden end.

"But I don't want her. *You* take her and let *me* be King Arthur."

"I don't want her either. *You* take her. Or by order of I, the King, I shall have you banished from the round table and Camelot as well. For*ever*."

"You're not playing fair, Sydney. And I'm not going to play with you anymore" says the little boy as he drops his sword and walks away. "But next time," the boy turns around and adds, "I'm going to be Merlin. And Merlin is more powerful than King Arthur."

"No he's not. He can just see into the future because he lives backwards. *His* future is *our* past."

The boy dismisses Sydney and continues on his way down the stone steps. But young Sydney is suddenly fascinated by this extraordinary gift of Merlin's.

"Wow. To know the future while experiencing the past" he contemplates in a soft voice to himself.

Looking down to the inner ward he imagines what it might have looked like in medieval times when the castle was alive and bustling with lords and ladies, noblemen and faire maidens, weavers, dyers, iron smiths, and every other kind of craftsmen, tradesmen, and artisan his imaginative young mind can think of, all plying their trades. He can see and hear the songs and voices of the minstrels, troubadours, and even a court jester. And he sees children at play with balls and hoops, as well as livestock and fowl roaming freely about. Just then, through the portal of the majestic gatehouse a group of chivalrous knights in shining armor astride their colorfully adorned horses gallop in with all the pomp and pageantry one would come to expect.

It was at this moment in Sydney's life when the seeds of what would become his lifelong passion were planted.

He then saw the same young lad engrossed in a book while lying on the floor of his childhood home next to a crackling fire within a fireplace. It is a cozy home with old world charm, but notwithstanding most of the modern conveniences afforded to the middle class homes of the mid-twenty-first century.

"Put the book down, Sydney, and come to the table" so says his mother, a thin woman with scarlet hair and simple but sweet features that matched her timid voice.

Assisting her with setting the evening meal on the dining table is his sister, although much older in appearance than the youngster he saw her as earlier.

"Come along, son" his father tells him as he takes his place at the head of the table. "Do as your mum says. You may continue with your reading after you finish your supper."

Here he remembers his father as a tall well-mannered man with an average build. He had the face and hands of a man who had spent much of his life working outdoors. But his rough exterior could not mask his amiable nature, nor his smile that had a way of warming the hearts of all those who came to know him.

Sydney's thirst for historical knowledge would continue well into his teens as evident by the next memory he saw of himself sitting atop of the Round Tower at Manorbier Castle while absorbed in still another book. From this high vantage point he was finally able to recognize where the location of his childhood home lay. Nestled in Southwest Wales in the county of Pembrokeshire he could see behind him the tiny quaint village of Manorbier only a short stroll from the castle. To one side, atop a ridge beyond a narrow valley, he could see

The Church of St. James, active during the Norman period when Manorbier Castle was established. Then, looking straight ahead, lies the sandy beach coastline of Manorbier Bay, and beyond that the Irish Sea. This was his home, now familiar to him in every direction, until that day came when he set off to pursue his calling within those prestigious halls at the University of Oxford.

Sydney saw images of the handsome young man he used to be sitting amongst his fellow students in classes where his ambition to learn were unparalleled with any other happenings in his life at that time. He saw himself meandering along the campus grounds with his nose in an open book and his shoulders weighted down with book bags. He saw himself roaming from one gallery to another within The Ashmolean Museum of Art and Archaeology, scribbling notes and always with that open book, until his presence became as much a permanent fixture as the statuary within the ancient Greek exhibit.

Surrounded with the literature by thousands of authors in the Bodleian Library, his favorite place to study and contemplate, Sydney's returning memory brought him back to a conversation he was reluctant to indulge in with a school chum who called into question his steadfast academic work ethics.

"You know, all study and no play will lead to a lot of regret when you're a crotchety old man" his friend warned him in a whisper.

"And it can also lead to a life filled with the joy of doing what I love to do" Sydney reminded him.

"And what's that? A life learning about the dead? What about experiencing life with the living?"

"I'm afraid the past is far more interesting."

"Says you. That's only because you've never bothered to venture out and partake in the pleasures awaiting you in the present."

"Oh, but that's where you're wrong, my friend. I happen to find *great* pleasure here in the present learning about how our past has brought us to where we are now. And if I can pass that knowledge on to others, and perhaps unearth a few new discoveries about our past along the way, then what better pleasure is there than that?"

"Boy you need to get out more."

Sydney chuckled.

"I'm serious" his friend continued. "What good is there in learning about all this past tense stuff?"

"Because, in the words of that philosopher George Santayana, 'Those who cannot learn from the past are condemned to repeat it.'"

"Or in the words of John Fletcher, 'But what is past my help, is past my care.'"

"George Savile, Marquis of Halifax, 'The best way to suppose what may come, is to remember what is past.'"

Determined not to let Sydney have the final word on this contention of quotations, his friend pondered earnestly for a quote that would bring him down into submission.

"Cole Porter, 'If you want a future, *darling*, why don't you *get* a past?'"

Sydney surrendered with a loud burst of laughter that echoed throughout the library bringing about a host of twisted looks from disgruntled fledgling intellects.

"Shhhh" reprimanded his friend. "Do you want to get us kicked out? Although for you it would probably be the best thing that could possibly happen. And being the good friend that I am, that's exactly what I'm going to do."

"You're going to get me kicked out of the library?"

"Even better. You're going out with me tonight. We're going to hit every pub on High Street and drink 'till we're well away. And if we're lucky we'll even raise a wee bit of hell along the way."

"You're crazy."

"*I'm* crazy!? *You're* the one who hasn't been laid in God knows how long."

From this point onward the memories bubbling up from what had been a black void began to accelerate. The images, although clear in every detail, were now all too brief. Only tantalizing snippets of his extraordinary life playing out in his mind like a trailer to an old forgotten movie. At what first appeared as flashes from his night out pub-hopping with his friend, culminated with a moment from that evening that made his heart dance.

She approached them with a tray of brew held high above her head, never spilling a drop as she gracefully maneuvered her way through the throng of merrymakers to a table next to where they sat. Her long silky ash-blonde hair was pulled back and tied with a light blue ribbon that matched the top she wore, a top that Sydney was quick to notice how it accented every inch of her voluptuous curves. There was a loose lock of hair that hung down to the bridge of her nose which gave the notion of just how exhausting her work was. But that genuine smile on her pretty face revealed the joy she found in her job in spite of its drudgery.

"What can I get you boys?" she asked after serving the neighboring table their drinks.

"A couple of pints, Marge" answered his friend in a loud voice.

"Of course! Why did I even bother to ask?" Marge said with a wink.

Sydney's friend mimicked a kiss in response as the two of them watched her disappear into the crowd.

"You know her?" asked Sydney with an unconcealed great amount of interest.

"When you've been to this place as many times as I have, one can't help but to get to know everyone who works here."

"How *well* do you know her?"

"Not *that* well, unfortunately."

As Sydney's eyes scanned the room in search of her his friend witnessed a look of enchantment on his face he had never seen before.

The memories then seemed to fast-forward through a successive montage of archaeological sites and digs throughout the world where Sydney would broaden his knowledge in the years ahead. Egypt, the whole of Europe, Central and South America, Southeast Asia, India. In all these places there was one person ever-present. Marge. His memory would always recall the sight of her with a camera bag slung over her shoulder and a camera in hand while focusing her lens on a myriad of archaeological splendors or on Sydney himself as he would brush away the earth from one of his many fascinating treasures that time had kept hidden for centuries. The perfect team, as so they appeared. A team whose features matured notably over their long period of exploration and discovery.

These images segued into memories of a classroom where this time he saw himself as the teacher. A not quite so surprising turn for a man with the unique background of being both an archaeologist *and* historian. With their eyes fixed upon him he saw the faces of countless pupils, among them, Jessica Wynn.

Hers would be the only face he would recognize in what immediately followed - a rapid barrage of people and places unfamiliar to him. They came at him in an overwhelming pace with no apparent chronological order. From childhood to old age and every memory in between, like thousands of snapshots of his life strewn about, they swirled through his head faster and faster in a dizzying delirium until it would at last come to an abrupt halt on those same familiar flames spiraling upward toward a starlit night.

Sydney rose up swiftly from his bed with hastened breaths, his heart pumping with an accelerated beat, and fine beads of perspiration formed across his brow. The lights in his hotel room were still on, just as they were before he had fallen asleep. Nothing at all changed in the room, yet, for a moment, a mere instant, the room was an unfamiliar place to him. The photos surrounding him were of faces he had never seen before. Only the memories from which he awoke remained entwined with his confusion. But before a sense of alarm could infiltrate his state of mind the full memory of Roger Owen, the man he was, came surging back.

The hotel's cocktail lounge adjacent to the lobby was the perfect spot for Sydney to call for an impromptu rendezvous with Jessica and Cyrus. Ideal for being located in the same hotel where Sydney and Jessica resided, and also for the simple fact that a tall stiff drink was precisely what Sydney yearned for following his adrenaline pumping dream. Although it seemed to him that this dream had consumed the entire evening, in reality he woke to discover that he had been asleep for no more than an hour. He felt pensive, agitated, and worried that if he fell asleep again he might awake with his life as Roger Owen sponged from his memory permanently.

Sydney sat down at the bar and ordered a double Gin and Tonic. As Roger he was never a heavy drinker, except for those benders he would indulge in with his friend Jeremy during his college years. Still, Roger had always enjoyed his beer with a good ball game, a glass of wine now and then to relax, and a Gin and Tonic during those infrequent cocktail parties he and Laura would attend. And so it came as a surprise to himself when he immediately changed his order.

"On second thought" he told the bartender, "make that a Brandy Stinger. A double. On the rocks."

The words just blurted out, before he was able to think about what it was he was requesting. Roger had never liked brandy. He never even knew what ingredients made up a Brandy Stinger. Yet, he suddenly felt this strong desire to have one.

After the bartender placed the cocktail down in front of him, Sydney stared at the drink for a prolonged period that was noticeable to the bartender.

"Anything wrong?" asked the bartender.

"No. Nothing at all. You can put it on my room tab" Sydney responded as he slid the bartender his room key card.

Wearily Sydney then raised the glass to his lips and sipped. It tasted strong and minty. *Rather like cold medicine*, he thought at first. But after another sip he was astonished to discover that he actually liked it, and surmised that it must have been a favorite of the Professor's.

The lounge he sat in touted a stately elegance. Rich mahogany, polished brass, and etched glass were all around. At the opposite end from the entrance there was a female pianist tickling the keys for a small number of patrons who had gathered for conversation and a nightcap. The drink and atmosphere put Sydney at ease, but not completely. He needed to share the event he had just experienced with Jessica and Cyrus and felt it could not wait until morning. And so it was shortly after eleven when Jessica arrived. Cyrus followed approximately fifteen minutes later. They moved to a corner table in an effort to yield themselves a little privacy. Sydney ordered another Brandy Stinger, Cyrus a beer, while Jessica settled for a cup of hot tea - feeling unmotivated for anything alcoholic since being roused from her bed to join them.

It took nearly a half an hour for Sydney to relate to them in explicit detail every recollection from his dream. He felt it essential not to leave anything out.

"Of course, some of the places I didn't recognize" he concluded. "Just as there were some faces...quite familiar to me,..but I couldn't tell you their names. For instance, that fellow in the library I told you about who took me clubbing. I assume we were close school chums. Yet I can't for the life of me recall his name."

"I wouldn't be too concerned about that" said Cyrus. "How many of us can remember the names of every person we've ever known? The good news is, it's all starting to come back."

"And the bad news is, it's all coming back at a price" responded Sydney as he began to tell of that single frightening moment when he awoke with no remembrance whatsoever of his life as Roger Owen.

Jessica could see the anxiety on Sydney's face mount as he spoke of this. When finished he downed the rest of his drink, which was half full, and gazed down at the empty glass for a prolonged moment of tense silence. When he finally looked up he saw for the first time a look of similar concern in Jessica's eyes over the likelihood of losing not only the memory but also the personality of this man she had come to know and adore.

The obvious shift in mood prompted Cyrus to once again speak out with optimism.

"At least the memory of your wife has returned. Margaret was her name, right?"

"But everyone called her, Marge" Jessica remembered.

"Except for me" said Sydney with a faraway look. For it was Jessica's remark that brought to his mind a flashback.

"I called her, Margie."

"Margie!?" the pretty young barmaid replied with a smile. "Either you're quite drunk, or incredibly presumptuous, Mr. Hamilton. Or perhaps it's just the noise in this pub and you didn't hear me correctly. I said, my name is Margaret, but everyone just calls me, Marge. *Not* Margie."

"You're wrong on one account, Margie" said young Sydney, leaning against the bar feeling so debonair. "I actually heard you perfectly.   But you're right, I *am* a wee bit drunk, and it *was* presumptuous of me. Although I'm not always like this. In fact, this is a first. Just ask my friend over there."

"That won't be necessary. I know your friend. He's in here all the time. And I've never seen you in here with him."

With that said, she picked up a tray of drinks and turned away from him ready to disappear into the throng of students.

"Then you won't mind if, with all due respect, I call you Margie. You're just so pretty. So alluring. So incredibly lovely to look at. Margie just seems.....*fitting*."

Turning around facing him she reacted slightly taken aback prior to her droll response. "Why Mr. Hamilton, you are just about the most *brazen* fellow I've ever met."   A flirtatious smile and wink then followed. "But don't stop."

"Call me, Sydney."

"No. I'll stick with Mr. Hamilton. It just seems....*fitting*."

"From that day forward I always called her, Margie."

Jessica and Cyrus were held spellbound with every word Sydney spoke, not so much for the story he was recounting, but rather over the uncertainty of not knowing who it was who was speaking to them. Roger or Sydney?

"And did she continue to call you, Mr. Hamilton?" asked Cyrus.

"No. It was always Sydney after that. The following night I returned to the pub where she worked, asked her out, and we were together ever since."

"Sounds like love at first sight" Cyrus beamed.

Jessica, however, was less enamored. "Is there really such a thing as *love* at first sight?"

"You're quite right" Sydney agreed. "I'm sure it was more *infatuation* at first. But I know that love soon followed after our first date."

"*Who* knows?" asked Jessica, leaning in closer towards him from across the table as if trying to peer deeper into his soul.

An inquisitive look flashed across Sydney's face.

"Who's speaking to us now?" Jessica continued.

"My misfortune is *not* that of having a split personality, Jessica. You know that as well as I do. But I understand what you're asking. And the answer is, I'm still Roger Owen in mind and spirit and Sydney Hamilton in body and voice. You see, what I observe,...these flashbacks,...they appear to me as,...well..." Sydney pondered a moment and then sighed. "Oh, how best can I explain this?...It's like *deja vu*. I see places I know. Faces I know. But as Roger I know they are places I've never been to, and people I've never met. And unlike your typical *deja vu*, with these images I feel emotions. And I know that they are the emotions of what Sydney was feeling because I'm fully aware that they are *his* memories, and *I* am *him*. And except for that instant when I awoke as *only* him, I'm beginning to find the whole experience...." He paused in search of the right word. "...*intriguing*."

"I know I've said it before but I'll say it again. *Fascinating*" Cyrus exclaimed. "With each day you become more and more fascinating."

"Here you are" interrupted their elderly waiter as he approached them with a tray of drinks. "Another beer for you, sir. A Brandy Stinger for the gentleman. And another tea bag for the lady."

"Thank you" said Jessica. "Sydney, in light of what you just told us, I suspect that the emotions you feel when you dream of those flames might have nothing to do with the life of Roger Owen, but instead....Sydney Hamilton."

Jessica saw again in Sydney's eyes that faraway look.

"Sydney, what do you see?" she asked.

"It's not what I see. It's what I hear. It's that song."

Jessica, Cyrus, even the waiter looked over their shoulders at the pianist. And it was the waiter who immediately recognized the song as George and Ira Gershwin's, *Our Love Is Here To Stay*.

"Some songs have a timeless appeal" said the waiter with a smile before leaving their table.

"Especially when it's our song" whispered Sydney.

"*Whose* song, Sydney?" asked Jessica.

"*Our* song!?" laughed Margie.

The small London cocktail lounge was dimly lit and nearly empty aside from the bartender and a trio of male musicians on stage; a drummer, a bass player, and a vocalist on piano, making it a romantically ideal setting for a young couple on the threshold of love.

"And since when did it become *our* song?"

"From this moment on" young Sydney answered tenderly.

"It's unfamiliar to me. Why *this* song?"

"All you have to do is listen to the words to know why."

Margie closed her eyes, swayed subtly to the beguiling melody and words being sung by a velvety voice, and smiled.

It's very clear,

Our love is here to stay.

Not for a year,

But ever and a day.

The radio and the telephone

And the movies that we know

May just be passing fancies,

And in time may go.

But, oh my dear,

Our love is here to stay.

Together we're

Going a long, long way.

And a long, long way indeed is how far Sydney and Margie's love for one another would take them. Beginning with a myriad of dates that would reveal wonderful and exiting new discoveries about each other.

"With photography as your major, what type of career following school do you expect to make a living from?" asked Sydney during one such date while picnicking in the University Parks.

"I'd love to have a successful career as a photo journalist. But I realize that field is a difficult one to break into. So, realistically, I'll probably wind up making a *living* as a commercial photographer."

"Commercial photographer? You mean like..."

"Print ads" Margie broke in. "Practically every print ad you see has a picture. I can see myself most likely working for an ad agency."

"But rather than taking pictures of consumer products for ads that will probably generate no emotional or lasting impact, *if* they're noticed at all, why not utilize your talent by taking photographs that will fire the public's imagination while serving to educate all at the same time?"

"And what type of photos might those be?" Margie asked with a sly sense of knowing where he was going with this.

"Archaeological discoveries cannot be properly documented by words alone. Think of taking a picture of a place or artifact that has never been photographed before, much less been *seen* by other humans in hundreds or even thousands of years! And then imagine sharing that photograph with scholars and students, and most importantly the average ordinary individual who would never in their lifetime see in person this place or artifact. Or never even knew that such a place or artifact ever existed. And then, because of this photograph, this photograph that *you* took, their minds would be opened to learn. To learn something of *our* past. Now how could a picture of a hamburger, or shampoo, or some pain medicine that's new and improved, possibly compare to the satisfaction that a photographer, such as yourself, would gain from the imaginative and educational impact one single snapshot could have on a person?"

Margie smiled. "If I'm not mistaken, I'd *swear* that you're about to proposition me to join you on some archaeological dig."

And join him she did. Throughout the rest of their school years, during semester breaks and summers, and after graduation when their travels would take them to the far-flung regions of the world, they would become an irrepressible dynamic team and highly impassioned lovers as well. It was only natural that their wedding would be held in The Church of St. James across that narrow green valley from Manorbier Castle.

Then there was that birthday of Margie's, Sydney recalled, when the newlyweds lived in their tiny South London flat. Sydney presented her with the gift of a turn of the twentieth century Ansco Junior, Model A, box camera. It would be the first of many.

In time a new career, a new home in a foreign country, and the birth of their only child would follow. Although this chapter of their lives together would be an evident departure from their adventurous days of extensive travel and discovery, it was no less rewarding in its own wonderful way. With his life absorbed in his teaching, along with writing books and lectures on demand, as well as Margie achieving her own level of success with her published photographs, they would still find time to entertain their small circle of friends with cocktail parties and barbecues. But above careers and entertaining friends their greatest joy and devotion would be to their daughter, Angela. And that same love and attention Angela would reap from her parents would again be heaped upon the birth of their grandchild, a boy, named William, whom they would all call Willie.

Surely whatever bumps Sydney and Margie might have encountered along their road through life together, they were all overshadowed by the good times and loving memories they shared. And it would be the song that Sydney dedicated to his love so long ago in a small dark cocktail lounge in London that only after their separation upon Margie's death would it become all the more hauntingly prophetic.

In time the Rockies may crumble,

Gibraltar may tumble,

They're only made of clay,

But our love is here to stay.

SEVEN

"It's like falling in love all over again."

Even though Sydney's statement was off track from their usual question and answer session about Roger, Cyrus had no need to ask Sydney who he was referring to. For it was noticeable to Cyrus from the moment they got together the following afternoon that Sydney's thoughts were on the memory of someone else. And trudging through Times Square in the biting cold left Cyrus feeling less willing to engage in conversation regardless of whether it be about Roger *or* Sydney. Still he did so out of courtesy.

"Is it something you'd like to discuss? Perhaps somewhere indoors? Where it's warm?" Cyrus asked through his chattering teeth.

"Now you *know* I'd much rather we spend these valuable moments together walking rather than sitting cooped up in some stuffy room. And yes, it *is* something I'd like to discuss with you because even though you're not my psychiatrist, I always get the impression that Jessica is annoyed whenever I speak lovingly of Laura, or now Margie. I don't know, maybe it's just me. I could be wrong. In any case, these emotions I have for this other woman, Margie, leave me with the strange feeling of being unfaithful towards Laura. It sounds crazy, I know. After all, they're both gone now. But in my heart they're still very much with me in every sense of the word."

"You know, in light of how much I hate shopping with my wife I never thought I'd say this, but, how 'bout if we take this conversation inside a department store? That way you can tell me about Roger and

Margie and anyone else you have on your mind while you marvel over all the crazy new things the twenty-second century has to offer. How does that sound?"

Sydney stopped suddenly at the sight of someone crossing Broadway in their direction.

"Sydney? How does that sound?" asked Cyrus a second time.

It was unmistakable. The person crossing the street was the same mysterious man who pursued him through Boston Common and the Beacon Hill district. Dressed in the same long black coat and hat, the man glared at Sydney with those cold beady eyes as he stepped onto the sidewalk and continued directly into a public building. Sydney hurried towards the building ahead of Cyrus until he stopped at its large front windows to peer in. What he found was a cafeteria on a mammoth scale. And being the lunch hour it came quickly to Sydney's mind the old phrase, *needle in a hay stack*.

When Cyrus caught up to Sydney he saw nothing in his behavior that struck him out of the ordinary, which begged him to question the obvious.

"You're hungry?"

There was no misinterpreting Jessica's anger as she paced the floor of Sydney's hotel room while Sydney and Cyrus sat calmly by and watched.

"I can't believe you never told me about this guy!"

"I didn't want to needlessly worry you."

"*Needlessly* worry me!? This guy stalks your house, chases you through Boston Common and Beacon Hill, and then shows up again here in New York and you call that a *needless* reason to worry!? Well thank you, Sydney Hamilton, for considering my feelings, but I *am* worried." She then turned her wrath on Cyrus. "And *you*! You didn't even see what this guy looked like!?"

"Let me think. A man in a dark trench coat crossing Times Square during lunch hour in the middle of winter. You're right, he should have stood out like a sore thumb. How on earth did I miss him?"

"This is no time for sarcasm" chided Jessica.

"Alright, alright you two" Sydney jumped in. "Let's come together on this. Now it's obvious that this mystery man is following me. And there has to be some sort of a motive behind it. Perhaps he has a vendetta against me, or I have a connection with him, or....I don't know. With my memory gone there's just no way of knowing.... *Unless*....Why don't we phone Mrs. Deere? Maybe I told her something about this man before I lost my memory that might shed some light as to what he wants with me."

"We'll use my phone" offered Jessica.

She placed her mobile phone on a table and verbally called up the number using Sydney's name and "Home." At the very instant Mrs. Deere answered the call a four inch beam of light projected up from the phone opened a six inch square backless hovering screen with a clear and sharp moving image of the other caller - a standard feature on all phones of the time.

"Well hello, Dr. Wynn. And you too, Professor."

Sydney and Jessica responded their regards.

"And the gentleman behind you, I don't believe I've had the pleasure..."

"Cyrus Owen, ma'am."

"Oh yes. Dr. Wynn told me about you."

"I'm sure" Cyrus grinned.

"Mrs. Deere..."

"Yes, Professor?"

"Do you recall if at any time before Sydney...Before *I* suffered my accident, if I made any mention of someone following me?"

"*Following* you!? Like a stalker? Heavens no."

"You're sure?"

"Oh I'd remember if you told me something such as that. If I may be candid, Professor, you've never been one to share with me anything that might be troubling you. We always spoke of the good old days, or idle chitchat about the day's happenings. But never anything deeply personal or troublesome."

A moment of dashed hopes amongst the three pervaded until Mrs. Deere struck upon an afterthought.

"Although..."

"Yes?" Jessica responded.

"Well, it's nothing I hadn't already told the police. Or you as well, Dr. Wynn. It's just that before the accident I noticed, Professor, that you appeared deeply upset."

"Upset about Margaret's passing?" Sydney assumed.

"No. Although there were always many times when it was quite obvious that you missed her. This time, however, was different."

"How so?" asked Jessica.

"I don't know. The only thing I can suppose is that you, Professor, were upset about the passing of Dr. Wesley."

"Who's Dr. Wesley?"

"That's right. You don't remember. Well, Dr. Wesley was a dear friend of yours going back, oh, thirty years at least. He used to also teach at the university before leaving to work elsewhere. *Where* he later worked, I don't know."

"So he was sad about Dr. Wesley's death?" asked Cyrus.

"Not so much *sad*. But more like....*disturbed*."

Sydney, Jessica and Cyrus exchanged confused glances at one another.

"For example" Mrs. Deere continued. "When I asked you, Professor, how old Dr. Wesley was, you told me eighty-three. Yet, you acted as though his death was an untimely one."

"Untimely for an eighty-three year old?" questioned Jessica.

"It was the following evening, after I had gone home, that you...you had your *accident*. Thank God your downstairs neighbor Mr. Murphy heard the snapping sound of the branches that broke your fall, otherwise you might have froze to death lying there all night."

Sydney mulled over these latest facts. "Interesting."

"Well I do hope I've been somewhat of a help."

"Thank you, Mrs. Deere" said Sydney. "You've certainly given us something to go on."

"Good. And if I can be of any more help, just let me know. Oh, and *do* come home soon, Professor. It's been very lonely around here with you gone, and I miss our chats terribly."

"Perhaps this coming weekend, Mrs. Deere. I miss them, too."

After an exchange of good-byes the image of Mrs. Deere vanished followed by a moment of silence.

"There's a connection" said Sydney. "I don't know what it is, but I'm sure this Dr. Wesley's death has something to do with why this man is following me."

"And suppose this man's intentions go beyond merely following you?" questioned Cyrus.

"You mean that he might be out to kill me?"

"He has a point, Sydney."

"I don't know. If he wanted to kill me he would have had the perfect opportunity to do so in Beacon Hill. There was no one around."

"But there were windows" Jessica reminded him. "Someone might have seen him do it."

"Not in the park. There was no one in the park either. Just the two of us,....and some ducks."

"You shouldn't make light of this" Jessica begged with growing anxiety in her voice. "For whatever reason he chose not to kill you in the park or Beacon Hill doesn't mean he won't eventually catch up with you and..."

Too overcome by the thought, Jessica was unable to finish her sentence. But Sydney understood her implication and decided at this point to say what he had stopped himself from telling her earlier.

"...And push me out a window?"

It was an inferred comment that cast a chilling probability to the circumstances surrounding his fall, where before such speculation would have been viewed as outright ridiculous.

"We'll notify the police" demanded Jessica.

"And tell them what?" Cyrus protested. "Following someone without a verbal threat is not against the law as far as I know. But let's say we *do* go to the police. Do you really think they'll take him seriously after we tell them he can't remember who this guy is or why he *might* be trying to kill him because in his mind he's still the man he used to be in a past life? And even if they do, what do you suppose the chances are that he'll become the focus of media attention before they even put a lick of effort into finding this guy?"

"Well look who's being just a tad bit hypocritical. Isn't that exactly what *you* hope to do? Make Sydney *and* yourself the focus of media attention? Perhaps you're only afraid that if Sydney's statement gets out now someone else will cash in on his story faster than you can finish your book."

"Damn the book! If I felt there was any way the police could prevent the threat of harm coming to Sydney I'd march him over there right - "

"Enough already!" shouted Sydney. "We've traveled down this road before and I don't wish to go there again. I told you both about this man because I thought that together we might be able to come up with an answer as to who this guy is and what he wants from me. I *didn't* expect it to drive a wedge between you two by doing so. Now I agree with Cyrus that we can't go to the police. The minute they hear my story I'll end up right back in that nut house. Perhaps I should just confront him again, only next time I'll pin him against the wall and force him to talk."

"In one life or the other you watched *way* too many movies, Sydney. You do something foolish like that and you'll probably get yourself killed."

"I actually have to agree with Jessica there" Cyrus bemoaned reluctantly. "I'll do a search on this Dr. Wesley, see what I can find on him. Seems to me if there *is* a connection we'll at least have something concrete to bring to the police that will steer the focus away from your other.....*issue*."

With a pool of emotion welling up inside Jessica, she turned her face away from Sydney.

"*Issue* is certainly an understated way of putting it" Sydney said with a light chuckle. "And I think that's a great idea. Thank you."

Sydney's attention was then drawn to Jessica when he detected what he thought to be the faint sound of sniffling.

"Jessica, is there something the matter?"

"I just wish you had told me all this earlier. If something happened to you or *does* happen to you I don't know what..." When suddenly realizing the tear upon her cheek, she turned away from them again without completing her sentence. "I'll be in my room if you need me" she said with not so much as a glance in their direction before leaving the room.

For a moment Sydney stood silent and bewildered.

"What in the devil?" Turning to Cyrus he expected to find in him the same confused reaction. "Now what do you suppose that's all about? I certainly didn't intend this to make her so emotional."

"You never fail to amaze me, Sydney."

"What do you mean?"

"You've been married to two women, the first one for nearly sixty-four years and the second for thirty-three, still you can't see the obvious signs of a woman in love."

Sydney appeared dumbfounded over Cyrus' surprising revelation.

"*Love?* But.... Well, I assumed that at one time she had a silly little crush on me, or rather, the professor that is. But *love?*"

Sydney looked toward the door of his room with a feeling of uncertainty as to how he should respond. Cyrus felt there was little more to say other than to just allow the thought of what he said to sink in and leave.

"I'll phone you if I learn anything on Dr. Wesley" said Cyrus as he made his way towards the door. "And I'd try to stay in if I were you. Don't answer the door unless you're sure of who's on the other side. I'll talk to you later."

Sydney, still in his state of bewilderment, said nothing as Cyrus departed.

It took a moment before Sydney himself finally took the initiative to leave and make his way down the hall to Jessica's room. He hesitated before knocking as so did Jessica before she opened the door. Her eyes appeared slightly puffy from obviously crying.

"May I come in?"

Jessica lowered her head and stepped aside allowing him to enter. She felt too embarrassed to look at him. Sydney too felt just as uncomfortable. As both Roger and Sydney he never quite knew how to conduct himself when it came to crying females. He moved slowly to the only window and looked down to the streets below, never once looking back at her.

"You know I was thinking,...actually a few days back,... something you might find rather amusing. I was thinking about coming back in this life as a history professor. Of all the different sort of people and professions I could have come back as, *I* come back as a history professor. And then I thought, now why couldn't I have come back as a rock star? Or some acclaimed stage dancer down there on Broadway? Or...oh, I don't know...*somebody* famous. I'm sure that everyone at one moment in their lives has tried to imagine what it would be like to be a celebrity. Then I got to thinking, now if I was famous I'd at least be able to recognize the adulation people would bestow on me. They'd be more open and obvious when it comes to expressing it. But as a history professor, or even as a simple construction manager for that matter, I just don't *see* such things so clearly. Probably because, aside from with my two wives, I can't understand what it is that someone would find...." Stopping short of finishing his sentence he finally turned to her. "I wish you'd stop me because I really don't know where I'm going with this."

"I'm sure you do. And I'm sure now that *I* know that *you* know how I feel about you, I'm looking right now like the perfect fool."

"Not at all! My dear, I'm the fool for not seeing it earlier. When my own kin can see it but I..."

"Cyrus!?" she interrupted. "Oh God. I'm so embarrassed."

"Oh no! There's no reason to be. I certainly know how it feels to love someone. It's wonderful. It's powerful. It's delirious and sometimes even a little frightening. But it shouldn't be embarrassing. My only question is, *who* is it that you have come to feel this way for? Sydney or Roger?"

"As Sydney I've always found you terribly attractive, in a sophisticated, dignified way. But your personality, quite frankly, sucked. Intelligent, *yes*. Whimsical, lighthearted, vivacious? Hardly. Of course, in light of now knowing about the loss of your family I can understand why you always appeared so dispirited. I'm sure you weren't always that way. But then the personality of Roger Owen took over. Who, despite his own loss, exuded everything that Sydney's previous personality lacked. Together, as Sydney and Roger, you've become the man I've always dreamed of. You know, I've never been in love before. That's because I've never known anyone quite like you."

Again, unable to look into his eyes, she lowered her head. Sydney's heart swelled with a feeling of sincere endearment towards Jessica. It went beyond flattery that this beautiful woman would come to love him despite his irritability he felt he had been laying on her, due to the circumstances, from the day they first met. But if she had noticed any peevish behavior in his character it was obviously understood or she chose not care. This, coupled with seeing her standing there, head bowed, tears in her eyes, he could not stop himself from going to her, placing a gentle kiss on her forehead, and taking her in his arms in a caring embrace. Jessica held him tightly, not believing at first that she was at last finding herself in this position she so often dreamed of. Yet this moment of exaltation was not to last. For it was in the way he held her, along with that *friendly* kiss on her forehead, that she knew without a doubt that what feelings she held for him were not entirely mutual.

"I'm old enough to be your great great great grandfather."

Jessica laughed in spite of knowing that in actuality there was less than a ten year difference in age between herself and Roger, and that Sydney was no older than her father. Still she understood what he was implying by his subtle attempt to lighten the mood. They released their hold of one another and looked deep into each other's eyes. In hers he saw love. In his she saw nothing but a warm kindness and perhaps even a hint of yearning to feel in return at least a small fraction of the love she felt so dearly. Turning away from him she decided to say something that would let him off the hook and put them both at ease from what was becoming an uncomfortable situation.

"I know. If only at a different time in another place. But the irony is, for you this *is* a different time in another place."

"Jessica..."

"It's okay, Professor. School girl crushes on their teachers come and go. And so too will this." Feeling a surge of emotion boiling up from within like a volcano on the verge of exploding, her only thought was to get him out of the room as soon as possible before erupting into tears. Opening the door and standing aside she hoped a change of subject would hasten his departure. "Don't forget to use the GPS button on your phone should you get in trouble."

"I don't plan on going out and getting myself lost."

"There are several reasons for having GPS in mobile phones. The most notable reason is for crime enforcement. If an individual is in trouble, especially in a case of kidnapping, all the mobile phone user needs to do is press in 911 followed with the GPS button. The police are then immediately alerted with an *exact* position on the victim right down to an interior closet or vehicle trunk. Likewise, a caller can also phone an acquaintance and use the GPS if they wish to be located by the receiver,...say like in a large crowd."

"It's nice to know that GPS is now being used for more purposeful reasons than just finding directions" and after a moment added, "Well now if this isn't the day for learning all sorts of new things."

Sydney realized at once that his attempt to buoy up her spirits had failed. He understood that her silence was his cue to leave and walked slowly to the door, pausing under the threshold to turn to her for one last word, but Jessica was quick to say something first.

"I'll call you in the morning."

Sydney nodded and as an impulse softly caressed her cheek with the back of his hand before leaving.

After closing the door Jessica hurried to the bathroom where after closing that door as well she turned on the water faucets in the sink to drown out the sound of her crying and hunkered down on the floor in the corner and began to weep uncontrollably.

Lying on his bed Sydney was not sure what was troubling him more, the reemergence of this mystery stalker, or knowing that in the room down the hall Jessica was probably in tears with a broken heart over him. In both cases he felt helpless to do anything about it. Still, despite knowing this, he found it impossible to set his mind at ease. So there he lay staring up at the ceiling for one, two, three hours as the light of day from his window faded to darkness and the bright lights of the city cast their luminescent glow on the walls around him. But just as these heavy thoughts were wearing him down to the verge of slumber the hotel room telephone rang bringing him back to an alert state.

"Jessica..."

"No. It's Cyrus. And have I got some interesting stuff to tell you about this Dr. Wesley. Dr. *Frank* Wesley."

"Oh yeah?"

"Absolutely. The minute I got home I went on the computer and it didn't take me long to find out what we have. I would've called you sooner but just as I was about to Jasmine fell down and hit her head on the door."

"Oh no! Is she alright?"

"Oh yeah. Just a little bump. You know how kids are. Anyway, she cried herself to sleep and I'm finally able to lay this on you. Dr. Wesley used to be a professor at Harvard, no doubt it's where you two became friends. But fifteen years ago he took a job that was offered to him working for the CDC in Atlanta."

"CDC? You mean, the Centers for Disease Control?"

"That's the place. He became their top leading Virologist. I guess a position he just couldn't refuse. *Then* only one day before you had your little fall out the window incident it turns out that Dr. Wesley died."

"Yes, we've already established that."

"True. But it's the *way* he died that I can now understand would give anybody cause to be shaken up a bit. It turns out the good doctor was murdered with a Rad Gun."

"A *what* gun?"

"A Rad Gun. Short for Radiation Gun. Nasty things. When pressed up against the victim and discharged it sends a lethal dose of radiation throughout the body without breaking the skin's surface. The level of radiation is so high that it begins to cause an immediate systematic destruction internally of the body's cells until within *minutes* the victim ultimately drowns in his own blood. There's no surviving a Rad Gun."

"Who would invent such a grisly thing?"

"The U.S. Government! Who else? Of course it was meant for use by secret agents, you know, the ones with the missions that the Government doesn't want us to know about. But unfortunately for the Government these secret weapons didn't remain a secret for very long.

And once the public got wind about how horrible these weapons were there was a huge outcry to stop making and using them. Of course the Government, wishing to paint a rosy side to the issue, came out saying that the Rad Gun was invented as merely a *humane* way of killing in situations when protecting oneself from certain death from an enemy makes killing an adversary unavoidable. Frankly speaking, has there ever *been* a humane way of killing someone?"

"Dr. Guillotin thought there was when he designed the machine that was to bear his name. He later thought differently after some forty thousand people lost their heads at the height of the French Revolution."

"Now I'm speaking with Professor Hamilton."

"No. Still Roger. Just something I remember from a National Geographic program I saw on television once. So then what you're telling me is that the U.S. Government is responsible for Dr. Wesley's murder?"

"Not so fast. The U.S. Government eventually bowed to public pressure and agreed to stop making and using the Rad Gun. But not before some of the guns slipped out onto the black market and into the hands of the underworld. At least, so says the Government."

"So that still leaves us not knowing who Dr. Wesley's murderer was working for."

"And also *why* they would want to kill you as well."

"I'll better that question with another. Why did he push me out the window? Why not just use this Rad Gun to make my death certain?"

"Maybe the murder of two Harvard professors, one current and one former, who were also good friends would be too easy to link to the person or persons who ordered the hit."

"Good deduction."

"Say, we make a great detective team. Like Sherlock Holmes and Dr. Watson."

"Yes, but one thing still bothers me, Watson. Why didn't he try killing me again in the park?"

"Perhaps Dr. Wynn is right. The chance of being seen by someone was too great."

There was a hushed moment as the two of them contemplated all what had been spoken. Cyrus then added what would certainly have surprised Jessica to hear.

"I think we have enough here to go to the police with."

"Well, there's still a lot of unanswered questions. But I think you're right. I'll mention it to Jessica to hear what she thinks."

"How's she doing? Did you go to her after I left?"

"I did. And you were right about that too. She *is* in love with me, or rather, Roger *and* Sydney. Poor girl."

"Poor girl!? Are you telling me you feel nothing for her?"

"Not at all. Of course I feel something for her. I feel a great deal as a matter of fact. There's no mistaking the emotional bond ¬I believe we share. A bond that goes beyond just being doctor and patient. Whenever I'm with her I feel at ease with myself and with everything that's happened. When I'm with her I get the same feeling I used to get when I'd enter my house in Lauderdale. A feeling that I'm home. But when she's gone I feel even *more* alone than I already do on account of being separated from Laura and the kids, and Margie and Angela. On top of that she's beautiful. I mean you must agree that Jessica is a *beautiful* woman."

"Of course I do. Despite our differences I have to admit that Dr. Wynn is a very attractive woman. No doubt about it. So what's the problem? Why do you regard her as some *poor girl* because she's in love with you?"

"Because I love Laura. *And* I love Margie. I love them both, and I miss them both."

"And it's alright that you should. But they're gone now and you're still here. You've got to stop living in the past someday, Sydney. There's nothing wrong with *remembering* the past. But there's no going back to it. While you're still alive you have to live your life for the present and the future. Now for most people love comes just once in a lifetime. Or in your case, once in *every* lifetime. So I think you're pretty darn lucky to have someone like Dr. Wynn come along who wants to love you for the remainder of your life. And believe me, people nowadays are living a lot longer than they used to in your day."

"So I've been told" Sydney muttered recalling the same words spoken by Jessica. "You speak a lot of truth, Cyrus. And I appreciate you being so candid with me."

"Hey, that's what family is for."

Hearing this from Cyrus brought a rush of joy to his spirit. Family. How he longed to be considered as, and invited in as, a member of the Owen family once again. It filled him with a feeling of worth that his new existence in the twenty-second century had lacked.

Sydney's voice choked when he reiterated what Cyrus said. "Yes. That's what family is for."

His emotion did not escape Cyrus' detection, and wishing not to embarrass Sydney he chose to continue past that subject and close the conversation.

"Listen, I have to get goin'. But if you want to go to the police tonight just call me and I'll be right over to take you there. I don't want you leaving that room all alone. Not even if Dr. Wynn accompanies you. Got that?"

"Understood."

They bade each other good-bye and Sydney hung up feeling good with respect to how things were developing. With the police being made aware of his friendship with the murdered Dr. Wesley, the coincidence of his plunge from his window only a day after the doctor's death, and the stranger stalking him since then, he felt confident that it would be only a matter of time before this mystery man would be apprehended. He also felt good about his acceptance as a true member of the family that was once his in a previous life, regardless of the highly unusual qualifying factors involved. And thanks to Cyrus his heart was opened to the possibility of forging a new life with someone who loves him. With accepting the way things are, and dismissing any feelings of disloyalty towards Laura and Margie, he suddenly felt certain that by allowing Jessica's love in, his own love for her would evolve.

Uplifted, Sydney could not contain his eagerness to share these wonderful things with Jessica. He went to his door, opened it, and watched a folded slip of paper fall to the floor. It was a note.

My dearest Sydney,

I crossed the line. My feelings for you went beyond that
ethical boundary that is supposed to exist between doctor
and patient. For this I am so sorry. But I realize that I
am too emotionally weak to overcome these feelings and
still serve as your psychiatrist effectively.
You require and deserve a doctor who can conduct
oneself with the professionalism that I failed to adhere to.
I will be glad to offer you several referrals of
psychiatrists in the Boston area, if you wish.
Finally, I also must apologize for leaving you at a time
when this mystery stalker has again made himself known.
But I am quite sure that Cyrus will do everything within
his power to protect you. Although we clash on certain
issues I do believe in my heart he's a good kid. Although I
still think you should waste no time going to the police.
Take care of yourself.
Love, Jessica

Sydney closed the door and immediately went for his mobile phone and called up Jessica. It took several rings longer than it normally would when he would phone her before she finally answered. On screen behind her he could see the busy bustle of a train platform.

"Sydney, please, give it a few days at least before we discuss the letter."

"A few days!? I don't want to give it another minute! Now listen here, Jessica, you *can't* leave. I've got some important information to tell you about this Dr. Wesley."

"*That's* the only reason you phoned?"

"No. That's *not* the only reason. There's something else I want to tell you, but I don't want to do it over the phone."

"Well, you're just going to have to because I'm boarding my train back to Boston as we speak."

"Where are you?"

"Grand Central."

"Grand Central? Stay there."

"Sydney, do you see that behind me? It's a line. A line to board a train. And I'm in that line, Sydney."

"Step out of it" he said as he hurried about the room donning his coat, scarf and hat.

"I can't just step out of it."

"Sure you can. Didn't you tell me at the speed those trains travel there's one that leaves every hour? You can take the next one."

"Sydney..."

"Sixty minutes. Surely you can give me sixty minutes of your time in person before heading back up to Boston. That's all I'm asking. I'm leaving the hotel now. Where shall I meet you?"

Jessica, exasperated, mulled it over until finally stepping out of line with a groan.

"Damn you. Why can't you just let me make a clean exit? Do you know the big clock in the middle of the Main Concourse Level?"

By this time Sydney had already left his room and was headed towards the elevators.

"If it's the same clock I remember over a hundred years ago."

"Same clock. It's been there forever. Meet me there. And don't be late. Because whether you're here or not I'm getting on the next train."

"Somehow I don't think you're going to want to after you hear what I have to say. In the meantime can you do me a favor?"

"What is it?"

"Phone Cyrus so he can tell you himself everything about Dr. Wesley that he told me."

"I'll phone him right now and I'll see *you* at the clock."

By the time they hung up from each other Sydney had already exited the elevator and was making his way across the lobby.

The cab ride from the hotel on 44th and Broadway to Grand Central Terminal on East 42nd Street did not take long due much in part to the minimal traffic on this particularly frigid and blustery night. He stepped out of the cab into a gust of wind that kicked up a whirlwind of snow around him. The warmth that greeted him after he hustled into the terminal was a blessed relief. So too was the overall atmosphere of the terminal itself. As a preserved historical landmark stepping inside Grand Central Terminal was like stepping into a time capsule, or in Roger's mind, like journeying back to a time familiar to him. Everything was the same right down to the marble paved floors and buff colored stone walls, as well as the wainscots and trimmings of cream-colored marble. It was all there and still every bit as opulent as one would expect of a public structure built in 1913. Of course there were typically a few subtle reminders here and there that he was living in the future, but nothing imposing or that which could not be overlooked.

Sydney only took a few steps along the long corridor that would eventually lead to the Main Concourse when he stopped suddenly having taken notice of a small flower stand to his right. *Perfect*, he thought. *Flowers on such a miserable night as this. What better way to begin when I tell Jessica how I feel about her?*

He bought a small bouquet of short stemmed miniature red roses wrapped with baby's-breath in green tissue paper and then continued his way up the corridor, across Vanderbilt Hall, and over the two flanking ramps that lead down to the Lower Concourse Level. There was a vague smile on his lips and a certain glee in his stride, for he had fair reason to feel so joyful. At last there was hope for a future in this life. A future of his own making, not of someone else's that he can only remember in bits and pieces, or of another whose life abruptly ended where he knows he could not go back to pick up where he left off. As long as these memories of both lives remained with him as a solid anchor of some sort of past from whence he came, then he could move on and embrace the future, come what may.

Sydney entered the Main Concourse where straight ahead of him in the center of this extraordinary 80,000 square-foot space he could see the Information Booth, a circular marble and brass pagoda topped with a gilded four-sided clock. Next to it stood Jessica with her back facing him. The whole scene suddenly reminded him of an old black and white movie - the busy train station, flowers in hand, and a beautiful girl he felt destined to spend the rest of his life with waiting for him under the big clock. But this romanticized picture would be fleeting, for no sooner had his eyes caught sight of her when around from the ticketing windows to his left the mystery man in black stepped into view directly in line of where Jessica stood.

On previous encounters his face had always remained expressionless. But not this time. Sydney saw in those beady eyes a look of such he had never seen in a person before. It was a look to kill. And it was this very look that produced a flashback of when Sydney first faced this man.

Sydney had barely opened the door of his home when the man pushed his way in so forcefully that he nearly knocked Sydney to the ground.

"I won't tell anyone!" Sydney shouted at the man as he scrambled to get away from him. But the man pursued him unmercifully. With no escape possible and no means of fending off the intruder, Sydney ran to his window and threw open the sash. It was dark and he saw no one on the street below. Still, he yelled, yelled as loud as he could hoping someone would hear him.

"Help! Help! Someone help me!"

Now, in Grand Central Terminal, Sydney saw that same look that told him this evil being was intent on taking care of what he failed to accomplish before, regardless of the crowds around them.

Sydney turned away from him and ran. Back through Vanderbilt Hall he took a sharp left headed towards a corridor that would take him to what was called the 42nd Street Passage. He did not glance back to see if the man was following. There was no need to. Unlike the brisk and steady pace the man kept in the park, this time Sydney could hear his footsteps running behind him.

Sydney turned left on 42nd Street Passage and then a sharp left again into a men's clothing shop hoping to lose him. It worked. The man ran past the store just far enough to where Sydney could still see him stop just a few yards beyond. Sydney crouched down behind a rack of apparels without losing sight of the man who, with his back facing Sydney, looked down and then slowly raised his head to scan the area. Sydney took out his mobile phone and called up Jessica.

"Sydney, where are you?"

"I'm in a men's clothing store."

"You're shopping while I'm standing here at this clock?"

"Jessica, he's here. The man who's been chasing me is here in the terminal right outside the store."

At that very second the man suddenly snapped his head around to where he was looking directly at the store. There were two entrances to the store and Sydney began moving in a stealthy manner towards the northern-most entrance while his pursuer began his way towards the southern entrance.

"He's coming in. I've gotta get out of here."

"Sydney, don't hang up."

"I won't."

"Cyrus told me everything. You've got to get to the MTA Police. Their offices are on the Northeast side of the Lower Level."

"MTA Police. Northeast side. Lower Level. Got it."

The man entered the store just as Sydney made his escape. This, however, did not go unobserved by the man and once again the chase was on. Immediately upon exiting the store Sydney made a left down the ramp that would take him to the Lower Concourse Level. When he reached the bottom he glanced up to notice that his pursuer was no longer behind him. But Sydney did not stop to contemplate what move his foe might be playing. He continued into the Lower Concourse Level heading towards the Northeast end as Jessica instructed.

"Sydney, are you there?" came her voice over the phone.

"Yes, Jessica."

"Turn on your GPS so I can get a fix of where you are."

"I'm on the lower level. I believe I've lost him."

At that moment Sydney pressed the GPS button on his phone and Jessica immediately picked up a red blip on a three dimensional tri-level layout of Grand Central Terminal that popped up on her mobile phone screen. As she watched the blip move across the Lower Concourse she began to make her own way towards the East side grand staircase.

"Alright, I've got ya. I'll meet you there in a minute" she told him.

Sydney approached a long narrow hall that led to the offices of the MTA Police. Along the left stretch of this hall were three entries leading to the train platforms. And in the center of the hall stood the man in black. *Impossible!*, Sydney thought.

Nevertheless, the man had indeed gone beyond the ramp and made his way down the escalator near the entrance of the Grand Central Market which, in turn, brought him in closer proximity to the hall where he was now standing. Dodging through the closest entry to the train platforms and reentering the hall further down was Sydney's only hope for getting around him. Not surprisingly, his pursuer also entered onto the train platforms from the nearest entrance to him in an effort to head him off. It might have seemed a blessing to Sydney that at this crucial moment the train on track 102 was disembarking its passengers. Squeezing through the throng, he figured, may act as the necessary barrier he would need between himself and the man in order to get past him. But the man in black was not about to let the hindrance of several pedestrians stand between him and his objective. He pushed his way through the crowd until at last they were face to face. Sydney then saw the man pull from his pocket a strange weapon that was black in color and resembled a gun except that it lacked having a typical barrel. It looked similar instead to a scanner gun he recalled from his later years as Roger, only much smaller, like that of the tiniest cell phone from that period. Sydney finally dropped the flowers he was so determined not to let go of while for a mere instant he struggled with the man. He managed to push the man away, but his adversary rushed back at him as a young male train passenger in his early twenties happened to step between them. The gun fired without sound. The eyes of the young man widened in shock as the jolt of an uneasy but not yet painful sensation raced through his body. His attacker brushed the young man aside and continued after Sydney who doubled back through the crowd. But Sydney's escape at this nearness would prove impossible. Just as Sydney reached the platform edge of track 103 the man in black caught hold of him by the shoulder and swung him around.

Again, Sydney was struck with a flashback of that moment at his window after he yelled for help to anyone who might hear. He looked around just as the man in black charged towards him, and then after a frantic struggle his attacker managed to push Sydney out of the window. Sydney could still vividly remember now the man's face looking down at him from the open window as he plunged downward.

It was an image that eerily replayed itself again as Sydney was falling backwards onto the railroad tracks five feet below. He hit the tracks hard on his left side and for an instant was dazed by the impact. He then looked up and saw that the man had fled. Sydney did not hear the shouts from onlookers after he fell. It was not until he turned his head and saw the light of the train coming towards him on the very tracks he was laying across when their voices filled the air. *The train! Oh my God, someone help him! Get up! Get up!* By Sydney's perspective the train grew larger as it rumbled towards him closer and closer. Suddenly his adrenaline kicked in and he scurried to his feet. He heard the sharp hiss of the hydraulic brakes, but still the train grew closer at a speed that seemed much faster than it would have if he were not standing in the direct path of it. One hundred yards, fifty yards, twenty-five, ten, five, and then without a second or foot to spare Sydney suddenly found himself being lifted in the air by two Samaritans who, by risking their own lives, reached down and hooked their arms under his, thereby pulling him up to safety. With his heart pumping so fast Sydney thought he was nearly going to pass out as the crowds gathered around him.

A woman's shrill scream then drew the spectators' attention away from Sydney over to where the young male passenger had just collapsed to the ground. Sydney caught a glimpse of the lad lying there before the crowds surrounded him. *It was a Rad Gun*, Sydney realized. *No wonder he'd use that over any other weapon. It's silent, it doesn't leave an entry wound, and the victim doesn't immediately collapse, leaving the killer ample time to make his escape.*

Sydney picked himself up and at once felt a searing pain in his left hip. He knew it was not broken for he was still able to walk on it. But the pain only increased with each step. Regardless of the discomfort he knew he had to get away because his attacker could be lurking anywhere amongst the mass of people running to the scene. So he limped his way as quickly as possible due West passing track 104 and heading towards 105.

Just after reaching the bottom of the grand staircase on the Lower Concourse Level, Jessica also heard the woman's scream and without delay ran in the direction from which it came. So close did she come in passing the killer as he exited the platform area and reentered the Concourse that they nearly bumped into each other.

Once on the platform Jessica pushed her way through the spectators until she was able to look down on the lifeless body of the young man lying there with his blood filled eyes wide open and blood streaming from his ears, nose, and mouth. Next to his hand she saw red roses strewn about and assumed they belonged to the dead man.

Sydney exited the platform area just beyond track 105 and limped his way across the Concourse towards the East grand staircase. Midway across his eyes met with those of the man in black. Despite the pain he doubled his pace and ran up the stairs with his pursuer following.

With no sight of Sydney around her, Jessica zoomed in on the GPS blip which led her to track 103. The flashing red blip on her screen appeared to be coming from under the train.

"Sydney!" she yelled as she dropped to her knees at the platforms edge. "Someone! Someone help! I think there's a man under there!"

"No! It's alright! He got out!" responded one of the men who pulled Sydney to safety.

In his fall Sydney had dropped his phone on the tracks.

"Where did he go?" begged Jessica.

But the man could only shrug his shoulders. Jessica stood and scanned her surroundings in desperation, but there was no sight of him anywhere.

Back on the Main Concourse Level with the stairs behind him Sydney ran as best he could across the vast marble expanse, all the while pleading with everyone he passed.

"Help! Help! He's after me! He's trying to kill me! Help!"

But his pleas went ignored. There was little reason for anyone to heed his cries for help. For it appeared apparent to everyone that there was no one chasing him. The man in black, seeing that Sydney was limping and unable to run very fast, held back to his previously typical fast and steady walk. Killing Sydney with the Rad Gun when alone with him or amongst a mass of people is viable. Killing him in the wide open space with a fewer concentration of people would be foolish. So he trailed him at a fitting distance until Sydney unwittingly made a fateful turn into a Northwest passage that would take him to 46th and 47th Streets. The passage was nearly two city blocks long. Looking more like a tunnel, it had a low ceiling and bright yellow tiled walls. Running its length down the center were large square tiled pillars. Throughout the passage there was not another individual to be found. This was bad for Sydney, but good for the killer. Sydney increased his pace but the man in black did not. With no one around he decided to resort to an old fashion way of killing him, by pulling out from a breast holster hidden under his coat a pistol with a silencer. A quarter ways down the passage Sydney looked over his shoulder just in time to dodge the bullet by sidestepping behind one of the pillars. The pillars were wide enough making it impossible for the man to stare down the middle and still clearly see both sides. This at least worked to Sydney's advantage as he continued his way towards the opposite end while dodging in and out between the pillars leaving the killer no other choice than to also move from one side to the other while firing off shots.

Upon reaching the end of this passage Sydney hobbled down a flight of stairs that led to yet another very wide passage to his immediate left. He was relieved to find it not nearly as long as the previous one. At its end there was an escalator to the right which took him up to street level on Madison Avenue and 47th Street.

The cold outside air did not stun Sydney as he stepped onto Madison Avenue in the same way it had when he arrived at Grand Central Terminal due to all the running he was doing. The wind, on the other hand, was still as merciless as earlier. So too was Sydney's pursuer. After crossing 47th Sydney looked around to find, to no surprise, the man also stepping out onto Madison, although he was no longer brandishing his pistol. In spite of the windy chill there were still too many pedestrians on the street to risk killing *another* innocent bystander.

As Sydney crossed 48th he noticed how his energy was wearing down from the chase and how the pain in his hip was increasing. He knew his body could not hold up much longer if this continued. He needed to hide. But where? And how, with the man tracking so close behind him? But luck came to Sydney by way of a commuter bus. Twice as long as busses in the previous two centuries, and naturally modernistic beyond anything Roger could have ever imagined in his time. But the bus did not make its stop on 49th Street to take on passengers, only to wait for its proper moment to turn onto Madison Avenue. Regardless, boarding the bus was not an imperative move for Sydney anyway, for by this time he was on the north side corner of 49th Street while the man in black was to the south and the long bus merely created the perfect obstacle to slow his pursuer who was closing the distance between them. The size of the bus also acted as an ideal cover to hide Sydney temporarily from the man as he contemplated which way to run in order to lose him.

The late twentieth century skyscraper that spanned the entire block running from 49th to 50th Street was surrounded by a fifteen foot high chain-link fence topped with an additional foot of barbed wire. From the ground up a seven foot high plastic concealment wrapped along the fence masking from view the inside from the outside pedestrian traffic. There was a large sign attached to the fence stating that the 437 Madison Avenue building was slated for demolition.

Sydney made the decision to run along the length of the fence eastward along 49th Street. But he did not have to run far before he almost passed a small cutaway in the fence large enough, if he crouched down and pushed aside the flap made in the fence, to enter onto the property. *An abandoned skyscraper*, Sydney pondered. *What better place to hide until I can regain my strength and figure out my next move?*

He squeezed through the tight opening and found himself staring up at three story high stone arches and a recessed glass facade that wrapped around the bottom lobby level of the building. The first story was boarded with plywood, while most of the glass up from that was shattered. Sydney quickly surveyed the area but found no means of penetrating the building. Knowing that the plastic concealment would hide him from view of his pursuer, he hurried back towards the front of the building along Madison Avenue, hugging the plywood barricade as he ran hoping to find an entrance. After rounding the corner of the building along 50th Street he came upon a loading dock.

He was not surprised to find the large metal rolling doors closed. However, he was surprised, if not very suspicious, to find a solid door, next to the large rolling door, with its handle and lock broken off and evidence of the door having been pried open as if with a crowbar or similar object. *Obviously I'm not the only one who wants in this building*, he thought.

The door swung open easily. Inside was a long dark narrow hall and what appeared to be another door at the opposite end that was slightly ajar. Sydney entered and closed the door firmly behind him. This shut him in utter darkness except for the sliver of light emanating from the other end. He walked cautiously towards the light hearing only the sound of his footsteps and the scurrying of rats from all around.

Sydney reached the end of the hall and with the slightest touch of his finger gave the door a nudge causing it to creak open. What he saw astonished him. The immense three story high lobby resembled an ice palace. Illuminated by a pale blue glow from the city lights shining in through the shattered windows above the plywood he could see that everything was covered under a fine layer of snow that had blown in through those same windows. Sydney gazed up and was simply overwhelmed by the beautiful sight of translucent ice crystals floating downward after swirling inside by the howling winds. He moved slowly in wonderment towards the lobby's middle while almost forgetting what brought him to this place. At the central part of the lobby there was a circular concierge desk with an escalator directly behind it. The walls to each side of the escalator were flanked by a row of elevators.

Suddenly he heard the echo of a door shut. It was the outer door in the hall from which he came.

"It can't be" Sydney whispered.

Looking around he saw there was no place to hide in this wide open lobby. But the escalator stretched an impressive four stories high to what appeared to be a mezzanine level with a circular balcony and surrounding offices. Quickly but quietly he climbed the stairs of the escalator. While doing so he began to speculate how it is that this man was able to know in advance where to find him. Sydney was sure that when he entered through the fence the bus was still shielding him from the man's view. Yet, there he was, still trailing him by entering the building through the same door. And how did the man know to head

Sydney off in that hallway on his way to the MTA Police? Or suddenly appear in the direction Sydney was running when he arrived onto Acorn Street in Beacon Hill? Or for the matter, how did this man know that Sydney was even going to be walking through the park at all on that day and at that time? And how was it that he knew Sydney would be crossing that footbridge? And in a city the size of New York, how was this man able to know where and when to find Sydney in Times Square? Or know that Sydney was going to be in Grand Central Terminal before he even arrived there?

Always knows where to find me, and always knows in advance my every move.

Then, with each step up the escalator, Sydney began to recall flashbacks that would tie all these questions together into one obvious conclusion. They commenced with the clear voice of a man with an undistinguishable face speaking to Sydney in his home.

"I know you might think I'm paranoid for saying this, but I know I've been bugged."

Bugged? It brought to mind something Jessica told him in the mental hospital.

"I'm taking you out of this bug infested place."

Surely Jessica was not speaking of the same type of bug. But what if that mysterious person who approached his bed that night in the mental hospital and put him to sleep with that pen-like object to his temple - the one wearing the *long heavy coat* - also planted a listening bug on him? *But where?*

"I read it's only the size of a grain of rice, they inject it just under the skin surface and he won't feel a thing."

It was something he recalled Laura telling him during his birthday dinner at Mancini's when she was explaining to him the procedure for having their dog Baloo injected with a microchip identification system.

But where would have he injected such a devise?

"Now what's that you got on your neck? Looks like a mosquito bite" said the young orderly in the mental hospital the following morning.

Of course! And since that night in the asylum he's heard every word I've spoken. Furthermore, what better place to position this listening bug than on my neck, close to my vocal cords? This would explain how he knew in advance where I would be going. Like that day through the park.

"I've walked one end of Central Park to the other. Boston Common can't be much greater than that."

And reaching Grand Central Terminal before me.

"Where are you?"

"Grand Central."

"Grand Central? Stay there."

That's also why at the Terminal his attention was suddenly drawn directly to the store I was in at the very second I told Jessica, "I'm in a men's clothing store."

And how he knew to find a faster way to the MTA Police so as to head me off before I got there.

"MTA Police. Northeast side. Lower Level. Got it."

Sydney also recognized that he must have known something when the mystery man pushed his way into his home and Sydney shouted to him, "I won't tell anyone!" He figured that the man must have known that the fall rendered Sydney with amnesia, otherwise he would have taken the opportunity to do away with Sydney once and for all while in the mental hospital. *But why kill me if I can't remember anything? That chase through the park must have been a test to see if I did indeed lose my memory. A test I passed.* "I don't know who you are!" Sydney recalled crying out to the man while on Acorn Street. Then the man made a conspicuous absence for several weeks until that night in the hotel bar when Sydney told Jessica and Cyrus, "It's all coming back." The following day the mystery man again made his presence known on Times Square.

But what about those times when I spoke nothing at all, yet he still knew where to find me?

Global Positioning System was the answer.

"With the GPS button you can get an exact position of your whereabouts" he remembered Jessica telling him before he embarked on his trek through Boston Common. And then later, before leaving her hotel room only hours ago, she elaborated further on its capabilities by explaining to him that one can get "an *exact* position on the victim right down to an interior closet or vehicle trunk." It made sense to him now why he saw the mystery man, while in the 42nd Street Passage, look down before slowly raising his head to scan the area. He was looking at a hand held GPS tracking device.

Sydney reached the top of the escalator somewhat horrified over realizing that there was a listening bug *and* GPS microchip implanted in his neck. Just then he heard that same door he entered into the lobby creak open. At this point it made little sense to Sydney that he should try to hide from his pursuer. There was no place he could hide where he would not be found. Nonetheless, he knew he had to keep moving until he could figure out what to do.

There were no windows on that level making it more difficult to see, yet despite the lack of light Sydney was able to make out several doors lining the walls surrounding the circular balcony. All were closed except for the double doors at the opposite end from where he stood. He wasted no time hurrying over to these doors. Inside it was even darker, but from what he could make out he seemed to be in a reception area. He could see a receptionist's desk against the center wall and a door to each side of this desk. Both were open. He entered the door to the right and was again struck by another surreal sight before him. There was just enough light escaping from a row of offices to his left, all of which appeared to have shattered windows, that it made it possible for him to discern a vast open floor of cubicles. While some of the cubicles were positioned as though they might still fill with occupants the following morning, most were jumbled haphazardly about like playing cards. There were a few desks and chairs as well as some toppled filing cabinets, but no computers or phones or other such office equipment. Everything, however, was painted white with frost.

Straight ahead of him there was what used to be a conference room. Its windows to one side overlooked Madison Avenue. The glass in the windows was gone and an actual snowdrift had developed stretching as far as the center of the room where there was still a large conference table. A glass curtain wall once made up the partition between the conference room and the hall beyond the reception area where Sydney presently stood. But now only piles of shard glass lay at his feet. At that moment Sydney contemplated the unthinkable. Yet with the sound of footsteps now ascending the escalator he realized he had no other choice.

He knelt down and picked up a sharp pointed piece of glass that would be small enough for him to grasp firmly in one hand. Fearing that he might leave a trail of blood in this opaquely lit area, he

scanned his surroundings and found along the innermost wall to the
right of the cubicles a series of open doorways that he assumed to be
more offices. Inside they were dark and ideal for what needed to be
done. Sydney rushed over to the first of these rooms, entered, and
braced himself against the wall.

Pressing gently with his index finger he could actually feel the
microchip that, just as Laura said, was no bigger than the smallest grain
of rice. He knew he would not have to cut long or deep. Still, he knew
cutting into one's own neck posed a great risk. Cut too deep or too far
over and he might sever his jugular vein or carotid artery. To cut either
would mean he would probably bleed to death before his pursuer even
reaches the mezzanine level. But he had no options to weigh. He
needed to seek help and could not do so as long as this man remained
ahead of his every move. And so with a firm grip on the glass he
slowly raised the pointed end to his neck, drew in a deep breath that he
held, and then with just the right steady amount of pressure he pressed
solidly until the skin was pierced. With that the blood began to stream
down his neck as he drew downward a slit no more than a quarter inch
in length.

Nearing the top of the escalator the mystery man paused when
through his audio earpiece he heard what sounded to be a stifled moan
of pain. In his hand he held the GPS tracker which displayed the floor
layout of the mezzanine level and a stationary red blip coming from a
small room within. The man made haste up to the top of the escalator,
then along the balcony, and through the double doors into the reception
area. Once inside amid the cubicles he made his way directly to the
room that Sydney had entered.

Still holding the GPS tracker in one hand, he removed a small
flashlight from his pocket with the other and began to shine it in what
he discovered to be an old copier room. The copiers were gone but a
sign from untold years ago still remained tacked to one of the walls that
read; *If copier jams, please phone office manager at x112.* There was
shelving along the upper part of one wall, and below it cabinet doors
which he proceeded to open. Finding the cabinets empty the man was
confused by the situation. The GPS was showing that Sydney was in
the room, but as far as he could tell Sydney was nowhere to be found.
He then stepped on the microchip which caused a loud pop in his audio
earpiece and the red blip on the GPS tracker to go out. Shining his
light on the spot where he had placed his foot he found tiny fragments

of what was left of the microchip. Angrily he removed the earpiece, tossed it aside, threw the GPS tracker against the wall, and stormed out of the copier room.

The man then stood motionless while he searched for any sign of movement and listened for the slightest sound. But all was still, and except for the howling wind, quiet as well. Slowly and vigilantly he began to prowl the office area like an animal hunting his prey.

Midway across the room, pressing his bundled-up blood soaked scarf firmly against his neck, Sydney huddled himself tightly under a desk inside a cubicle. He knew the desk was positioned so that the underside where he was hiding could not be seen by merely looking into the cubicle. His assailant would need to enter completely into the cubicle in order to look under the desk. But as the man drew closer, peering into cubicles, glancing under desks, Sydney realized that the vapor emanating with his every breath might reveal him. He inhaled a deep breath and held it. Sydney came to the decision that if he is discovered he would not go down without a fight. And as the man crept up to his cubicle and began to enter, so close in fact that Sydney could hear him breathing, he realized that if he was going to make a move on him he had better do it now before his assailant could fire off a shot. Sydney's plan at the count of three was to reach out and throw his arms around his assailant's legs thus tackling him to the ground. *One....Two....* But incredibly there suddenly came a loud noise, like a piece of metal dropping to the ground, from the far opposite end of the building on the same floor. The man turned and ran towards the area from which the sound came as Sydney exhaled a tremendous sigh of relief.

Through the cubicles the man ran, past the conference room, and then through another maze of cubicles on the south floor of the building, to an open door along the innermost wall from which he saw a glow coming from within. He drew his gun and entered only to find what used to be a board room housing five transients varying in ages. There were blankets on the floor for beds, a few chairs, and in the middle of the room there burned a bright fire from inside a drawer that had been removed from a metal filing cabinet. The occupants were naturally surprised to find a man with a gun entering their secret abode. But they said nothing. Not finding what he expected, the man slowly backed his way out of the room with his gun still drawn. Once completely out of the room his attention was drawn to the sound of one of the reception area doors closing shut followed by the clamor of feet running along the mezzanine balcony. The man in black bolted towards the sound of the footsteps. By the time he reached the reception area he could hear him fleeing down the escalator. When he himself reached the escalator he heard the lobby door creak open shortly followed by the door to the loading dock slamming shut.

Sydney was still crouched under the desk when he too heard the running footsteps and the door to the loading dock slam shut. Moments later he heard the same door slam shut a second time.

Outside the man in black ran around to the front of the building and eventually back out from the restricted area onto the street, unaware that behind one of the stone arches he had passed a frightened elderly transient, breathing hard, clutching a bottle of booze in a brown paper bag, and looking relieved that he managed to evade this crazy stranger who was chasing him with a gun.

Silence brought a sense of ease to Sydney's frayed nerves. But he felt no urgency to leave his compact hiding place. Feeling both mentally and physically drained, and fearing that further exertion might worsen the blood flow from his neck wound, Sydney decided to remain situated. It took approximately thirty minutes until his heart rate began to pump normally again, and another thirty minutes before the tribulations of the day began to have an effect on his ability to stay awake. Although the thought was with him that if he fell asleep he might never wake up from either bleeding or freezing to death. Or both. *And God forbid if that should happen*, he thought, *who would think to find me here?* But a peculiar peace came over him as his thoughts shifted to pleasant memories of those ordinary events in an average day with his family that he so often took for granted. The laughter of his kids in the backyard while getting soaked from giving Baloo a bath. He and Laura planting spring flowers in clay pots, with the help of the kids, of course. Walks along the beach with his family and the joy in his children's eyes when they would find a sea shell even more beautiful than the last. Even those hot Florida days when his children would happily help him wash the car. And then there were those simple quiet nights with he and Laura lying on the couch with the kids on the floor and a big bowl of popcorn between them as they watched TV.

These memories were not limited to his previous life as Roger Owen. Happy memories of Sydney Hamilton's past also began to emerge out of nowhere like some forgotten dream. He recalled one of the many sunny days he and Margie would take their young daughter on a Swan Boat ride in Boston Public Garden. And cradling his baby grandson in his arms at one of his backyard family barbecues he loved to host on those delightfully warm New England summer days. But as these memories began to lull Sydney to sleep another memory surfaced that in contrast to the others was dark and painful. A memory that Sydney would have preferred to remain forever lost to his amnesia.

He recalled that sweltering summer night when he sat alone in his dark classroom at Harvard with only the use of a small lamp to light the several books on past historic pandemics he was mulling over. The air in the room was hot and stifling. The air conditioning in the classrooms had been turned off to conserve power since the summer classes were canceled due to restrictions imposed on public gatherings. Sydney had already lost his daughter, grandson, and son-in-law two months earlier. And like most all others in the world who had been directly affected by this cataclysm sweeping over the earth, Sydney felt that by perhaps adhering to his own lifelong belief that mankind can change the course of events by learning from its past, there might be something he might discover that will bring an end this nightmare already into its third month. However, Sydney was not foolish enough to believe that he was the only one desperately searching for an answer through means of studying the past. But in those desperate months where fear and vulnerability prevailed, there was also a feeling of helplessness. To curb this feeling many turned to doing whatever they felt might be within their power to help bring an end to the pandemic. While scientists and doctors offered theories. And others, like Sydney, studied the past. Most turned to prayer.

It was sometime between eight and nine that evening when Sydney's phone rang. It was Margie. She was at home on the living room sofa. Her skin looked ashen, her eyes weary, and when she spoke her voice sounded weak.

"Sydney, you better come home quick."

Aside from the sullen atmosphere that had descended upon the Hamilton household ever since the passing of Angela, their grandson and son-in-law, Margie otherwise appeared in fine physical health throughout the day. But after supper she spoke of feeling tired and urged Sydney to go forward with his plans to drop by the school for a few hours while she rested. He did so hesitantly. And then, only a little over an hour and a half later, came the phone call. There was no need for Sydney to ask why he was needed home quickly. He knew by seeing and hearing her over the phone what was happening.

The street scene throughout the city looked every bit as surreal that night as it did from the time the pandemic began. Pine coffins lined the streets. In some places where there was a large apartment complex it was not unusual to find one coffin stacked on top of another. Funerals were rare on account of the risks involved with attending such gatherings. And with the exception of those who already pre-purchased family or individual burial plots, availability in the cemeteries, particularly those in the cities and suburbs, was practically nonexistent. Cremation was the safest and, with the mortality rate being so high, the most efficient way of disposing of the dead. Each county was responsible for the supply and delivery of pine coffins to its citizens. Each day after dark a hearse, typically a black painted truck, would cruise the streets picking up its morbid cargo by men wearing hooded hazardous material suites, or *hazmat* suites, who were unfairly dubbed *grim reapers* by a large percentage of the public. This hearse would then transport its contents to an undisclosed cremation site far beyond the city limits.

It was not an unusual site for Sydney to find very few people out and about as he drove home that night. Those who *were* on the streets were either mourners crying over the caskets of their loved ones, or simply pedestrians who for one reason or another had a need to be out. One thing they all shared in common, including Sydney himself, was the white surgical masks worn over the nose and mouth to prevent inhalation of the deadly virus.

Sydney discarded his surgical mask upon entering his home. On the sofa he found Margie lying there in a delirious cold sweat. Her breathing was labored. And there was an unmistakable bluish hue to her face - an ominous sign of the virus.

"I'm here" he said as he knelt down beside her and took her hand in his. "I shouldn't have gone out."

"Don't be silly. You being here wouldn't have stopped this from happening."

"But I could have gotten you to the hospital sooner."

"Now you and I both know there's nothing doctors can do."

"That's not entirely true my love. I've heard that there are now some people recovering from this through the use of some new drugs they're experimenting with. Are you in any pain?"

"I have a terrible headache. I'm warm. And very thirsty."

"I'll bring you a glass of water."

While Sydney was in the bathroom he realized she was more right than he was willing to believe. But there *were* cases he had heard of where experimental drugs were used and the patients recovered. But were these isolated cases? Where did they occur? And did *all* hospitals across the country have access to these drugs? Sydney did not know the answers, and he knew time was running out. He needed to get Margie to a hospital as fast as possible and hope for a miracle. He opened a bottle of aspirin and spilled nearly half of them on the floor in panic.

He returned to Margie's side with the glass of water and held her head up to help her drink. "Here you are my love. Swallow these four aspirin. They'll relieve your headache and should help bring the fever down." When she finished he patted the sweat from her forehead with a cool damp towel he brought from the bathroom. "Now I'm going to take you to the hospital."

"Oh no, Sydney. Let me die at home. Please."

"Don't talk that way. I won't hear of it. You've got to be strong and positive. There's a chance these doctors might be able to offer you these new drugs. And where there's a chance there's also hope. Can you put your arms around my neck?"

Margie felt too weak to argue the point with him and complied, through a great deal of effort, to wrap her arms around his neck.

"That's right. Very good. Okay, I'm going to carry you to the car. Just keep a hold of my neck."

Through the front door and to the vehicle he carried her, placing her frail body gently on the back seat. After pressing his thumb to a laser sensory that started the vehicle by recognizing his finger print, Sydney then joined Margie on the back seat where he rested her head in his lap.

"Destination?" a computerized voice asked?

"St. Elizabeth's Medical Center. Emergency."

"Destination; St. Elizabeth's Medical Center. Emergency" acknowledged the computer.

"I don't know how this happened, Sydney. I haven't been out of the house in weeks."

"God only knows how this virus actually spreads." It was at that point a thought came to mind that would burden him all his remaining years. Sydney had heard of the possibility of some people having an auto-immunity to the virus. If this was true, and if he was one of those who had this auto-immunity, then could he have contracted the virus and passed it on to Margie without ever experiencing any of the symptoms himself?

"You should wear your mask" she said.

Sydney shook his head and tenderly kissed her on the lips, and then told her, "You're not going anywhere without me."

She smiled during what would be a moment of silence as they looked lovingly into each other's eyes.

"I'm not afraid you know" she assured him, still smiling. "Soon I'll be with Angela, little Willie, Joshua, and my parents."

"We'll *all* be together again someday. But for right now I still need you here with me. So I need you to hold on. You hear me, Margie? Hold on."

"You're a good man, Sydney. I'm so glad I was working that night you came into the pub."

"I probably wouldn't have gone back if I hadn't met you."

"We made quite a team, didn't we?"

"We still *are* a team. Wherever we go, whatever we do, we'll continue on as it's always been with us,...together all the way."

"I'm so cold now" said Margie as the smile left her face.

"We're almost there my love."

"Promise me you'll lay me to rest in the family plot next to Angela and Willie."

Sydney refused to think about such a thought, and instead directed his attention straight ahead to the road on which the vehicle was traveling and muttered in desperation, "Where the bloody hell is that hospital?"

They had been inseparable from the time they met as young adults. And now faced with the thought of losing her, of waking up without her by his side, of no longer hearing the sound of her voice, her laugh, or seeing that smile that never failed throughout the years to brighten even his darkest moments, struck him with a terrible fear. Together they had become one. Being apart was unimaginable. But as hard as Sydney tried to mask this fear, there was no hiding it from the woman who knew him so well. And so she did what she had always done at times when she saw he was troubled, she smiled and then managed to find exactly the right words to say that he needed to hear.

"Don't worry my love" she said. "Whatever happens, remember, in time the Rockies may crumble, Gibraltar may tumble..."

Sydney smiled. "They're only made of clay..."

And then together they finished, "...But our love is here to stay."

It was as though they both finally conceded the inevitable with their tight embrace that followed.

"Arrival; St. Elizabeth's Medical Center. Emergency entrance" announced the computer.

Sydney carried Margie from the vehicle and through the emergency doors into an overcrowded waiting room that was on the borderline of sheer pandemonium. The dying were everywhere. Lying on the floor, slumped in chairs, and some, like Margie, being held in the arms of their loved ones. There was sobbing by the ones who brought them there, and not surprisingly a few who were in hysterics.

"Where's your masks?" asked an exhausted middle-age female nurse who hurriedly approached them. "You both can't come in here unless you're wearing masks. John, get a couple masks for these two!" she called out to a young orderly.

In no time the young man was at their side reaching into a cardboard box full of surgical masks from which he retrieved two. Noting that Sydney's arms were occupied the orderly set down the box and proceeded to strap each mask over the heads of Margie and Sydney respectively.

"You'll need to answer a few questions for the intake nurse over there at admitting" said the nurse.

"Where can I set her down?" asked Sydney.

"Anywhere you can find a spot."

The nurse walked away leaving Sydney at a loss when he panned the room to find no available place to lay Margie down. But the sympathetic orderly felt obliged to assist.

"Come with me" he told Sydney.   "We're all out of wheelchairs I'm afraid."

"No problem. She's as light as a feather."

"You always say the sweetest things, Sydney" said Margie trying to ease some of Sydney's own fears through a show of lightheartedness.

He led them through the triage area, which appeared even more overflowing with patients than the waiting room, down a long corridor, and beyond a pair of electric sliding doors into an access hallway. Here too, as was with the triage, patients on gurneys lined the hall. The orderly popped into a supply closet and retrieved a pillow and blanket and then continued to lead Sydney and Margie a short way further to a vacant space on the floor against the wall.

"Unfortunately there are no more gurneys available either" he said while placing the blanket and pillow on the floor. "But she'll be alright here. You go back the same way we came, back out to the waiting room, and do your intake with the nurse. It'll only take a few minutes."

Sydney gave an appreciative nod to the young man and gently laid Margie down upon the blanket and rested her head on the pillow.

"I'll be back shortly. You just rest now."

"My entire body is beginning to ache."

"They'll give you something to ease the pain when you're seen by a doctor" said the orderly.

"Can't they give her something now?"

"I'm so sorry. She's gotta be seen by a doctor first."

"Then do you think in the meantime I can have something to drink?" asked Margie. "I'm still very thirsty."

"I'll bring you back a cup of water."

"I'll get her some water" said the orderly. "You go take care of the paper work."

"Thank you."

Sydney went back to the waiting room and to the admitting counter where he answered the typical routine questions rambled off by a nurse sitting at a computer - name of patient, age, address, purpose of emergency. Considering the number of patients packed into the waiting room due to the pandemic, the last question seemed rather redundant to Sydney, nonetheless he understood why it had to be asked.

"Your wife's number is forty-two" said the nurse.

"She's just a number?"

"Believe me, it's usually not done this way. But with so many patients waiting to be seen there's really no better way. Listen for her number to be called."

"How long will it take before she can see a doctor? I'm afraid she's failing fast and needs to be seen by one as soon as possible."

"I'm sorry, sir. But everyone you see in this waiting room needs to be seen by a doctor as soon as possible. Despite a full staff working around the clock we just can't see more than we can handle. Now we'll call your number. It shouldn't be too long."

Sydney was never one to make a scene, especially over situations that he knew were beyond anyone's control. Quiet and mild had always been his nature. And although he was certainly not satisfied with the answer, he made no attempt to dispute it.

"I'll need to be buzzed back through those doors."

"You can't go through those doors until your wife's number is called."

"But my wife is already in there. A young orderly brought us through to wait in a hallway."

The nurse hesitated a moment and then she shook her head and sighed. "Hold on. I'll have to get a nurse to escort you. We can't have you wandering around back there alone."

After she left Sydney reassessed the mass of those dying and grieving around him and pondered in astonishment over how it came to be that in the twenty-second century a sight such as this could still exist. Where man, despite all his medical advancements, can still be rendered helpless against microscopic organisms that have gone on killing since biblical times.

"Another nurse will be right with you" said the intake nurse as she returned to her station. Seconds later the door opened to the triage area.

"Mr. Hamilton?" inquired the nurse at the door. "If you'll come with me."

"Hello" he said as he entered through the door.

"Hi. Now why don't you take me to where your wife is."

"Sure. She's right over this way."

She followed Sydney as he retraced his way back to Margie. During this time he took it upon himself to inquire in a different approach the same question he had asked the other nurse, hoping to receive a more definite answer.

"With so many patients in the triage how is it they'll ever be able to see all the others who continue to fill up your waiting room?"

"Fast turnover."

The cold response brought Sydney to an abrupt halt.

"What are you saying? But what about those drugs I've heard about in the news?"

"*Experimental* drugs administered in laboratories God knows where. The fact is that only one in twenty who received the drugs have survived, leaving it to be questioned if it was the drugs at all that cured them or if they just had an immunity to the virus and would have recovered regardless."

"Then you mean to tell me that none of these patients will leave here alive?"

"Look, I really shouldn't be telling you any of this, but people come here expecting a miracle, and under any other *normal* circumstances the majority of patients who come to emergency would leave here cured. But this pandemic isn't normal. And the truth is...." She began to choke back tears as her stoic professional demeanor started to give way under the despair of so much death and the inability to stop it. "The truth is we can't do anything here except ease their pain with what little morphine we have left to spare during their final hours...or minutes. After one dies, another from the waiting room will take his or her place. It's all we can do."

She looked back at all the occupied gurneys in the triage and wiped the tears from her face. For Sydney her honesty hit hard as it dashed all last remnants of hope that Margie might leave the hospital alive. Knowing this made every *second* left with her crucial. He resumed his course, with the nurse following, and gradually increased his pace to a full run as an unsettling intuition began to emerge that his love might have already passed on.

When he reached the spot where he left Margie he found only the blanket and pillow remaining where she once lay. A painful sinking feeling struck deep within him. Panic ensued as everything that followed suddenly became a blur of events.

"Where is she? Where is she!? She was right there!"

He ran down the hall frantically searching all around in circles and then ran back.

"Sir. Sir!" the nurse called out.

"She's gone! Where did they take her!?"

"Maybe she got up and is walking around here somewhere. Now why don't you just come with me and we'll go..."

"She couldn't have gotten up! She was too weak to even walk! I only left her for a few minutes while I went and...." He then spotted the young orderly walking towards him. "You! I left her with you. Where is she? Where's my wife?"

The orderly looked down at the blanket and pillow and appeared as shocked as Sydney that she was no longer there.

"I don't know. I brought her a cup of water, held her head up so she could drink it, then rested her head back down upon the pillow and made sure she was comfortable. And then I got called away for a moment. I was just coming back to see how she was doing."

"Margie!" Sydney began to call out as he backtracked his way down the hall, through the sliding doors, along the corridor, and into the triage area. "Margie! Margie!"

The nurse ran after him but the young orderly stayed behind, staring down dumbfounded at the spot where he left the man's wife only moments before.

In a spinning nightmarish daze Sydney could find nothing but the dead and dying around him, but no sign of Margie.

"Margie! Margie!"

He then did the unthinkable by starting to remove the covers off of the faces of those who had died.

"Sir! Sir!" the nurse continued to call out. "Mr. Hamilton!" She called to a male doctor who was at that same moment hurrying over to Sydney to stop his erratic behavior.

"Sir. Sir?" pleaded the doctor. "Can I help you, sir?"

"Are you a doctor?"

"Yes."

"His wife is missing" said the nurse. "She was placed in the hallway and now she's gone."

"Okay. I'll help you find her. What's her number?"

"Her *name* is Margie!" Realizing that the doctor sincerely wanted to help, Sydney took a couple deep breaths to regain some composure and then continued. "Or rather, Margaret. Margaret Hamilton."

"Check with admitting and find out what her number was and if she has already been seen by another doctor" he told the nurse who dutifully complied. "Now why don't you come with me, Mr. Hamilton, and show me exactly where you last saw your wife."

Sydney led the doctor to the spot where he left Margie only to find the blanket and pillow both gone and a gurney with a new patient had been placed over it. He related to the doctor as calmly as possible the events that followed after he left her lying there. Moments after he finished the nurse returned with word of her findings.

"Doctor, admitting still had her chart and here it is. According to this Margaret Hamilton hasn't even been *seen* by either a nurse or doctor yet."

The doctor took her chart and glanced over it before taking the nurse aside.

"Excuse us, sir."

Sydney could not make out what was being said. He only heard a lot of whispering while the doctor repeatedly pointed to the spot where Margie had been. After the nurse left the doctor returned to Sydney.

"Mr. Hamilton, could you please come with me?" He led Sydney to a small examining room. "I'm going to ask that you wait in here while I get to the bottom of this. I assure you we *will* find your wife. But it won't help if you're wandering about. We need to know where we can find *you*. So please, be patient. And trust me, we'll find her."

Sydney made no objection to the doctor's request on account of the sincerity in his voice.

As Sydney sat there alone in that small examining room he feared the worst. The thought that she may have died alone, without him by her side to comfort her. He admonished himself for ever leaving her in the first place. But then tried to reason that he only meant to be gone a few minutes and, although very weak, never figured that her death might come so soon.

What must have only been the passing of minutes seemed instead like hours to Sydney until the door finally opened. It was the same doctor as before, only this time he was not alone. He was accompanied by another male doctor who looked to be approximately the same age as Sydney.

"Mr. Hamilton, this is Dr. Rease."

"Hello, Mr. Hamilton. I was the one who found your wife. And I'm sorry to tell you that Margaret passed on. Evidently, only moments after our orderly, John, left her side her body shut down. Her eyes were open which was what brought me to notice her when I just happened to be passing by. I can assure you that unlike many of the others here, your wife went quickly and therefore without any pain."

At that moment, with just those few words, Sydney's whole world had imploded. Dr. Rease allowed a moment to pass for it all to sink in before he continued.

"I didn't know who she was. There was no one around and no chart or tag beside her. So I instructed her body to be removed from the hall so as to make way for another patient. Apparently at the same time I was trying to find out who she was, Dr. Ash here was making the same inquiries."

"Where is she?" whispered Sydney.

"In the morgue, I'm sure. Whenever you're ready I can bring you down there to identify her."

The three men left the room together, although Dr. Ash went a separate way as Sydney followed Dr. Rease across the corridor and into an elevator. There were no further words spoken between the two as Sydney was led to the morgue. There were also no tears shed by Sydney at this time. He was simply in too much shock over the loss and over how quickly it all happened.

When they arrived on the basement floor that housed the hospital morgue, Sydney was stunned by what he saw. The elevator opened to a very long hallway where midway down to the right was a room where autopsies were performed, and across the hall from that another room, the morgue. Contrary to what Sydney expected to find, the morgue was a place bustling with activity. The hallway was lined with individual racks that reached practically to the ceiling allowing the accommodation of six corpses from bottom to top of each rack. These racks were filled to capacity with each corpse concealed within a white body bag. Still, there were other bodies on gurneys, and at the far opposite end of the hall he saw these body bags stacked high atop one another before being packed into a freight elevator by a crew of hard working men.

"What you see here is just the makeshift morgue. The overflow, you might say. Inside the actual morgue itself are the bodies that relatives have arranged to be picked up by their mortuaries. The others you see here will all be sent off to be cremated. This is done through either the family's wishes or because the bodies have never been claimed or identified. Now at this point I need to ask you what your wishes are with your wife's body?"

"We have a family plot. I'll arrange in the morning to have our mortuary pick Margie...." His throat tightened with emotion making it impossible for him to finish.

"I understand. I need to get back up on the floor. If you have a picture of your wife, Carl here will be able to better assist you in locating her."

Sydney nodded, removed from his pants pocket his phone, and brought up a photo of Margie for Carl to see. The morgue assistant, Carl, was a man probably no more than thirty who looked far older than his true years due to the stress of this never ending procession of death he had to deal with day in and day out.

"She would have been brought down fifteen, possibly thirty minutes ago at the most" said Dr. Rease. "Look familiar?"

"Fifteen or thirty minutes ago?" He examined the photo closely, but said nothing.

"His family mortuary will pick her up in the morning" Dr. Rease added.

Carl's eyes suddenly widened before turning to Sydney with a look of alarm. "Was she wearing a light short sleeved blouse, white, with a design of little yellow flowers near the top?"

"Yes. That's her."

Carl quickly turned his attention to the men loading the freight elevator, removed his mask and gave a loud whistle that seemed out of keeping considering the nature of their surroundings. "Hey you guys, the truck you were loading fifteen minutes ago..." he yelled to them. "Has it left yet?"

"It's leaving the dock now" one of the men hollered back.

"Get up there and stop it! Hurry! There's a body onboard that shouldn't be!"

"What are you saying?" Sydney asked in dismay.

Carl turned to Dr. Rease with a desperate explanation. "What was I to think? When she was brought down there was no identification on her, no one to claim her. You know yourself we get at least a dozen a day who walk in alone with no I.D. and then die with no one to claim their body."

Before the apologetic morgue assistant had even finished speaking Sydney was already running down the hall towards the freight elevator. But the doors closed before him.

"Where's there another way up?" he asked one of the men standing nearby.

"You can use the stairwell over there."

Sydney shot over to the stairwell and flew up the stairs taking three steps at a time to the floor above. When he flung open the door to the outside the freight elevator had also just arrived. But the black truck was already driving off through the well lit parking lot.

"Can you call it back?" he asked the elevator operator as the doors opened. But the man shook his head. "Can you tell me where it's going then?" But again the man said nothing and only shrugged his shoulders.

Sydney kept his eyes on the departing truck the whole time he ran around the side of the hospital to the front of the emergency entrance where he had parked his vehicle. By the time he entered and started his vehicle the truck had already disappeared down the street.

"Destination?" asked the computer. But Sydney immediately threw it into manual drive.

"Manual drive initiated" said the computer.

With Sydney now in control of the steering and acceleration he was successfully able to relocate the truck as it wound its way through the surrounding streets towards Interstate 90, the Massachusetts Turnpike. Still it was not until they both entered onto that particular highway traveling west that he was finally able to catch up to the truck. But his repeated blasts of the horn brought no sign of slowing from the vehicle ahead. In fact, the truck began to speed up, but so did Sydney. He wondered why the truck would be heading in a westerly direction right towards the heart of Boston until the truck changed its course and turned south onto Interstate 93, the Southeast Expressway. Sydney's attempts to pull alongside the truck met with no response from the driver to either pull over or even slow down. It was not even possible for him to view the driver for the windows were tinted as black as the truck itself. But Sydney knew that the truck would eventually have to reach a destination, and wherever that destination might be he was determined to be there.

For approximately eight miles Sydney followed the truck until it began to curve eastward past the intersection with route three. For a little over another two miles he traveled until the truck finally veered off on exit five going north onto route twenty-eight. *The Blue Hills Reservation?* Sydney wondered. *But of course!*

They were named The Blue Hills by early European explorers who, while sailing the coastline, noticed the bluish hue on the slopes. In 1893 the land was purchased by the Metropolitan Parks Commission as a recreation area of unspoiled wilderness only minutes from the bustle of downtown Boston. And so for two hundred and thirty-two years the vast 7,000 acres of upland and bottomland forests, swamps, marshes, ponds, meadows, and the twenty-two hills in the Blue Hills chain, the tallest hill reaching a height of 635 feet, allowed daily visitors the opportunity to commune with nature by offering a wealth of year-round activities from boating, camping, fishing, golfing, hiking, horseback riding, rock climbing, swimming, ice skating, as well as downhill and cross-country skiing. But that all changed the summer of 2115 when two months into what was the height of the pandemic the reservation was closed off to the public for secretive reasons. Most people speculated, justifiably so, that the government wanted to prevent citizens who could not afford or find a cemetery for their loved ones, and did not want them to be cremated in mass at an unknown location, from performing their own burial on the grounds of the reservation. But Sydney realized there was a far bigger reason the government wanted to close off Blue Hills Reservation when he reached the bottom of the exit ramp and turned right heading north into the reservation where he was promptly brought to a halt by armed military. The gate through which the truck had entered was as far as Sydney was allowed to travel.

"Sir, I'm gonna have to ask you to turn right back around. This area is restricted to the public" said the military guard.

"Listen, I've got to get to that truck. My wife's body was accidentally placed onboard. She's supposed to be buried in our family plot."

"That's impossible, sir. Now I'll ask you again, please turn this vehicle around and leave the area immediately."

Sydney ignored the guard and stared straight ahead as he tried to figure out what, if any, options he might have.

"Sir....*Sir!*"

The military guard raised his rifle just as three other guards approached his vehicle while also raising their fire arms just a bit higher. Sydney realized at once that pursuing the issue further, much less breaking through the gate, would be futile and suicidal. He looked at the guard, nodded, and then slowly backed his vehicle before making a full turnaround.

Entering back onto the highway westbound, Sydney only traveled a couple hundred yards before pulling his vehicle over to a stop along the side of the road. He remembered hearing that the perimeter of Blue Hills Reservation was heavily patrolled by military vehicles, aircraft, and searchlights. But taking in the size of such a perimeter, Sydney gambled that he would be able to penetrate the boundary line nevertheless. And there was no moon that night which made the likelihood of being seen seem quite dubious.

As he had hoped, crossing into the woods posed no problem. But the visibility factor offered a different challenge all together. Groping his way through the dense forest in near total darkness made for a slow trek as he headed in a northeastwardly direction back towards route twenty-eight. He knew that it was necessary to get himself within sight of the road in order to locate the final destination of the truck. He also correctly assumed that by the time he reached the road the truck would be long gone. But as he continued through the brush alongside the road he was not surprised to see yet another black truck speed past him heading northbound in the same direction. It was not until approximately a quarter mile up the road that he saw the red rear lights of the truck turn left. Onward he trekked trying to keep a steady pace despite being slowed down by the obstacles of branches, fallen trees, and rocks that he would stumble over in the dark.

The road the truck turned onto was no more than a narrow gravel pathway that disappeared into a black void. Sydney knew he would need to hug close to the path or otherwise risk becoming lost. And being lost in the middle of 7,000 acres of dark wilderness without so much as a flashlight played heavily on his fear. But as fate would have it, getting himself lost was exactly what happened when after traversing just over a mile he realized that the path must have taken a turn northward. It was just too dark for him to notice this until it was too late. He stood motionless hoping to hear one of the trucks passing in the distance. But all was silent until suddenly nearby the sound of yapping from a pack of coyotes echoed through the forest. He knew it to be the sound they make after a kill. *At least they'll stay close to their food and away from me*, he told himself.

Sydney's memory told him that there were several large hills not far ahead of him if he continued in the same direction he had been traveling. From atop of one of those hills he would be able to reestablish his location. But the oppressive heat was causing him to languish. Still he pushed on, even finding himself at one point trudging through a swamp in water halfway up to his knees. Then, at last, he came upon the base of a hill that arose approximately three hundred feet. *Not the highest point of the Blue Hills, but high enough*, he thought to himself with some relief.

Ascending the hill was challenging due to its rugged and rocky terrain. His breathing was labored to the point of near collapse when he finally reached the summit. It was not until he was able to steady his breathing and look up that he saw towards the north, in between where he stood and the lit skyline of Boston eight miles in the distance, an orange glow emanating from the valley floor below. With the sight of this a rush of adrenaline shot through his body. He knew where to go, and he needed to get there quickly.

Down the slope of the hill he raced, stumbling a few times, but picking himself up and continuing on without delay. When he reached the base of the hill he found himself once again amid a black forest. But this time Sydney knew the direction he needed to travel. And it was not long before the orange glow he saw in the valley began to appear through the thicket of trees. As the light became brighter Sydney ran faster until he was brought to a sudden halt by a ten foot high chain-link fence. The fence encircled a meadow roughly the size of a football field. To his right he saw the gravel path that led through an open gate. In the center of the meadow he counted no less than six black trucks with their cargo of bodies being unloaded by workers wearing hazmat suites. They were stacking the bodies like cordwood, some in body bags, others in pine coffins, onto large wooden pallets. Sydney then witnessed an enormous forklift that dwarfed the trucks around it raise one of these pallets stacked with the dead and carefully lower it into a colossal bonfire that reached the height of a five story building.

There was already a Blue Hill Cemetery southwest of the reservation. But a year after the pandemic ended it would become known as *Old* Blue Hill Cemetery, and the secret of what happened in the Blue Hills Reservation during those dark days of the previous

summer would become known to the public with the opening of the
Blue Hill Memorial Cemetery located in the very meadow where
Sydney now stood. Yet that would be a year away, and for now, on
that particular night all Sydney could do as he clasped his fingers
through the chain-link fence was watch in horror the magnificent
billowing flames of amber and gold soaring upward until they filled the
night sky with dancing sparks and plumes of orange-gray smoke.

EIGHT

There was no cold sweat, no anguish, and no tears this time when Sydney awoke. Only empathy and some sadness for the old professor who had to go on living with the grief of losing his beloved in such a tragically horrific way. A grief he was never able to fully heal from. And with the flood of memories, emotions, and love for this woman surging back to him within the past couple of days he was at last capable of understanding why.

It took a moment before Sydney remembered where he was and why he was there curled up under an office desk and freezing. But when it all came back to him he decided to wait and listen for any possibility that the man in black might still be lurking about. The wind had stopped and with it the howling that precipitated it. He could not recall a time in either life when he had experienced such a profound silence. He moved his limbs slightly only to confirm that he was still able to and that they had not succumbed to frostbite. His clothes where covered under a layer of frost that made a crackling sound when he moved. There was frost on his hair and eyebrows as well, and his skin was a pasty white. Sydney knew that he needed to get up and start moving about or risk rendering himself immobile due to a lack of circulation from the cold. He stood and was relieved to notice at this point that his neck had stopped bleeding. *No doubt the icy cold helped*, he figured. After giving his arms and legs a shake he cautiously retraced his steps through the building and out the door from which he had previously entered.

_____

The winds from earlier had ushered in a light snow storm. With an absence of the wind-chill factor thus making the outside temperature slightly more bearable, and no sign of the mysterious stranger who has been trying to kill him, Sydney felt a slight sense of ease that his troubles were over...for now. But he was not, however, complacent and maintained a wary eye for the man after he left the restricted area through the same opening in the fence and made his way back up Madison Avenue.

As he walked Sydney began to think of Laura and their children, and how fortunate Roger was to have died before any of them, thereby being spared the pain of loss that Sydney had to endure. Then, as he thought about it further, he realized that by fate or phenomenon, as Jessica called it, he had not been spared that same grief over their loss at all. Although he had agonized over this very thing before, this time he was able to compare his heartbreaking emotions to what Sydney had gone through. And then the unthinkable began to happen. Although he could see the faces of his children as clear as if he had just seen them the previous day, their names he could not remember. He then saw images of what he remembered from his life as Roger gradually begin to fade, like a light slowly growing dimmer until all was dark.

"Oh God, no" he said with a trembling voice.

When he reached the corner of Madison and 50th he saw on the northwest side of the intersection a sight that gave him hope. A hope when at this desperate moment he saw his life as Roger slipping away. It was a welcoming sight indeed. Opened in the spring of 1879, the Gothic facade of St. Patrick's Cathedral stood out in conspicuous contrast to the glittering glass towers that encircled it. The gray stone of the entire cathedral itself, from sidewalk level to the top of the two 330 foot high spires, was cast aglow in a pale blue from its surrounding flood lights.

Sydney crossed Madison Avenue and walked west on 50th Street alongside St. Patrick's to where he was able to ascend the ten steps leading to the south transept access and enter through the large ornate double bronze doors.

Inside there was no hint of anything modern from the twenty-second or twenty-first centuries. The original beauty of the enormous cathedral was the same as it had always remained for over the past two hundred years.   There was the massive stone groin vaulting and the grandeur of the side-aisle pillars in the nave of the cathedral, each with their elaborate imposts from which their magnificent arches arose. Also the stunning stained glass windows and tracery recessed within their ornamental tympanums.   Along the walls of the north and south transepts the life-size marble statues of various Saints.   And all along the other walls of the cathedral, from the vestibule to the apse, niche altars each with their own marble high relief's of biblical scenes and thousands of votive candles burning before them.   And then there was the marble and gilded opulence of the cathedral's centerpiece, the Sanctuary, and beyond that the High Altar with its glorious golden crucifix shining brightly in view from every angle of the cathedral.

The one thing that stood out with Sydney was that in a place so great in size he could not find another individual anywhere.   By all appearances he was completely alone and wondered to himself if this was a sign of the times in which he was now living, where religion had become nonexistent in society.   He hoped not and reasoned that it was, after all, late in the evening with inclement weather that no person in their right mind would step outside and face.   *Besides*, he quipped, *somebody had to light all these candles.*

Sydney crossed over to the front of the Sanctuary and looked up at the crucifix before glancing back over his left shoulder to the rows of pews where, for a moment, he recalled the little boy Roger used to be sitting in a pew along with his parents and siblings in the small and modest Cleveland church that they attended regularly.   But like the other fading memories of his past life, this sentimental image began to grow dim.   First to disappear was the background, followed by each brother and sister one by one, and then his mother and father, until all that was left was a black void.   With the blink of his eyes Sydney was returned to the sight of those pews in the cathedral knowing that he had just lost the memory of something very dear to him, but he had no idea who or what that memory was of.   He moved closer to the pews, took a seat, and then stared at the pew he was sitting on hoping that whatever it was he saw would return.   But nothing came to mind.   He knew what was happening.   Little by little all traces of Roger Owen were vanishing as the missing puzzle pieces in the mind of Sydney Hamilton were beginning to reassemble.

He then saw three black children.   Two boys whose ages he guessed to be nine and fourteen, and a little girl no more than a year old.   He knew not who these children were, only that he loved them immensely. Then, gradually, the clarity in their faces began to blur and dim. With desperation, anguish and tears Sydney dropped to his knees and fixed his eyes upon the crucifix on the High Altar.

"I know You're here. You've been with me throughout both lives. You know everything that's happened, and everything that *will* happen to me. And You know that over time I've finally come to accept this curve ball You've thrown at me. The memories of two lives, and with both lives the painful loss of all my loved ones. But I've dealt with this fate as best as any man could, and in spite of it, and in spite of this nightmarish ordeal I've been going through with this man who's trying to kill me for what reason only *You* know, I've nevertheless chosen to forge ahead and start a whole new life with Jessica. Still that's not enough. Now You have to hit me with the cruelest blow of all by taking away the only thing I have left of the family I love so dearly. First You erased my memory of Margie and Angela and everyone else I've ever loved in this life, and then You graciously gave them back to me. But in doing so You've decided to take away all the memories of those I have ever loved as Roger. *Please* don't let this happen. Without my memory of them, all the films and photographs of their faces will mean nothing to me. *Nothing!* Oh God, I ask You, I *beg* of You, please, *please* don't purge my mind of these memories! Allow me to go on living and remembering and loving all those I love from *both* of my lives. Oh God, hear me. I beg of You....*Please.*"

Sydney bowed his head until he suddenly sensed the presence of a stranger dressed in black standing in the aisle to his left which drew his attention.

"Sorry for sneaking up on you" said the young priest. Sydney was surprised by his youth. No more than his mid-twenties he assumed. His amiable nature was matched with a kindly face. "We don't see many people in here this late at night. I just wanted to let you know that if you need me for confession, or wish to seek counsel, or simply share what's on your mind,...your story,..you can find me up there behind the High Altar."

Sydney paused a moment feeling somewhat amused over the friendly priest's thoughtful offer. "Even a man such as you, Father, would find my story hard to believe."

The priest was only slightly fazed by Sydney's vague response. But it was what Sydney asked next that downright befuddled the well-intentioned lad.

"Would you happen to have a phone I may use?"

"Uh...Well, yes I do. Of course you may."

While the priest reached into the pocket of his cassock for his phone, Sydney felt his own pockets for his wallet. Both phone and wallet were brought forth at the same time. Sydney took out of his wallet a small slip of paper on which a phone number was written.

"An important number in case I lost my phone...Which I did."

The priest handed Sydney his phone.

"Thank you. This won't take a minute."

Jessica was still at Grand Central Terminal along with Cyrus. He had joined her shortly after she phoned him with the urgent news regarding Sydney following her discovery of the dead man on the train platform. The immediate area of the incident was roped off by the police and the victim was being wheeled away on a gurney past Jessica and Cyrus when her phone rang with a call from an unknown number.

"Hello?"

"Jessica, it's Sydney."

"Oh my God, where are you? Are you alright?"

"Yes, I'm fine. For now. I'm in St. Patrick's Cathedral."

"Stay there, Sydney. I'm here with Cyrus and we'll be right up to get you."

"Fine. But listen to me, Jessica, there's something I need to tell you. I'm losing Roger. It's all fading away. You've got to help me. Surely there's *something* you can do to stop what's happening."

"We'll see what we can do about that later, Sydney. For right now let's just concentrate on getting you back safely and over to a police station. Until we get there try to keep yourself well hidden."

"Oh I don't think he'll be able to find me again anytime soon. I've taken care of that."

"Good. Then we'll be there in a few minutes."

The conversation only furthered the priest's confusion. A confusion made apparent to Sydney by the look on the priest's face.

"Like I said, you'd find it hard to believe." Sydney handed the phone back to the priest and as he did so something captured his attention directly over the priest's shoulder. On the wall behind him, set within niches, were the life-size marble statues of four Saints. Two Saints were standing and below them the other two were seated. It was the seated Saint on the bottom right that Sydney's eyes became fixed on.

"Well, once again," the priest went on to reiterate, not noticing at first where Sydney's attention was focused, "...if you'd like to talk, or confess, or...use my phone, I'll be right up there behind the...."

As though not listening to a word the priest was saying, Sydney rose up from the pew, passed the priest, and crossed an aisle and then through another section of pews until he came to stand directly under the statue, never diverting his eyes once from the face of the Saint. Then the priest also stood and silently watched for a moment, puzzled by Sydney's fascination with this particular Saint.

Seated and wearing robes, the Saint held in his left hand an open book, with his right hand raised slightly from his lap as though offering a blessing. And at the base of this statue in gold lettering his name; *ST BASIL THE GREAT*.

"He was a prolific writer" said the priest. "He wrote quite a bit about the Holy Spirit and its relationship in the Holy Trinity. Born in Caesarea in Cappadocia in either 330 or 329 AD I believe. If you have an interest in St. Basil the Great I can print off the computer for you some of his texts."

Sydney shook his head. "That won't be necessary. He just bears a striking resemblance to someone I know. But I don't know who."

At that point the young priest took a deep breath and gave up. The old man was simply too perplexing to try to figure out. Sydney never turned around to watch as the priest walked away. His focus remained on the face of St. Basil. *That face*, he pressed himself hard to remember. *Where have I seen that face?*

That face of the elderly looking Saint he gazed upon was narrow with a long thin nose, deep set eyes, a heavy brow, and high cheek bones. He was bald except for the wavy hair on the sides that grew down below his ears. A moustache and a curly beard that covered his neck completed the look of this man from nearly two millennia ago who bore a striking resemblance to the same man who Sydney now remembered sitting in his current Boston home on Commonwealth Avenue. A man who was his friend. And aside from the absence of being adorned in robes, the two men could have passed for identical twins.

"Are you sure I can't offer you a glass of port, or brandy perhaps?" Sydney asked his friend. "You certainly look as though you could do with a glass of one or the other to calm your nerves."

"No thank you, Sydney. I'd rather just get on with saying what it is I came here to tell you."

Sydney's friend drew in a deep breath which did nothing to steady his hands that noticeably began to shake. Beads of perspiration formed heavily on his brow as he glanced to the window acting pensive and anxious.

"Could you close those curtains?" he asked Sydney.

"Of course."

After doing so Sydney's friend then expressed a change of mind.

"On second thought, a glass of port *would* be helpful."

Sydney gladly commenced with pouring them each a glass. Afterwards, Sydney sat down in a chair across from his friend and they both took a sip of their port.

"Alright, Frank, now tell me what's troubling you."

Dr. Frank Wesley hesitated nervously and then took another sip of his port before starting in.

"It was the spring of 2115 when the CDC received a report of a very small village in Zaire where the entire population had been wiped out by an unknown disease. The CDC was called out to investigate. Before our team arrived we speculated that it might be another outbreak of Ebola. After all, it was in Zaire where the Ebola virus had its origins. But then there were also the odds it could perhaps be the Lassa or Hantaan virus, or anthrax, or even bubonic plague. There was any number of possibilities really. When we entered the village garbed in our hazmat suites we found not a single survivor among the small population. Upon initial examination of the dead we were able to clearly rule out Ebola as well as the other diseases we previously considered. The bodies, all marked by a strange blue cast on their faces, had bloated in the humid heat, still, we performed an on-the-spot autopsy of one of the dead and found no correlation to anything we had ever seen before, except for some similarities to the historical *written* autopsy records of 1918 influenza victims. Along with lungs choked with blood and other body fluids, another unique feature in particular was the presence of heliotrope cyanosis, where the lungs become so desperate for air that they literally deplete oxygen from blood vessels in the face thus causing that bluish tone. Because there were no survivors to relate to us the symptoms each victim experienced before death, there was really nothing else for us to go on at the site. So to prevent further spread of the disease the village was burned along with its dead. Blood and tissue samples were brought back to the CDC in Atlanta for epidemiology studies. And what we discovered was a whole new virulent flu strain. Possibly one more lethal than the 1918 flu virus.

Now let me explain to you a little something about a virus, Sydney. It's so small that thirty-thousand can sit on the head of a pin. It survives and thrives only by invading cells. And it reproduces itself inside of these cells. Without a cell to infect, it would die within hours. It's an organism with a strand of eight genes. But these eight genes are not locked in a fixed structure. Instead they exist as separate fragments allowing a virus the ability to change their permutations. Because these eight genes mutate endlessly they're able to circumvent our immune systems attempt to stop it. And every thirty years or so a mutation comes along that results in the creation of a *super virus*. A virus that spreads efficiently, replicates well, and transmits successfully from one person to another. A pandemic strain that is beyond our body's ability to protect us and so powerful that it renders vaccines ineffective. Although such pandemic strains have been introduced to the human population since 1918, nothing had ever come along in one hundred and ninety-seven years that equaled the devastating magnitude of the flu virus that swept over the world in that year. Scientists in my field had always felt that such a global catastrophic event was long overdue. And by 2115 we were well over one hundred and fifty years overdue. Somewhere out there was a ticking time bomb. And on that day in that little village in Zaire we found it and brought it back with us to the U.S.

Of course the only concern of the U.S. government at the time was that if this strain ever landed in the hands of the wrong people who are unaware of just how powerful this lethal contagion is, they might use it for biological weaponry that could unleash death beyond the borders of their intended victims. But we didn't need the government to pressure us into finding a vaccine. We already knew well before it was brought to their attention that a vaccine needed to be discovered as soon as possible because of the likelihood that this new virus hadn't been confined to that one village alone. And if it ever made its way from a village to a major city with mass transit there would be no containing it. But finding a vaccine presented a formidable challenge. Mainstream science acknowledged that beginning as far back as the early nineteen-eighties antibiotic resistant strains of bacteria were emerging. The last half of the twentieth century even saw antiparasite drugs grow powerless against such killers as malaria. And so naturally when it came to viruses, with their high degree of inherent mutability and rapid reproduction rate, it was only eventual that antiviral resistant influenza strains would also emerge. Within the first twenty years of the twenty-first century nearly ninety percent of all antibiotics, antiparasitials, and antivirals became useless against diseases and infections. For science it was like starting from scratch in their haste to discover new drugs to replace those that were no longer effective. And since then it's been a never-ending race to keep one step ahead of the drug-resistant strains that inevitably develop. Therefore, it was met with no surprise, but disheartening nonetheless, that this new flu virus was resistant to every single antiviral drug we threw at it.

Now it was about at the same time that all of this was happening when a young biologist came to work for the CDC. His name was Michael Baines. Only in his early twenties and fresh out of college, he fit the typical mold of so many other youthful intellects that begin their careers at the CDC. He was full of ambition, ideas, and eager to prove to everyone that his purpose for being there was to find the next great cure for some dreaded disease that has eluded science throughout the history of medicine. Naturally this new mystery virus was just the thing for him to sink all his time and energy into. Baines' expertise was botany for medicinal uses. An expertise in which, I must admit, he was profoundly skilled at. And where he excelled most was his depth of knowledge with plants in the Amazon rain forest. Granted, throughout the past two centuries scientists have turned to the Amazon rain forest time and again in search of botanical chemicals that can be used for medicinal purposes, but have found through their efforts that many identified bioactive compounds end up as having no human use. Still, nearly all biologists will agree that an estimated forty-five million species of terrestrial flora, fauna, and microorganisms living in the

world's rain forests have yet to be identified. Baines learned of one
such plant deep within the rain forest south of the Amazon River close
to the Colombian and Peruvian borders in a valley called Javari. He
heard that anthropologists in that region had observed a handful of
indigenous Indian tribes, notably the Korubo tribe, recovering at a
miraculous rate from bouts of the flu, a disease brought to them by the
white man, after eating the leaves of a plant that they used for that
reason and other medicinal functions. Photos that Baines had viewed
of the plant suggested it to be of the Cucurbitaceae family, similar to
the Momordica charantia, or *Bitter Melon* plant which had long ago
been tested and found to contain a huge list of chemicals with
properties and actions that purportedly range from being antiviral,
antibacterial, anticancerous, and an immune stimulant, among others.
And worldwide its ethnomedical uses are too numerous to count. But
this particular plant looked to be a whole new unidentified species
within the same family. And with *that* deduction, and the possibility
that it might hold the key chemical element that can destroy this virus,
the CDC wasted no time in granting Baines' request to travel to Brazil
and into the rain forest interior to locate this plant and bring it back for
analysis. But on the eve before his departure a terrible accident
happened.

Certainly it wasn't the first time an accident had occurred while
handling a lethal virus with potentially devastating consequences. For
example, in 1976, in the Toxic Animals Wing of Proton Down,
Britain's equivalent to our own CDC, a scientist's hand slipped when
he was injecting a syringe containing Ebola-infected guinea pig blood
from one guinea pig to another. The needle penetrated through three
layers of latex gloves into the tip of his thumb. After six anxiety filled
days his temperature suddenly shot up and his blood tested positive for
the Ebola virus. Proton Down was immediately shut down. Its
employees ordered home and put under surveillance. The English
scientist was taken to North London's Coppetts Wood Hospital while
its hundred and sixty other patients were evacuated to alternative
infirmaries. The entire medical staff tending to him was placed under
quarantine. His wife and two children were placed under quarantine.
Even several of the scientist's friends were put under home quarantine.
For forty-nine days his life precariously hung in the balance while
doctors attacked the virus with everything they had available including
large doses of human interferon that was injected twice daily.
Miraculously he survived and none of the people he came in contact
with became infected. England had been spared an Ebola outbreak.

Then in 2005, another accident occurred when samples of the deadly H2N2 Asian flu strain which killed four million people in 1957 were mistakenly shipped by a company called Meridian Bioscience to more than four thousand labs in eighteen countries and territories on behalf of the College of American Pathologists as part of a test kit that would enable laboratory personnel around the world to measure their proficiency in detecting various stains of influenza. It was the association's policies to never have these kits include micro-organisms that can harm people. Yet, *somehow* H2N2 was included, and only by sheer luck was the mistake realized and all the samples destroyed before anyone became infected. So accidents *do* happen. And in 2115 we saw that even a maximum-security laboratory was susceptible to deadly mishaps. Although in Michael Baines' case the accident was coupled with plain stupidity on his part.

The CDC has three levels of laboratories. The P1 facility is your basic laboratory such as you would find in a science department at a university. The P2 facility offers a higher level of security where only trained and authorized personnel can enter, and where work is performed under hoods that suck air away from the experiment through ventilator ducts, past chemical scrubbers, and ultraviolet light that disinfects the air, and microscopically gridded filters. Then we have our maximum-security laboratory, or P3 facility. Only with a security pass can one enter through the several guarded locked doors to where, after showering with disinfectant soap and donning a set of head-to-toe protective clothing with gauze face mask, double latex gloves, and a radiation badge that monitors the levels of exposure to isotopes occasionally used in research, you would then pass through two more air locks lined with microbe-killing ultraviolet lights before entering the inner core. The core itself is pressurized with the air forced in through microscopic filters and then sucked back out past additional layers of filters, high heat sources, ultraviolet lights, and chemical scrubbers. Handling samples of a virus, whether it be in test tubes, pipettes, or petri dishes, would all be done within a glove box where one would need to insert their hands into a large set of thick rubber gloves that are permanently installed on the clear-plastic front wall of the hooded box. The samples of the virus in Vacutainer tubes are stored in deep freezers. When removed for study the tube is transferred into the glove box where it will thaw prior to it being analyzed.

Now on that evening before his departure, Baines worked late, long past the time when everyone else had gone home. Only a staff of security guards was present in the building when he decided to do some final research of the mystery virus before flying down to Brazil the following morning. Inside P3 Baines removed a Vacutainer tube of contaminated blood from the deep freezer and was walking it over to the glove box when the tube accidentally slipped out of his hand and shattered on the floor. Shards of glass and frozen blood were strewn around his feet. Baines knew immediately what needed to be done. He sprayed disinfectant on the area before crouching down to clean up the scattered pieces with a sanitized rag. In his crouched position he lost his balance and by placing his left hand on the floor he was able to brace himself from falling over. But in doing so a fine sliver of glass punctured through the two layers of latex on the tip of his index finger. The sliver was so small he could barely see it. But remember what I said about how thirty-thousand virus organisms can sit on the head of a pin? On that sliver of glass there was frozen blood. And in that blood were organisms of this virus. And it only takes one, just *one* single organism of those thirty-thousand or more to enter into his body, quickly thaw in his warm blood, get rapidly pumped throughout his system by his anxiety induced adrenaline, and enter into a solitary cell where it could begin to replicate. That's all it would take. One organism and one cell. But although Baines definitely felt a prick to his finger, he saw no blood. And then there was the good chance that the disinfectant had landed on that particular sliver of glass before it pierced his glove. Still, not taking any chances, he at once removed the two sets of gloves and submerged his hand into a disinfectant tank and held it there for a good five minutes. After which, feeling confident that he was out of danger, Baines finished cleaning up the remnants from the shattered tube and disinfected the entire laboratory before going forward with his intended research with another sample. After completing this research Michael Baines went home. And *that* is where he made his stupid and ultimately fatal mistake. If he had followed proper procedures he would have reported the incident to the Laboratory Safety Office where he would have been given a thorough examination before being allowed to leave the premises. And considering the fact that he might have been exposed to a lethal virus we really knew nothing about, chances are that they would have quarantined him in that lab for several days to monitor him and make sure he didn't show any symptoms before releasing him. But the Safety Office was closed. So what Baines *should* have done was to simply stay there in that laboratory, over night if need be, until the safety team arrived back at work the following morning. But he didn't. Instead he went home.

Whether he had a good night's sleep or not we'll never know. But there are three things that we *do* know for certain. He began that day feeling fine, he never told anyone at the CDC about the accident, and by nine AM he was on a flight to Brazil accompanied by a colleague named Beth Livingstone. For whatever reason he chose not to tell anyone at the CDC of this accident we'll never know for sure, but can only assume that it was because he felt that being the new kid on the block a mishap such as this would have discredited him. But I'm more inclined to believe that he didn't want anyone to know for a far more selfish reason. Baines knew that if he told us about what happened he would have been quarantined in that laboratory for several days at the least, while in the meantime we would have sent someone else to Brazil in his place. Someone who, if this plant proved to be the thing that could kill this virus, would take all the credit as being the discoverer of a vaccine against the most lethal virus to come along in two hundred years. So he took a gamble with millions of lives at stake and lost. We *all* lost.

While in flight to Belem, their jumping off point to the Amazonas region, Baines had already begun running a fever. In the cab to their hotel his breathing became labored in conjunction with a deep bronchial cough. By the time he entered his hotel room he was too weak to unpack. It was then, while lying on his bed with his face gradually taking on that horrific bluish cast, that he told Livingstone of the accident that happened the previous night. Minutes later Baines was dead. Livingstone immediately phoned me from her room and recounted everything that Baines had told her before he died. We both knew that Brazil's Federal Department of Public Health needed to be contacted right away so that Baines' room, her room,...the entire hotel for that matter, could be quarantined. She volunteered to take on that responsibility while I conferred with CDC Director, Dr. Benjamin Sands on the situation and how we should go about alerting the airline and other people who Baines might have come in contact with. Sands, however, hesitated to act, wanting first to bring this to the attention of the U.S. Secretary of Health and Human Services, Barbara Lansing, in Washington. And although Sands came around to siding with me that an alert needed to go out at once, Lansing argued that it might create a panic, not to mention how it will look on the U.S. to have brought a deadly contagious virus to the doorstep of another country. She pressed upon us to wait until she spoke with the President. Both Sands and I, however, adamantly contended that every second wasted brought us closer to seeing a pandemic that we have no resources to stop. But

Lansing was equally adamant about stalling any public announcements or quarantines without administration approval, citing the logistical, economical, and above all, political ramifications this could have. She went even further by demanding that she speak personally with Livingstone over the phone before going to the President. But when we couldn't reach Livingstone on her phone or even through the hotel phone, we feared she might have already fallen ill. After all, she had been in direct contact with Baines since they met at the airport that morning. It wasn't until much later into the pandemic when we learned that Livingstone *did indeed* succumb to a fever after speaking with me. Delirious, she was never able to make that call to Brazil's Federal Department of Public Health, and in fact probably died within the hour. Unlike the 1918 flu that was initially called the *Three Day Fever* because it typically took three days before the person died, the 2115 flu hit hard and killed fast, often within the same day of showing its first symptoms.

Now, back to that fateful day. After we were unable to contact Livingstone on the phone, Lansing finally conceded to the urgency of the situation and promised to take it directly to the President without delay and that we would be notified very soon what to do. While Sands and I waited I remember him expressing to me his regrets over notifying the government officials first before taking actions on his own. But now, any actions he took would be going directly against governmental orders. So we were left with nothing to do but wait. And we didn't have to wait long, a couple of hours at the most, before Sands and I eventually looked at one another realizing the same thing. It's too late. By that time the other passengers on that flight, including flight attendants, airport employees, the cab driver, and hotel staff, had nearly all been infected and had by now probably passed it on to their families, friends, other passengers and guests. Its global spread was now inevitable. A killer had been set loose from its cage. And an apocalyptic event beyond anyone's imagination had begun."

Sydney was standing beside the table where photographs of his family were displayed when Dr. Wesley finally finished speaking. Stoic and silent he gazed down upon the photos for a prolonged moment until eventually, without turning to look at his friend, he asked the obvious question, "Why are you telling me this?"

"I've always felt terrible about what happened to your family, Sydney."

"I know that, Frank. Still, I'm not the only one you know personally who lost his entire family. And besides, it wasn't your fault. So what's the *other* reason you're telling me this."

Dr. Wesley looked down at his empty glass and held it up to Sydney in gesture. "May I?"

Without a word, Sydney crossed over to the end table next to the chair where he had been sitting earlier, picked up the bottle of port and filled his friend's glass. After a long sip Dr. Wesley went on to explain.

"Dusk was approaching when Sands and I began to receive reports through the wire of a strangely large number of Brazilian citizens centered in and around the city of Belem, as well as a smaller but, nonetheless, significant number in other major Brazilian cities, who are falling ill to a mysterious high fever and respiratory ailment. We rushed to relay this information on to Lansing's office, though we were unable to speak with her directly. Shortly afterwards, more reports started coming in of passengers arriving in other countries on flights that originated from Brazil who were also showing the same type of symptoms. This information was also relayed to Lansing's office and within the hour we finally heard from Lansing herself. She appeared and sounded stressed beyond measure, just as Sands and I felt at the time. And after an apology for the delay and a vague explanation of bureaucratic dickering from all branch levels over what should be done about the crises, she was finally given the go-ahead to inform us to act immediately at doing whatever possible to stop the spread of this virus. We were told to put out an alert to all foreign countries, friend or foe, explaining to them where this disease has originated from and to suggest that they do whatever needs to be done to halt all transportation coming into their countries from Brazil. Likewise, Lansing went on to say, the U.S. Department of Transportation has already stopped all air and sea traffic coming into the U.S. from the entire South American continent until this thing can be contained. But she cautioned us with one stipulation that we were given no explanation for. By no means whatsoever were we to tell *anyone* about Michael Baines as the carrier of that virus to Brazil. Definitely no foreign countries, no one within the CDC who might not already know, and for those who do, not even our family or spouses can ever know. She ordered us to destroy any records of Baines and Livingstone's trip down to Brazil, and instructed us to come up with an alternative explanation to their families regarding how and where they died. And because repatriation of their bodies back to this country was at the moment impossible, not to mention extremely dangerous, this meant falsifying a reason to their families why they can't retrieve their remains. She concluded with this ominous warning that this incident was to be considered a top classified government secret and any violation towards exposing it would be handled with the severest punishment.   Within a half hour after speaking with Lansing, Sands and I were paid a visit by two men from a governmental department I can't recall, who wanted from us the names of every individual who knew about Baines' trip to South America and the circumstances that followed. Because we were only hours into the crises there were only a handful of people who knew. Myself, Sands, of course Livingstone who we presumed was already dead, a Molecular Pathologist named Gabriel Velasquez, an Epidemiologist named Cynthia Brice, and medical researcher, Dr. Avery McKenna. Aside from Lansing we had no way of knowing how many other people on the political end knew.   And we can only presume that the President was fully aware of it. As for Velasquez, Brice, and McKenna, they where then also questioned by the two men and given the same verbal warning of strict secrecy with what they knew and the dire consequences if they *did* tell anyone."

"But *why* the big secrecy over Baines?" Sydney implored.

"It didn't take long for each of us to figure it out. And when we all got together privately one time and questioned it amongst ourselves we were not surprised to find that we had all drawn the same conclusion. You see, in March of 1918, while World War One was raging over there in Europe, one hundred American soldiers in Kansas fell ill while in training at Camp Funston. One week later that count rose to five hundred cases. Then they began to die. In that same month eighty thousand U.S. soldiers crossed the Atlantic to Europe. The following month nearly a hundred and twenty-thousand followed. And when they arrived in Britain, so too did this mysterious flu. British civilians began dying in epidemic numbers. And soon our international allies were falling dead to the disease as well. By June it even reached epidemic proportions among the ranks of the German enemy. And back in the states Camp Devens in Massachusetts was reporting one hundred soldiers dying *per day*! Yet, even after it reached the point to where over two hundred thousand recruits had been hit with this flu, all moves to quarantine the camps throughout the U.S. were rejected. No matter what the cost, the war demanded reinforcements. And so they continued sending them. By August a quarter million doughboy's, as the young soldiers were called, were pouring into Europe each month.

The flu itself came in three waves. After a few weeks the number of deaths would subside until the second wave hit, and then the third. Each wave more devastating than the last. And with each wave it spread further and further until not a single country on earth was spared. And so for the rest of the twentieth-century history taught us that the great influenza pandemic of 1918 began in America and was brought to Europe by our United States soldiers where it then spread throughout the rest of the world. Is it any wonder that the press made so little of it after it was all over? America wanted to be known as the ones who went over there to win the war to end all wars. Not the ones that brought the deadliest pandemic in recorded history that claimed more lives than the war itself. And so it wasn't until the turn of the twenty-first century when a discovery was made that might at least place the *origins* of this flu squarely on the soil of another country. Back then bomb scarred medical records where found that told of a two and a half month period beginning in December of 1916 when a respiratory ailment struck the British Army's largest transit camp in a little backwater village called Etaples, located in northern France. With a constantly shifting population of over one hundred thousand soldiers, Etaples grew to the size of a small city. A real melting pot that included divisions from the Highlands, Wales, Ireland, New Zealand, Australia, and the West Indies. During that short period more sick than wounded were being treated. And in February of 1917 the first soldier of twelve to follow died of this mysterious flu-like illness. Service medical records indicated that they died with the same type of dominant symptoms that later arose at Camp Funston a year later. If this *was* the same flu virus that would begin killing millions in a year, we have no way of knowing how it made its way from Etaples, France to Camp Funston, Kansas. Without doubt it was the U.S. soldiers that brought it to Europe, but there is no solid evidence that proves that it didn't originate in the U.S. as well. Even though the 1918 virus' genetic code was deciphered way back in 2005 using the tissue from a 1918 victim exhumed from Alaskan permafrost, with no *pre*-1918 tissue samples in existence from those who died in 1917 to substantiate that the virus that killed those soldiers in France was the same virus that began killing soldiers in Kansas a year later, we're left without having the influenza genetic material to link the two. Therefore, history has then, as it still does to this day, affirmed that the 1918 pandemic originated in the United States of America. And so the bottom line as to why the U.S. Government wanted us to keep silent about Baines' fateful trip to Brazil is because they didn't want America to be blamed again for another 1918."

Sydney could only stare at his friend in disbelief over what he was hearing. "But if this is supposed to be a classified U.S. secret, then I ask you again, *why* are you telling *me*?"

"Because you're a historian, Sydney.   And you rightfully believe that when it comes to history only the *truth* should be told. And as far as I know, only I, and now you, know the truth behind a world catastrophe that will be taught and discussed for generations to come."

"What about the others?"

"As far as Barbara Lansing goes, everyone already knows that she contracted the virus during the early stages of the outbreak and died. About two years after it ended my good friend Benjamin Sands informed me that he couldn't keep the truth from the people any longer and was going to go public with what he knew. But before that could happen he reportedly committed suicide. To this day I still find it hard to believe that he would take his own life. Sure he was burdened with his own feeling of guilt. But speaking out with the truth was, as he told me, going to free him of that guilt. Besides, Sands had everything in the world to continue living for. He had his wife and kids. It just doesn't make sense to me that he would end it all and take everything that he knew about the pandemic with him. And then another two years had passed after Sands' death when I heard from Gabriel Velasquez who wanted to inform me that he had begun writing a book about the pandemic that was going to be a tell-all, and that *nothing* was going to be left out. He wanted to know if I would collaborate with him on it. I told him no, and warned him against it. But he didn't listen to me. The following day he and his wife were murdered in their home. Their house had been ransacked which led police to eventually close the unsolved case as a burglary-homicide. Then only a year ago this month I received a phone call from Avery McKenna telling me that Cynthia Brice had phoned him to say that she was asked to guest on a nationally syndicated news program to speak on the 2115 pandemic. She wanted him to watch the show because she was planning on live television to finally, in her words, *"blow the whole lid on this."* Brice never arrived at that television station that day and was never seen or heard from again. And a year later her disappearance still remains a mystery. This brings us to McKenna, who, I tell you with mixed emotions, died a month ago of natural causes, a heart attack. And he took his secret to the grave. This leaves just me and now you. And you, being an author of so many books, is who I was hoping would be the one to write that book that Velasquez wanted to write and that Sands and Brice wanted to tell the world about."

"But surely *you're* better qualified than me. *You* write it and I'll piecemeal it to my publisher."

"Sydney, I'm dying. I have pancreatic cancer. I know what you're thinking, but pancreatic cancer is treatable now. True. But only if it's detected in time. And to be very honest with you, Sydney, I've known. I've known for awhile but I just don't want to go on. I'm old. And I've seen a lot of death. And I've had enough. I'm tired. Then when I heard that McKenna died I realized that I was the only one left who was aware of the truth, and if I take that secret with me as McKenna did, then no one will ever know the truth. But with my cancer now in the advanced stages I've got only weeks, if not days left. Now I've kept a journal hidden in my house all these years stating everything I've told you. I didn't dare bring it with me. You see, I know you might think I'm paranoid for saying this, but I know I've been bugged, *and* followed ever since this all began. I want to give it to you, but it would be best if you come to my home in Atlanta to receive it. And better that we not travel together. I'll fly home today and you follow tomorrow or the next. It would be safer that way. Are you with me, Sydney? For the sake of history?"

For the sake of history. From the time he was that little boy swinging a wooden sword atop of the battlemented curtain wall at Manorbier Castle everything Sydney ever learned and taught, worked for and struggled for, fought for and believed in for his entire life had been for the sake of history. Now he was being handed the opportunity to *rewrite* history. To refuse would be an injustice to future generations. To refuse would be unthinkable. Accepting his proposal Sydney nodded his head and then finished off the small amount of port that remained in his glass.

"Thank you" said Wesley with a smile of relief.

"One more question" Sydney asked as an afterthought. "The plant. What was learned about the plant?"

Wesley grimaced and shook his head. "Obviously it wasn't the cure we hoped for. We found it to have no antiviral compounds whatsoever."

Sydney glanced over again to the photos of his family and wondered to himself if they might still be with him if they had only already known that this plant was ineffective.

"It could have been worse, Sydney" came a sympathetic voice. "In 1918 the world population was just over 1.8 billion. And whether it was forty million or a hundred million that perished that year, in comparison to the hundred and fifty-two million that died in 2115 when the world population was a staggering *forty-two* billion, ...it could have been worse. It could have been a *whole* lot worse."

But those figures offered no consolation to Sydney as he continued to stare at the images of his loved ones who were no longer with him.

That night Dr. Frank Wesley arrived at his home in Atlanta and was murdered. Sydney learned of it the following day and that his friend's home had been ransacked, suggesting to the police that he entered upon a burglary in progress. The next day a mysterious man in black would arrive at Sydney's home and attempt to orchestrate what police would assume to be a suicide.

Sydney turned his face away from the statue of St. Basil and realized that his life at last had come full circle. There were no more missing pieces to the puzzle. No more blank memories of the events that brought him to the place where he now stood. Sydney Hamilton was back, but he still understood the reason for Jessica and Cyrus' involvement with him. He knew he had a past life. And he knew he was a man named Roger Owen with a wife named Laura whom he loved dearly. He also knew he was a family man who lived a wonderful life. But that was all he knew. Nothing more.

Sydney suddenly felt overwhelmed by an inner-peace that he had not known since the years prior to 2115. But he cautioned himself against feeling too complacent. His life was still in danger, and the sooner he exposed what he knew the safer he would be.

In the silence of the cathedral there suddenly came a faint thud that echoed throughout. It seemed to come from the vestibule area. Sydney knew it had to be Jessica and Cyrus and wondered why it had taken them so long to finally arrive. He strode assuredly down the side isle past a line of alters along the north wall.

The vestibule in St. Patrick's Cathedral is no less impressive than the cathedral itself with its massive ornate bronze double doors serving as the main entrance to the cathedral. Along a portion of each wall to the north and south of the vestibule is an alter with burning votive candles. Above each alter is a life-size statue. On the north wall, St. Paul. On the south wall, St. Peter. And next to each of these statues a set of large double wooden doors with windowpanes of obscured glass that each lead to side antechambers. Both north and south antechambers also have identical wooden doors that open directly into the cathedral, as well as a set of doors that serve as alternate entrances into St. Patrick's.

As Sydney approached the double wooden doors of the north antechamber that opened to the cathedral he saw a sight that stopped him cold. Through the obscured glass he could see the dark silhouette of the man who has been trying to kill him. *But how?* Sydney wondered. *He must have been lying in wait outside the office building and then watched me as I entered the cathedral*, was the only rational explanation Sydney could think of. But there was no time to dwell on any further possibilities. He knew he needed to get away from him, and *fast*! Outside those bronze doors was 5th Avenue and no doubt plenty of people. That is where he needed to place himself, among people, among *witnesses*. Sydney rushed towards the vestibule, but as he did so the double doors of the antechamber that lead directly into the vestibule flew open and the man in black charged after Sydney with his Rad Gun in hand. In the center of the vestibule the man caught hold of Sydney and swung him around to where they were face to face. Then he pressed the Rad Gun against Sydney's abdomen and fired. Sydney's eyes opened wide as a burning sensation shot throughout the inside of his body. In shock and in pain he grasped a hold of his assailant's shoulders. But the man grabbed Sydney's hands firmly and removed them and then fled the cathedral through the bronze doors. Sydney looked down to where he fired the gun into him and pressed his hand against the spot, but found there was no hole and no blood. He became lightheaded as his legs began to tremble. Then his legs gave out and he crumbled to the floor. *This isn't the way it's supposed to end*, was his only thought. *It <u>can't</u> end this way. There's so much I need to tell. I <u>must</u> tell someone. <u>Anyone</u>.*

Sydney dragged his body across the marble floor to the bronze doors. Blood began to stream from his nose as he pulled himself up by clutching onto the door's inlaid artwork. Back on his feet he then pulled the heavy door open and staggered to the outside.

It was still snowing when Sydney looked out onto a 5th Avenue that was eerily devoid of any street traffic and pedestrians. With his lungs filling with fluid his breathing grew heavy and he began to cough up blood. Gradually disorientation set in as he lurched forward and stumbled down three steps that were only a couple of feet in front of him. Lying on his back on a snow covered stone pedestrian walkway - which was elevated another four steps above street level - Sydney now found himself facing the cathedral and staring straight up at the monolithic facade of this gothic work of art. Lavish ornamental stonework of the highest detail, exquisite traceries, and those two magnificent spires reaching towards heaven, all towered over him in a most imposing way. And set within a deep tympanum those glorious bronze doors with their inlaid high reliefs of six Saints, the twelve Apostles, and Christ, all of whom, in his delusional state, seemed to be looking down upon him. But in contrast against the structural might the cathedral displayed there were the delicate snowflakes drifting lazily down to earth that brought him an odd sense of serenity.

So this is dying, he marveled.

Then, in a sight more welcoming than angels themselves, the faces of Jessica and Cyrus appeared over him.

"Sydney....Sydney, we're here" said Jessica, stunned by the sight of him. "Oh my God, Sydney. What did he do to you?"

Cyrus had already begun placing an emergency call on his mobile phone. "We have a man badly wounded here and needs an ambulance *fast*! He's at St. Patrick's Cathedral. Outside. 5th Avenue side. Hurry, please!"

"Sydney, can you hear me? You're going to be alright. Help is on its way. Just hold on."

They watched in horror as blood began to stream from his ears and the white of his eyes began to turn red. Then Sydney coughed up blood and began to choke.

"He's choking on his blood" said Cyrus. "Turn his head to the side."

Jessica lifted Sydney's head and followed through allowing a copious amount of blood to run from his mouth.

Meanwhile, Cyrus felt him over quickly. "There's no entry wound" he told Jessica. "Was it a Rad Gun, Sydney?"

Aware of everything that was being spoken to him, but unable to speak, Sydney nodded yes. Cyrus looked at Jessica and shook his head, knowing that with such a weapon Sydney's outcome is fatal. Over the sound of his gargled breaths and beating heart, Sydney heard the bell of St. Patrick's begin to slowly toll away the twelve hours of midnight. Then in a surprising move, Sydney reached up his hand, grabbed Cyrus by his coat and pulled him down to where his face was close to his. With great difficulty and his voice garbled from the emission of blood in his throat, he spoke.

"The government doesn't want us to know..."

Cyrus glanced at Jessica and then looked back down at Sydney and asked, "Know what, Sydney?"

"Michael   Baines.....CDC....a   lab   accident.....he   was infected......and then went to Brazil where it spread....."

Sydney released his tight grasp of Cyrus' coat and coughed up the greatest amount of blood yet. It was enough to allow him, for only a moment, to draw in a deep breath. In doing so he resumed his head, still held raised in Jessica's hand, back to its straight position. Cyrus reacted with bewilderment over Sydney's broken statement, while Jessica, overwhelmed with grief and tears, took hold of his hand in hers, leaned in to where her face was gently touching his and whispered, "Don't you leave me, Sydney. I need you, you hear me? There's so much ahead for us. You've just got to hold on. Please, Sydney. Don't go. *Please* don't go. I love you."

Sydney looked into her eyes with empathy, but also with an acceptance of what he knew was to follow. And with a voice so weak and barely audible he said softly, "It's now *my* time. And you'll go on. You've *got* to go on."

Then, as though someone had called to him to do so, he turned his head away from them both and looked to his other side. A flash of amazement graced his face and his eyes lit up with joy at the sight of something. But there was nothing there that Jessica and Cyrus could see. At that moment Sydney simply smiled and said, "You're all here." And with that the life passed from his body as the bell continued to toll..... *Ten..... Eleven..... Twelve.*

NINE

Roger opened his eyes to a room brightly lit by the morning sun. He turned his head to the left and saw a vacant pillow. He then turned his head to the right and saw on the clock that it was ten after eight. He reflected on how good it felt to sleep in and how he wished he could do it more often than on weekends alone. After a long deep stretch Roger laid there for a moment and ruminated on how well rested he was feeling after having such a good night's sleep. Then he threw back the covers, stepped out of bed, slipped his feet into a pair of slippers, and clad in only boxers and a loose fitting T-shirt, entered into the bathroom where he splashed his face with cold water before heading downstairs.

Entering the living room Roger came upon Justin sitting on the sofa in his pajamas watching cartoons on the television. He mussed the top of his head as he passed behind him and continued into the kitchen where he found Natalie sitting in her highchair gnawing on a slice of buttered bread. Standing in front of the stove he saw Laura frying up bacon with Bagheera, their cat, affectionately rubbing up against her legs. After placing a gentle kiss behind her ear, which gave them both reason to smile, he reached down and gave Bagheera a little scratch on his head before pouring himself a cup of coffee. Then, crossing over to the kitchen table situated within a bay window style breakfast nook, he paused first to give Natalie a kiss on the forehead before taking a seat.

Glancing out the window he could see Tyler throwing a tennis ball across the backyard for Baloo to fetch. After taking a sip of his coffee he then picked up the Sun-Sentinel newspaper placed in front of him.

Roger Owen would never remember anything of the glimpse into his future that he experienced on that night of October 22, 2011. He would never know of the life he will live after his present life is over. There would be no recollection of the British History Professor he will become, nor will he know anything of the mystery that will swirl around his death on the steps of St. Patrick's Cathedral. There would be no remembrance of a woman named Jessica Wynn or of a great great great grandson of his named Cyrus Owen. Nor would Roger ever know about the book that will be written about his life and his family a hundred and fourteen years in the future, or about the success and prosperity that book will bring to Cyrus and his family. He would never know of the tragic pandemic that will come, the truth he will know of its origin, or of the cryptic message he will tell Cyrus before his death. A message that Cyrus, although unable to decipher, will include in his book, thus prompting readers worldwide to speculate on its meaning. A speculation that will be voiced by the public first as a whisper and then eventually grow to a roar prompting an unyielding multinational investigation that years later will finally reveal to the world the shocking truth behind the 2115 pandemic. Because of this the professor who lived his life for the learning of history and teaching of history will himself *become* a part of history that historians like he will speak of and write about as the annals of time continue. Finally, and most poignantly, he will never know that the son born unto Cyrus and Sarah will be named in honor of him, Roger Sydney Owen.

Outside of his home that morning, beyond his property, past the waterways, over the coastline, and high above the sparkling sea, brilliant rays of sunshine shone through cotton-like clouds on what would be for Roger Owen, the dawn of *just another day*.